More to Life

a novel by

Janet Nichols Lynch

Legacy Book Press LLC
Camanche, Iowa

Table of Contents

To Marsha, my lifelong friend

1

"So this is where you've brought me to die."

"Mom."

"An old folks' home."

"Assisted living."

"A meadow is not shady. There may be trees around it, but not on it. It's in full sun."

"Mom, Shady Meadow sounds nice." My daughter Brooke pauses in her task of unpacking a cardboard box to use the back of her hand to push her oversized glasses up her ridiculous chopped nose. In her late forties, she still wears her hair like a teenager, draped down her back nearly to her waist. She has to color it now. Her lips are swollen with Botox. Fashion has always been a girl's worst enemy.

"It's too expensive here. I could live to a hundred-and-four like Beverly Cleary. That would take a chunk out of your inheritance."

"Mom, I don't want your money. I want you to be safe and comfortable. Oh, these are nice." She holds up a pair of pink floral panties before folding them and setting them in a dresser drawer.

I gaze out the window at the gray, bleak sky, the bare branches of a tree, black sticks. January is the cruelest month, not April, bursting with green and sprouting new life. Oh god, spring! How will I ever endure until spring and on and on in this depressing hell hole? Oh Al, where are you when I need you the most? He would have never stood for my moving in here, despite our shattered marriage.

I hang up the few clothes I've kept, ones I usually wear, out of several closets full of clothes I had that I might wear. The hangers on the bed rattle like a pile of bones. That will be me, soon enough, not soon enough—I have become ambivalent about this issue. This room is so small it seems the dirty pink walls are pressing in on me. The carpet is brown to hide food stains, shit, vomit, blood. My stomach heaves. "What a dump," I mutter under my breath.

"Mom, this was your choice."

"Sort of." When I was released from the hospital and Brooke came to take me home, she brought me to her house instead of mine. She said my house had been sold, something, she said, I had agreed to, even though I have no recollection of it. A sorry lesson the aged have to learn: careful whom you give power of attorney to, especially if it's your only kid who happens to be an attorney. We toured several other assisted-living residences in the Sacramento area before I decided on Shady Meadow. The cheaper ones smelled like pee, old people's pee. That's where I draw the line. The gorgeous, luxurious ones which allowed pets cost an arm and a leg.

Brooke crosses her arms and tilts her head to accesses our progress. "This place isn't so bad. It's really starting to look like home."

"Do you think prisoners ever say that about their cells?" My full house of seven rooms has been compressed into one. Crammed into this room is my bedroom set, recliner, music cabinet, and shadowbox of cat figurines. That's it. My photo albums have been reduced to some damn lighted digital frame that changes photographs seconds before I'm able to focus on the previous one. Gone, too, my walls of books. True, I would have never reread them, but they are like old friends I will never see again but know I have. I had hoped to skip this stage of life. My fervent wish was to peacefully drift into death in my own home. "What am I supposed to do here?"

"You'll make friends," Brooke chirps.

"*Old* people live here."

Her face blooms into a smile. She has a beautiful smile, everyone has always said so.

"I could play the piano." I reel my head dramatically about the room. "Where is my piano? Honey, someone has stolen my Baldwin grand."

"Oh, Mom, you barely touched that piano."

This is a sensitive subject with me, tinfoil against a filling. I need my piano with me, the broad smile of the keyboard so comforting, the arrangement of white and black familiar, organized, the hulking piece of furniture filling up most of my living room, my life.

"Too bad they didn't take the music cabinet with it," Brooke muses. "Then you could fit in your other nightstand."

I peer at her from the tops of my eyes. "Why two nightstands? I'm just one person."

"It would make the room look symmetrical." Brooke points an accusing finger. "That mahogany cabinet doesn't match your walnut bedroom set. Why do you want to hold on to a bunch of old music books?"

"You're right, my darling. Appearances are everything. Where are my mother's symphonies?"

"I told you—in storage."

"Storage as in the recycle bin?" I imagine a young composer erasing my mother's crackling, yellowed scores and replacing them with new notes, although I know recycling music doesn't work that way. It's unlikely the world will ever hear my mother's brilliant music again.

"Storage as in storage."

"It's generous of you to wait until I'm dead before you trash grandmere's music."

"What, Mom?" Brooke is ready to bolt, her purse strap slung over her shoulder. She is plunged deep into the recesses of her phone and is poking around in there. She isn't gone, but her mind has left the building. That's always been her way. At Disneyland, she'd be asking when we're going to the zoo.

"Where's Willy Whiskers?" I lean against the bed, bend down, and extend my hand. "Here kitty, kitty, kitty." I wonder if my sarcasm could be mistaken for dementia.

"W.W. is in good hands. He's probably found a new companion at Best Friends Animal Society."

"Like I'm already dead."

"We'll see if we can get him to come visit." The cheer in Brooke's tone sounds forced.

I snort. "Cats do not visit. They have the memories of ants. Thanks to you, W.W. has already forgotten all about me."

Brooke's face crumples, her puffy lower lip jutting out. Good. This girl has caused me plenty of heartbreak over the years. "Mom! I'm trying to take care of you as best I can. You know we had to make some concessions for your condition."

"Fuck my condition!" I go over to the dresser, pull out a pair of socks. I unbundle them, lift my right foot, teetering on my left.

"Mom! Sit down to put on your socks."

"Don't tell me how to put on my damn socks!"

"Mom!"

"Brooke!" Dumb name. Just one of my many regrets. Why not River or Stream? Muddy Ditch. "Trickle," I try aloud, telling myself a joke.

"What, Mom?" Her thumbs flash over the text she is composing. She sends it off and pockets her phone. "Gotta run. Don't overdo. Get some rest."

"That's all I have to do."

"See you soon, Mom." She kisses my cheek and escapes out the door.

"'Bye, Trickle." I remove tuxedo kitty from his shadowbox compartment and stroke his head, singing softly, mournfully, "Out in the wide world, kitty, pretty, kitty."

2

I awake with a start. *Where am I?* Oh, yeah. Parked in fucking Shady Meadow like a dilapidated old car up on concrete blocks. I wonder if I can escape. Could I walk out the door of my room, and out the building, then keep walking and walking until…? The problem is I have no place to go. I roll my eyes to the illuminated digital clock on my nightstand: 9:43. Just 9:43. I'm tired, but not sleepy, a familiar state. I've never been much of a sleeper and aging doesn't help.

Think of something lovely. Yellow daffodils bursting from the ground heralding spring. Willie Whiskers pouncing on my chaise lounge, pressing his head against my leg or into my palm. I loved lounging and reading and dozing, basking in the sun, even though everyone tells you it's the enemy, run for cover. I loved my backyard, my pool, my flower beds, my own dirt beneath my nails, the pink, fuchsia, white blooms, rewards for my toiling. All gone now. Not such a lovely thought after all.

What else? Notre Dame, Westminster Abby. I got to step foot into both. When everyone thought I'd marry my high school/college sweetheart Mike, I ran away. I bummed through Europe with Tony, a guy I was casually involved with and certainly not married to, something nice girls didn't do in those days. Mother called me a whore. Too bad. Once she was resigned to my plan, she thought of ways of using it. "See if you can make some connections when you're across the pond. You're bringing more than hippie clothes, I should hope, at least one nice dress. Maestro von Schuller in Frankfurt will remember me." Mother always had trouble understanding where she ended and I began. I knew there would be no connections for me, no concert career. But I toured Mozart's house in Salzburg and Beethoven's house in Bonn. I went to St. Stephen's in Vienna, St. Mark's in Venice, St. Peter's, but not the Sistine Chapel. It was closed for the Assumption, a Holy Day of Obligation. I figured I'd never get back to the Vatican and I was right. For some things in life, you just get one chance.

Still wide awake. I'm in for a long night. I do enjoy lying in the peaceful dark. I used to be afraid of it, but that stopped when I lost my faith, never any consolation to me, just fear and guilt. The music of faith is good though: Bach and Palestrina, Gregorian chant. "Praise God from Whom All Blessings Flow," "Oh, Mary, We Crown Thee with Blossoms Today." I hum "Amazing Grace" softly to myself, a wretch like me.

I drift off, but am jolted awake by yelling blasting through the wall. A crazy-sounding woman rants in a gravelly croak, mixed with phlegmy, throat-clearing. "Where's my cigarettes? You said you'd bring my damn cigarettes."

"You aren't allowed to smoke in your room, Mom," says a calm male voice.

"I don't smoke in my room. These people are goddamn liars."

"Your room smells like smoke," says another male voice, deeper, more strident.

I could switch on the light and read, but instead I lie here, eavesdropping on real-life drama. It's not like I have to strain my ears.

"This bed is crap." The woman coughs and harrumphs. "Your dad has the best bed. I want you to swap us beds."

"Mom, this is the bed you wanted," says the deeper voice. "It took three of us to shove it in here."

"No, I wanted the bed we had in the guest room. That's what I said but you boys don't listen. Lumpy bed, crap for food. I hate this fucking dump. Get me out of here."

Oh, take me, too, please, but not the same place as you take her.

"You asked us to move you in here," says the guy with the sweeter voice. "Remember? You picked this place because you have friends here."

"Just Sally now that Ethel has passed. Third resident this week. Alotta deaths here."

The deep voice chuckles. "Well, you gotta expect that, Mom."

"I'm not talking natural causes, cancer and stuff. There's rumors flying about a staff member snuffing us seniors out."

"Now, Mom, you can't believe everything you hear."

"You know how easy it is to snuff an old, weak person? Just hold a pillow over their face a couple minutes and they're gone."

"Mom, Mom, don't start imagining things," says the softie. "You'll upset yourself over nothing."

"Let's see," says the deep no-nonsense voice. "You got the staff nurse, the staff physical therapist, and the staff snuffer. They charge extra for that?"

"Oh, fuck you!" screeches the woman. "I'm serious! Someday you'll walk in here and I'll be stone cold, and then you smart asses will be sorry."

Both men are laughing now, seemingly uncontrollably, putting a smile on my face.

"How about some ice cream, Mom?" says the nice guy, his tone high-pitched and lilting like he's humoring a petulant child. "Let's go get you a McDonald's caramel sundae."

"Good. We can stop at Walgreen's for my cigarettes."

I hear the group troop past my door, down the hall, the woman still crabbing, "Where's Ricky? How come Ricky and Lauren don't come to see me?"

Because no one can stand you.

The quiet seems especially still and void after the uproar. The image of a pillow descending over my face causes me to shutter. No chance to even scream for help. That old bat probably knows everything that goes on around here. I slip out of bed, tiptoe to the door, and jiggle the locked knob. Turns out, I'd like to live a little longer. See what comes of it.

3

I have nothing to do. Most of my life I was too busy, budgeting every minute of the day to get everything done and now there's this dreadful idleness. I just eat and sit around. The food here isn't bad, but the community meals are weird. You have to rub elbows with people you don't know and make small talk. You have to be pleasant and appear happy to be here. I did meet this one woman, Margaret, at breakfast who is nice enough, but we have nothing in common.

A book is good company. I love to read and read, but I can't read all day. Sometimes I go on Netflix to peruse what's available in case I feel like viewing, like in the old days when I strolled through bookstores when there were bookstores, picking up books, running my fingertips across their shiny jackets, scanning the flap copy, then setting them down, having no time to read. Viewing is not as good as reading. It doesn't take up my whole mind and makes me fidgety for something more to do. When I listen to audio books, my mind wanders and I miss out. I prefer to do my own work of making meaning of the text, seizing the words, seeing for myself how the sentences lie on the page.

As I read, I doze. Sometimes, as I'm drifting off, a dread descends over me, an awful feeling, a kind of panic, and I claw my way to consciousness, snap my eyes open, straighten in my recliner. Memories flood my mind, regrets. I should have gotten Brooke a dog. She begged and begged for one her whole childhood. On her eighth

Christmas, she cried when she didn't get one, truly believing her letter to Santa would deliver. On New Year's Day, I bought her a hamster as a consolation, which she named Beethoven, not after the composer but the dog, even though Beethoven the hamster was a girl. I was constantly stressed out that our cat would get her. I didn't know hamsters live less than two years. The poor thing developed a tumor in her throat and had to be put down. No more hamsters.

There are things about Brooke I've never understood. Like how could me, a cat person, raise a dog person? Brooke needed that dog. Lots of my preconceived notions about parenting were wrong. You can't go back and change anything. I would if I could, but then would Brooke be the same person? Was I too strict? Probably. She has been "in therapy" for years, moving from one shrink to the next. Some of them tell her all her problems stem from the fact that I was a bad mother. I can always tell when Brooke is seeing a you-had-a-bad-mother type of therapist because then I really pay in her recriminations.

The digital frame flickers as it turns from one photo to the next, my life all in a jumble: Grandson Carter holding a middle school Cyberquest trophy, Pre-schooler Brooke in a flouncy scarlet velvet dress playing her first quarter-sized violin, Al and I hiking the Grand Canyon decades ago, Carter's first day of Kindergarten, Brooke's high school prom. I don't have the emotional stamina for this tsunami of memories and turn the frame to the wall.

I shift in my chair, stretch my legs. I chide myself: stop moping around. Get up, you lazy ass, get out! I love to walk. It makes me feel so much better, but I can't seem to root myself out of this damn recliner. I feel stuck. I thought retirement would be different. I thought I'd have all the time and freedom to go to all sorts of places, have all sorts of adventures. I tried to bolster friends to travel with me, but they just wanted to stay home. I found out it takes courage I don't have to venture out on my own.

So here I sit. Three hours until the dining room opens. The afternoon weighs on me. My lap feels empty. Probably Willy Whiskers has forgotten all about me by now. You can't expect much from a cat. Dogs are smarter, more dependable, but too needy. The cats in my life chose me, just showed up like Willy Whiskers. So many cats, overlapping sometimes. Groucho was black and white with a mustache. A car ran over his tail, and he was so desperate to get away that his tail was pulled clean out of his body and lay in the road for me to find, like a flat, dead thing, like poor, miserable Groucho himself within a month. Beach was the color of sand and died of a urinary blockage. Mable had orange around one eye, black around the other eye, and a white stripe down the middle. Doris liked to play pee-a-boo behind the shower curtain while I sat on the toilet. Ralph allowed feral kittens to suckle on his teats. Max was a Manx who lived to nineteen. Mable, too. Nineteen years is a long time for a cat, but not long enough. It's sad to see an old cat lose its life force. A couple of them I should have put down sooner. More regrets. I used to think nature knows best, but it doesn't. Nature is a cruel bitch.

I yearn for the furry comfort of Willy Whiskers, the vibration of his purr. I lift my hand and draw it across the air pretending to pet him. My hand grows heavier and heavier. I drift off. When I awake a young woman is bent over me. The hair at my nape bristles. I release a small "Ach!"; a scream caught in my throat. I wriggle out from under her and stumble to a standing position. "Wha-what do you want? What are you doing in here?"

The woman rears back, palms in the air. She is short and plump, certainly not strong enough to take a pillow and—what nonsense! She tips her head. "Sorry to disturb. I knock and no answer." She is wearing black capris and a pale blue polo with the Shady Meadow insignia. She offers me a timid smile, the corners of her almond-shaped eyes crinkling. "I am Marisol. I clean."

She obviously means well, but still she's a jarring invasion of my privacy. I've always done my own housework. I objected when I saw the housekeeping fee on my Shady Meadow contract, but state health regulations require all rooms here to be professionally sanitized.

Marisol stretches an inviting hand to my recliner. "You sit, lady, relax. I start in bathroom." She pushes her cart past me.

I sink back down, my arms crossed tightly. How can I relax with an intruder in the room? I lean back and my legs shoot forward. I take a deep breath. Abruptly, invasion morphs into rescue. Someone is cleaning my toilet. After all the years I've done for myself, my husband, my daughter, my grandson, someone is doing for me. How about that? "Uh, thank you!" I call after Marisol.

"No problem!"

I wish people would say "you're welcome" instead of "no problem." Marisol begins to sing under her breath in a foreign language. It isn't Spanish, probably Tagalog. She does look Filipino. I'm curious to know for sure, but you can't ask such things of people these days without being called racist. Her voice is high and sweet, the melody lilting. I close my eyes and am transported to a tropical island with mango trees and turquoise waters.

4

I've made a new friend, or rather, Margaret has made a friend of me. She's gone out of her way to take me up, and I find that I'm flattered. In past friendships, I've been the one to do most the work, until I flat out gave up on some of them. I just couldn't hold onto to everyone in my life who had once meant something to me. It seems if I don't see a person regularly, through work or an activity, we lose contact. I suppose it's the natural progression of things. Now that I'm stuck at Shady Meadow, why not have a Shady Meadow friend?

Margaret has lived here only six months, but already she seems to know everybody and everybody's business. She slips my hand into the crook of her arm, presses it against her warm, doughy side and leads me through the place, introducing me around. I'm surprised how comforting this is. Apparently, I've been starved for attention.

Together we attend yoga class, Margaret's orange Lululemon pants bulging and indenting in unexpected places. I don't have any yoga clothes; I've never warmed to the activity, although I've tried it several times. My body doesn't bend in the right places, but then most of the other yogis at Shady Meadow aren't any more limber than I, so I fit right in.

Margaret invites me to join the bridge-playing ladies. No men—I don't know why. I haven't played the game in years, but I like the way it wakes up my brain. It's fun, except with Bonnie, who can't remember any of the cards that have been played and makes outrageous bids. The other players are too gracious to say anything, except for Margaret who scolds, "Pay attention, Bon, for cripes' sake!" as if she's capable. Iris is hard of hearing. Conversing with her, Margaret looks like she's playing charades. "Pies? What kind of pies?" bellows Iris, as if the louder she talks the better she can hear others. "Not pies," corrects Margaret. "Drive! Drive! Are you gonna drive to your daughter's?" She holds up two fists and moves them up and down like she's steering a car. Margaret cracks me up. I haven't laughed so much in three years as I have in the past three days. It feels good to laugh.

Pandora has the best memory for what cards have been played. When I am introduced to her, my eyes widen and my chin dips, no doubt like dozens of people who have met her over the years. I try to think of a polite way to ask, "What the hell were your parents thinking?" Instead I say, "Were you named after somebody?" Pandora shrugs her narrow shoulders. "Lots of trouble, that's me. When I was little, everyone called me Dora. I didn't know my complete name until my first day of Kindergarten when the teacher called roll. When no one owned up to Pandora Prentice, she bore down on me and scolded, 'Child, don't you know your own name?' I burst into tears."

Margaret cuts the deck, bends the cards in a fine arch, and riffle shuffles with a satisfying whoosh and snap, something I've never gotten the hang of. "The nuns who taught me could be scary," she says. "I was afraid to even sneeze in class. But I sat there thinking how glad I wasn't a boy. The nuns just hated boys." She makes a motion of rapping a child's knuckles with a ruler and has a good laugh over it. Like Margaret, I went to twelve years of parochial school, but we turned out way different. She is still a devout Catholic; I've fallen-away. She raised seven children to my one. I have a master's in reading; Margaret has a GED. She's smart though, and resilient in a way I've never been. "Don't wear your heart on your sleeve." "You have nothing to cry about." "Would you look at her making such a fuss over nothing?" "Oh, now, here come the alligator tears." I've heard all of those expressions.

As Margaret and I piece together a jigsaw puzzle set up in the sunroom, she confides, "I was a stay-at-home mom, then a stay-at-home grandmom. When Murray passed last spring, Robbie and Dawn and their kids wanted to move in to take care of me. Right, more like they wanted me to be a stay-at-home great-grandmom. Murray was a manager in the cardboard industry, good with money. He left me sitting pretty, so I let myself out to pasture. A very nice pasture, I'll say. I know my Murray is looking down on me from heaven saying, 'Put your feet up, Maggie. You deserve a good rest.'"

I raise my eyebrows and wrinkle my nose. "So you like it here?"

"Are you kidding me? Someone else doing all the cooking and cleaning for a change! I sold Rob the old house and everything in it for half of what it was worth. Made everyone else mad as hell because they were thinking that was their inheritance, but what was I gonna do? It needed too much fixing up to even think about putting it on the market."

"When my house sold, my daughter bullied me into liquidating," I say. "Brooke is against any excess stuff lying around. If she has two spatulas, she gives one away."

Margaret gasps. "That's just wrong. A spatula for cookie sheets is completely different than the kind you use for browning hamburger. Plus, if you're flipping a rack of ribs you need two spatulas at once. I had a whole drawer full. One Christmas when I had little Lily and Lucy over and we got out my whole collection of cookie cutters and—I had the kids because Tommy and Darlene were on the outs trying to decide if they should divorce or stay together because—"

Away Margaret goes. She starts a story, which reminds her of another story about something else, and then I have to hold in my mind the place where she made the abrupt digression, in hopes of hearing the end of the first story. Her chatter is both engaging and exhausting. During my first conversations with her, I tried to clarify relationships, but her web of family and friends is so extensive, I figure it will become clearer as we go along. I busy myself assembling a tiny windmill of about ten brick-red pieces. I never thought to do a jigsaw puzzle at home, but here I like having something to do with my hands, and when I fit two out of a thousand pieces together, I feel a teensy charge of dopamine erupting in my brain.

"That's Sam for you! What a hoot!" Margaret sways her head as she laughs.

She has rambled from long ago Christmas cookie-making to a current Shady Meadow incident, and I somehow missed the segue so I don't know what she's talking about, but I pretend to. "Who's Sam?"

"Oh, he's the life of the party around here. Another thing he did, when the guys were in the sauna, he hid all their clothes! They had to dash through the pool area in their little white towels, their cheeks all rosy. These ones, I mean." She presses her hands to her face.

"You'll have to introduce me to this Sam."

She lowers her eye lids and peers at me suspiciously. "And have you snatch him out from under me?"

"He's your boyfriend?"

"Hardly. Let's just say I have a little crush." She wriggles her ample bottom in emphasis. "But with so many available women around here, I doubt if he'll ever give a gal like me the time of day."

"Don't sell yourself short. With your winning personality, you're a hell of a catch!"

Margaret's face explodes in a wide grin. "I am? You're not just saying that 'cause we're friends?"

"Hell, no. And count me out. I'm done with romance."

"Oh, shucks, how come?" Margaret looks stricken, as if I've doused her face with cold water.

I flutter my fingers like I'm warding off a fly. "Falling in love is for young girls. Ever notice how many older women are single? Most of us realize a good relationship is hopeless."

"Heck, why is that? We're still kickin'."

Outside, on the circular drive, an ambulance rolls up, lights flashing.

"Uh-oh," says Margaret. "I wonder who that's for."

We watch the action out the window for a few minutes before resuming work on our puzzle. "Murray was your high school sweetheart, right?"

"Yeah. So?"

"That's the difference between you and me. I had a number of boyfriends before I got married. I tried dating after my divorce, but all those guys bored me to death or else they were looking for some gullible woman to support them. Good god, one of them even lived with his mother."

"So?"

"So romance has been beaten out of me. Taking up with a man also means taking up his baggage. Besides, old men are so unattractive."

"Colette! Not all of them."

"Hair hanging down from their nostrils, sprouting out of their ears. They got hair growing everywhere but where it belongs on top of their heads. Most go in for the Santa Claus look, white beard down to here." I press the side of my hand above my breasts. "Are these old geezers too lazy to shave or have they just given up?"

"Not all the men around here are old." Margaret nods toward our in-house physical therapist, Dr. Martinez, who insists on going by Raul. He's a cheerful sort, with black flashing eyes, a lock of curly hair dangling over his brow, a ready smile full of bright white teeth.

I snort. "I doubt if he'd be interested in dating his grandma."

Margaret shrugs. "You never know."

Raul helps a very old woman get out of a chair, not because she has an appointment with him, but because he happened by and saw that she needed assistance. The bulky old bag of beans is trying to get out of an armchair by hoisting her butt first. Raul urges her to ease back down, then instructs her to scoot her body to the edge of the seat, position her hands at the ends of the arms of the chair, plant her feet firmly on the floor, lean forward, and heave herself up. With much groaning and weaving, the woman manages to rise to her feet, huffing and puffing.

"Success!" Raul exclaims, with a clap of his hands. "Now, we go again."

"No, no," protests the woman.

He pushes down on her shoulders to get her seated again. I imagine his strong, firm hands encircling her throat and squeezing. "Practice makes perfect," his voice rings out cheerfully.

The woman again tries to rise up, butt first.

"No, no, like I told you. Like you did last time." He repeats his instructions, and the woman follows them, this time taking longer, giving Raul a chance to glimpse his slight, but perfect build in the mirror behind him. He can't resist flexing his well-formed bicep with appreciation as his protege grunts and groans and breathlessly rises to her feet a second time.

"Excellent!" exclaims Raul. "You are sensational. We go one more time."

"Leave me the fuck alone!" The woman shakes her cane at him in a menacing way and stomps off.

Raul turns, notices another woman, nods to her yellow sweater, and says, "Oh, I like that bright color on you. Very flattering."

"Oh, do you think so, Dr. Martinez? Really?" The woman titters.

"Raul. Please, you must call me Raul!"

"Quite the ladies' man," I comment to Margaret under my breath.

"I think he's very sweet. Makes the ladies feel good about themselves, very generous with his time. He didn't have to stop and help Shirley out of her chair."

"Yeah, against her will."

"She was going about it all wrong."

I nod. "Okay, he's good at what he does." I can't help thinking it's the nice guys you least suspect who are sometimes the murderers in who-done-its. "Tell me more about your Sam."

"Not my Sam, not yet," says Margaret, "but he has been flirting with me. He patted my bottom in the elevator."

My eyes snap up at her. "That was okay with you?"

Her face flushes fuchsia. "Well, yeah." She leans into me confidentially and whispers, "I'm interested in sex. I've only slept with one man my whole life. I wonder what a different one would be like."

I can't resist teasing. "How would Murray looking down from heaven feel about that?"

She sits back in her chair and grins. "He'd say life is for the living. There's no jealousy in heaven. I wanna be cherished again."

I blow air through my lips. "Cherished! Ha! I've never been cherished."

She slaps my arm. "Oh, you have, too, Colette! What about your husband?"

I shrug and roll my eyes. "We had an every-man-for-himself kind of marriage."

"A what?"

"Al wasn't that into togetherness. But I knew what I was getting. He was the right one to marry. No regrets there. I chose Al, I went after him, and eventually he gave in to me. We had a no-drama, low-maintenance marriage, maybe too low because I didn't retain him. I've racked my brain trying to figure what I could have done differently. What about you? Didn't you ever feel lonely in your marriage?"

"With seven kids, are you kidding me? Lonely would've been a luxury."

Margaret makes a joke out of what I consider a serious issue, but I forge on. "I think everyone feels lonely in a marriage sometimes, men and women both, sometimes in the same marriage. Go figure. Al didn't want to do stuff with me so I found other people to go places with, girlfriends, my daughter, sometimes for get-away weekends, sometimes longer trips."

Margaret presses my wrist. "Couldn't you *make* him take you places?"

"Aw, it's no fun going someplace fun with someone who doesn't want to be there with you. Al would say 'Go, have fun.' He seemed happy to have the house to himself. I sometimes wondered if I didn't come back would he care one way or the other."

Margaret bats the air. "Oh, go on!"

I shrug. "Anyway, I was happy enough to stick it out. Then, just as we were approaching our golden years, Tabby comes along. She wanted Al, she went after him, and eventually he gave in." I hand Margaret a yellow puzzle piece she can use on the flag she's working on. "Good luck with Sam. I wish the two of you much happiness together."

Out of my peripheral vision, I sense movement out the window. I straighten in my chair to watch the EMTs wheeling a gurney. The sheet is drawn over the supine person's head. "Margaret, have you heard any rumors about deaths around here that aren't quite natural?"

"You mean, like there's a snuffer-outer among us?"

I study her expression, but can't tell if she's joking. "Yeah."

She shakes her head. "Nothing to those rumors."

"Then you've heard them?"

"Don't worry about it, Colette. It's just later than we think around here."

Out the window, we watch the EMTs tilt and slide the gurney into the rear of the ambulance and slam the door shut. "Too late for some," I muse.

5

Busy at the jigsaw puzzle again the next day, I nudge Margaret and tilt my head toward a Santa in the corner easy chair, blissfully snoring and drooling in his beard. "Looks to me like the guys in this place are more likely to have a drawer full of Depends than a medicine chest full of Viagra."

"Don't be too sure of that. Sam has vitality! He's the champion pickle ball player around here. All the guys want to be his doubles partner."

"Pickle ball? That isn't even the real thing."

"What do you mean?"

"Isn't it just geriatric tennis for old duffers?"

I meant to get a laugh out of Margaret, but she narrows her eyes instead. "You don't like men much, do you?"

My response is slow and when it comes, it sounds forced even in my own ears. "'Course, I do."

Another Santa, sans the bowl full of jelly, wears a herring bone driver's cap and thick, tinted, horn-rimmed glasses, his shirt splayed open at the throat with enough wiry white hair spilling out to knit a sweater. He's seated alone at a card table, his forehead nearly touching a page which he studies through a magnifying glass. From where I'm seated, I can see that it's a musical score.

I tap Margaret's wrist, lean across our table and whisper, "That poor man can't see."

21

She responds in her regular speaking voice. "Harry? Sure, he can, just not too good."

The man is drawing on his music with colored pencils, connecting the notes like a child's dot-to-dot. The colors he has selected are blue and green: earth and sky. I close in on him, take a seat at his table. I can't seem to help myself.

He straightens to acknowledge me. "Hello, young lady."

"Hi." I cock my head to peer at the music. It's Bach's Fugue in C Minor, from Book One of the *Well-Tempered Clavier.* I've played that one.

"I suppose you're wondering what I'm doing." The man slides his glasses down his nose to peer at me, the corners of his mouth turned up. His breath flows a bit faster in anticipation of mansplaining.

I can see that he is tracing entries of the fugue subject in blue and the countersubject in green. I point to the last line of the score. "You missed one."

He takes up his magnifying glass. "Oh, so I have! Overlapping statements."

I reach into a cupboard deep in the recesses of my memory. Its hinges creak, but I grab the word I'm searching for. "*Stretto.*"

"So it is." He rears back to access me fully. His eyes are a striking cornflower blue.

I spring to my feet with an unexpected buoyancy, probably due to a close encounter with Bach rather than—who did Margaret say?—Harry. Probably bald under that jaunty cap.

6

Margaret has got me thinking about my old boyfriends. I sit in my recliner, open my laptop to Facebook, and look for Mike, a coward's way of checking up on old lovers. There might be a way to know who visits your Timeline, but I'm not tech-savvy enough to know it. Over the years, every decade or two or three, I have phoned Mike or emailed. "I'm married," he told me the first time. I know, dude, so am I; I'm not after you.

Ah, here he is, another Santa Claus. I lean toward the screen, squinting to see beyond the white whiskers, in search of the sixteen-year-old face that used to make me weak in the knees. I recognize him around the eyes, the corners of his mouth. I wonder what my life would have been if I'd married him instead of Al. He was a good high school/college boyfriend, the right guy to discover sex with. We had a blast together, rambling around in his beloved, souped-up '64 Mustang. "His car is loud," Mother had complained. Daffodil Hill to Bolinas to Fern Canyon to watching the frogs not jump at Angels Camp. Mike sometimes sat on my piano practice room floor figuring complicated math problems that took a whole page of binder paper. He attended all of my recitals, and when I totally bombed, he held me and let my tears wet his shoulder, my mascara imprinting little butterflies on his blue work shirt.

I see that Mike doesn't use FB much, not many posts. Same interests over the years, cars and the Giants. I know his wife is named

Pam, a woman who already had three kids when they met, whom they raised together. I could have given Mike his own kids. I click on Pam's name to go to her Timeline. Her intro: "Plastic canvas brings me joy." No personal photos, just memes: "God sends us exactly what we're ready for at the exact time we need it" and "Advice from the ocean: be shore of yourself." Photos of miniature plastic canvas furniture she has made for her plastic canvas dollhouse. She seems very sweet. Maybe she's had a lobotomy. Colette, be nice! She's probably very intelligent, a retired nurse. Probably a good life companion for Mike, never causing him the grief I did.

The longer Mike and I were together, the more Mother hated him. What wasn't to like about him? He was a good guy. He made her daughter happy. Didn't that count for anything? "No ambition," said Mother. "You'll have to support him and that will be the end of your concert career." I would have no concert career. It took Mother the longest time to realize that. The day I received the rejection letter from Julliard, she asked, "Do they know whom they are dealing with? Have they any idea who your mother is?" Love is blind, especially when it comes to parents and their offspring. My mother believed my talent rivalled hers. I went to Sac State. Mother claimed it was because I was "chasing" Mike. I knew it was because a state college was where I belonged.

During our college senior year, Mike and I decided to date other people. It was my idea, actually. I didn't know what I was getting into. There were jealousies, recriminations, long, late-night phone conversations. Really, I thought no matter what I did, Mike would still love me and we would end up getting married and raising a family together. He showed up at my senior recital with a dozen red roses and his date Sally. I had a memory slip in my Brahms because her face loomed up in my brain rather than the tricky modulation I was supposed to play. After graduation, I tramped off to Europe with Tony. When I returned two months later, Mike was too hurt to get back together. I cried and cried, but what could I have done differently? Twenty-one was just too young for me to be settled for life. By twenty-six, I started to panic. That's the way young women were pressured to marry back then.

I thought Tony understood I was just hanging out with him for the adventure of Europe. I might have broken his heart. I probably didn't even consider his feelings, so self-centered I was back them. I moved on to a succession of okay-for-now guys, still believing there was a way I could get back with Mike, even though we had separate lives in separate towns, San Jose for me and Elko, Nevada, for him.

I met Cameron at a gym where all the women wore leotards and tights and leaned against rotating barrels with knobby surfaces to break down their cellulite. I wore a T-shirt and shorts and became interested in powerlifting. God knows why. All the guys working out at the gym were in awe of Cameron because as a younger man he had won a bunch of bodybuilding titles. What a hunk. Among all the willowy, leotard types, he chose me, coached me on my bench press. I didn't even know if a woman pressed the bar above or below her breasts. No YouTube back then.

Cameron was a cardiologist, fifteen years older than me. I thought older men would appreciate me more than guys my age. I think now they appreciated my youth. On our first date at a health food restaurant, I asked him about his family and hometown, and he said such information really had nothing to do with him. I should have realized right then, he wasn't about to let me into his life. I thought I didn't care, his being only an okay-for-now. In bed, I discovered a glossy scar on his stomach where he said a bullet grazed him. I didn't ask about the circumstances; I got that he wouldn't tell me. He said he was a Sufi who could bilocate, but he had a flicker of a grin when he claimed that. His man-of-mystery thing was bullshit, but he was absolutely gorgeous. I loved running my hands over his muscles.

Cameron was a kind of a doctor without borders, but not that specific organization, who volunteered his services in third world countries, which is what they were called them. By the time he left for several weeks, I was head-over-heels. How was I supposed to know it was possible to fall in love with an okay-for-now? Wasn't I a rational person, the master of my own emotions? Nope.

I wrote him witty letters on flimsy, light-blue paper that folded into an envelope with red-and-white-striped edging. I learned to spell Afghanistan—three letters of the alphabet in succession. My life felt small in comparison to his. Practicing the piano six hours a day seemed stupid, repeatedly showing little kids where Middle C is. I wondered what I could do to impress him. I wondered how I could become a woman whom he would want. I wondered if he would return to me. He did.

Days passed between his phone calls. I learned that men ran on different clocks than women. On the in-between days, I fantasized about him constantly, mostly in bed, and he wasn't even much good there. I couldn't relax with him. He was all wrong for me. I wanted him knowing how miserable he made me. I didn't understand how badly I wanted to be in love. To be loved. It can creep up on you, overtake you. For one date, I dug out hot rollers from the back of a cupboard. That changed nothing. Sometimes he called to ask me if he could prescribe me a painkiller, which was really for him. I said yes. Bodybuilding crushes the body. When I got the nerve to declare my love for him, he said, "I am your friend." That's it. When he left for good, it took me a year and a twenty-pound weight gain to get over him. Decades later I searched for him on the Internet. I found him posed on the covers of long-ago muscle magazines. I gathered other information about him: his birthplace, where he earned his MD, the name of his lifelong partner whom he never married. I had known so little about him. He isn't on Facebook now or anywhere else. At age sixty, he blew his brains out. Coward. He could squat half a ton, dodge bullets in war-torn countries, but he couldn't face old age.

With a sigh, I log off Facebook and close my laptop. I check my watch and rise from my recliner with a grunt. I go through my leg stretches, straight to the front with foot grabs, knee to chest with ankle rotations, leg cocked in back. Use it or lose it. I stand in front of my closet, trying to decide what to wear to dinner. Community living requires me to be more cognizant of my appearance. Dressing for dinner makes me think of those characters in an old Agatha Christie mystery, one of them invariably landing face down in the soup. I select burgundy slacks and a paisley rayon blouse to match. At home, I wore the same T-shirt and jeans for days. At home, I jumped into the pool to cool off without bothering with a swimsuit. Let the neighbors peek through the fence at my saggy old white butt, that was their business, while I wondered if ceasing to care what people think is a sign of impending senility.

I put on fresh underwear, just in case I have body odor that my own nose can't detect. I must say, in general, Shady Meadow does a good job of keeping down old people stink, so I do my part. As I pull socks out of my dresser, I notice three odd-shaped, reddish-purple splotches on my right forearm. With the slightest bump or scrape, I bleed beneath the skin, another sign of old age. I dig my thumbs down the sides of a sock and bunch it up. I steady myself on both legs, then transfer my weight onto my left leg. I raise my right knee as high as it will go, point my foot, and plunge it into the sock. Success! The left one is a little trickier. I don't balance as well on my right leg for one thing, and for some reason my left knee can't rise up as far as the right. Success again! The day I have to sit down to put on my socks, I will be old.

I pick up my comb, bracing myself: I'm about to look in the mirror. Peering back will be an old woman resembling my mother. It's natural to look old; I've been old for many years. I don't feel old. I don't appreciate the mirror reminding me of the fact. I check for food between my teeth, crumbs at the corners of my mouth, dried mucus beneath my nose. My hair is the same chestnut brown it's been my whole life, except now it comes from a bottle. I've been to the Shady Meadow salon to have my roots done, my eyebrows waxed. The technician also mitigated my nanny goat whiskers. Why does nature think old women should grow beards? I apply eyebrow pencil, blush, lipstick. Such a bother. I never did this at home, but here I must satisfy an old woman's vanity. I stare back at my reflection and practice a smile. Not too bad, not yet.

7

As much as I appreciate Margaret, she doesn't make a good walking companion. She is so slow it hardly counts as exercising. She shuffles and yaks. She halts to complete a thought, as if she can't move her feet and get to the end of a sentence at the same time. This morning I slip out of the building alone at the break of a pink-clouded dawn, when I seem to have the whole wide world to myself. I think how the smartest little pig sneaked out to get apples an hour before the wolf. It saved his life. If Margaret wants me to walk with her later, I'll go out a second time.

I have found a good two-mile route. I take the pathway snaking through the adjacent park, circle the Shady Meadow community, passing the tennis courts, pool, and gazebo, then I cross the hump-backed wooden bridge over a little creek leading to a miniature fake waterfall and cement wishing pond with coins shimmering at its bottom. The rose garden is on an incline, dotted with ceramic gnomes, mushrooms, and houses, which cries out peewee golf, and yet I can't be too cynical about it because I'm a sucker for this sort of kitsch.

This morning I push my pace, my breath milky and ragged, my heart beating faster. I imagine the endorphins popping awake in my brain, coursing through my nerves. I feel the same as when I was a school girl pumping my bike to school. Over and over, I have to remind myself how old I am. Recalling an event, I get the time wrong: that was thirty, no forty, no fifty years ago. We begin our lives young, and we are young so long, we develop a young mindset. Feeling old doesn't come naturally.

I'm crossing the road to the park when I feel a familiar rumble and pressure in my gut. That's one damn thing about aging. It oftentimes takes exercise to get my bowels moving, and when they do the impulse is quite insistent, whether I'm close to a toilet or not. I hold still, squeeze tight, wait for the churning in my innards to pass. I turn around, take a short cut across the lawn, burst through a side door of the Shady Meadow main complex.

Usually, I make it to the toilet in time. I think I'm going to this morning, when a man lunges out before me and grasps both of my hands. He has a caved-in chest, scrawny limbs, a wide stance for balance. A large, jeweled crucifix swinging on a heavy chain is the most robust thing about him. He appears so frail he doesn't seem long for this world. I'm not one to yelp sexual harassment every time a man touches me, but this guy's grip is vise-like and he reeks of a strong cologne, and—goddamn it—I gotta go. His burning, crazed eyes peer into my face. Who was it that said religion was like opium? Oh, yeah—Marx.

"Have a blessed day," he chirps.

"Uh, yeah, you, too." I wrench loose of his hold and dash down the hall. I pause at my door, squeezing, squeezing, willing the surge in my gut to halt for a few precarious moments. In my room, I fumble with the drawstring of my Spandex leggings as I dash toward the bathroom. I'd like to wash my hands clean of Blessed-day Man's cloying stink, but there's no time. I yank down my pants, and my ass hits the toilet seat in the nick of time. Safe, like home plate.

When I hear piano playing coming from the dining room, I nudge aside the drawn accordion doors to peek inside. It's Harry playing his Bach on a lovely, ebony Yamaha grand. Well, he's sort of playing it. I creep into the room and slide into a chair, hoping not to be noticed. Harry leans forward, his nose inches from the music rack. He lifts his magnifying glass and peers through it and his thick glasses. He places his hands over the keyboard, his fingers long and curved. He plays through the first statement of the subject, quite musically, a lilt to the contours of the phrase, but when the left hand enters, he falters. Abruptly, he swivels his torso around, startling me. He taps the frame of his glasses. "Macular degeneration."

"That's a shame."

"I can read the notes once I know what they are." He resumes playing, gets a bit farther in the music before he breaks down again. He chuckles as he takes up his magnifying glass. "Luckily, pianists memorize."

"Right, but fugues are the devil."

"I like what polyphony does to the brain. Keeps the wires straight."

"Yes. It kept insanity at bay for Robert Schumann, at least for a while."

"Do you play?"

"Not anymore." I shift to the edge of the chair to rise up. "Excuse me for intruding. I just heard the piano and, well, I'll leave you to it."

He twists his torso and his whole face blooms into a smile. "Please, stay. It's good to know another Classical pianist around here."

I just told him I don't play, but I nod. "All right. For a little while."

He's not ashamed of his limitations. I admire that, envy it. I've always been challenged in forgiving myself for falling short of my own expectations. "You can't be great at everything," Al used to tell me, and I'd say, "I'd like to be great at something, just one thing." Al would take me in his arms and try to hug and kiss away my feelings of inadequacy. He was a good husband until he wasn't. "You're a great teacher," he told me. "Those that can't, teach," I quoted, and he countered, "And there are those who can't teach." I know that, but I've always felt teaching is a pedestrian talent.

Harry lifts his music off the rack, and holding it close to his face in his right hand, plays the left-hand part of the fugue's exposition. Then he shifts the music to his left hand and plays with his right. He replaces the music on the rack, and leaning forward, attempts both hands with some success.

I am so engrossed in his process that I don't realize someone else has entered the room. I smell her presence first, cigarette smoke and essence of perspiration and pee.

"Stop that racket, you old shit!" the woman screeches. She wheezes, clears her throat, and coughs. I recognize her voice immediately, my next-door neighbor. This is the first time I've gotten a look at her, standing beside me now, weaving on unsteady feet. Her moon face is puffy, her wild hair a pinkish color with white roots. She wears a baggy housecoat, stained with dribbles of food and coffee. "Stop embarrassing yourself. Use the keyboard and ear phones in your own damn room."

Harry seems to know who is addressing him without even glancing over his shoulder. In an even, calm tone he says, "I like this piano. It has a nice touch. It's the one they're going to use for the talent show."

The woman snorts. "That leaves you out."

Harry resumes his piano playing as if he doesn't hear her.

Incensed, she raises her voice. "I'm going to complain to the management."

Harry drops his hands into his lap and turns to her. "You do that, soup thrower."

"I hate you! I hate you!" the crone screams in frustration. She turns and staggers out of the room.

Harry twists on the piano bench and says sheepishly, "Sorry you had to witness that."

"Soup thrower?" I repeat incredulously.

"Didn't like it, I guess." Harry's comment is so dry, I burst out with a loud guffaw. "No joke for the family. They had to pay for the carpet cleaning."

I shake my head. "That's pathetic!"

Harry slightly lifts one shoulder. "A sad state of affairs. I feel sorry for her."

I look to the door and back to Harry again. "She's my next-door neighbor, I think. I hear her through the walls ranting like a crazy woman. I hope my body goes before my mind does."

"Oh, I don't know. The folks with Alzheimer's can create their own reality, they can time travel, see dead people they've missed for so long. It might be fun."

"And they can be mean, violent. I hear her though the walls ranting to her sons."

"Dottie doesn't have Alzheimer's. She's a drug addict. Opioids."

I shift my feet, wondering if I should speak my mind or let it go. "That's no excuse," I blurt. "It's horrible the way she treated you. You shouldn't have to put up with her verbal abuse. They should kick her out."

"She can't hurt me." Harry returns to his Bach.

After a few more minutes, I quietly slip away without disturbing him.

Relaxing in my recliner that afternoon, I think of Harry, his unwavering patience with his dogged attempts to play music he can't see. I imagine myself seated at the dining room Yamaha, my fingers poised over the cool, firm keys. Of course I'd never play in such an exposed area, but I can fantasize about it. What could I possibly play? The Mozart Fantasy in C Minor, part of it. Schumann's *Scenes from Childhood,* some of them. Sections of Beethoven's Sonata in D Major, Opus 28—how did I possibly remember the Opus number?—which I labored over for an entire school year in preparation for my senior recital.

My mind plays the subject of Harry's Bach C Minor Fugue, and softly I hum along. I rise to my feet, and open the top drawer of my music cabinet. Some musicians organize by era—Baroque, Classical, Romantic, Contemporary—but I prefer the alphabet. Either way, Bach is on top. I open my marked-up score of the C Minor Fugue and trace each subject statement with my finger.

9

As Margaret and I cross the main parking lot on a short afternoon walk, I see Iris getting into a car. Not the passenger's seat, but the driver's seat.

I gaze after her and nudge Margaret with my elbow. "I wish I could do that."

"Do what?"

"Get in a car and drive away."

"Why not? I can."

My head snaps from watching Iris to peering into Margaret's face. "You have a car here?" I ask incredulously.

She laughs. "Well, sure. This isn't a prison."

"It's not?"

Margaret sweeps her arm toward the parking lot. "See all these cars? A lot of residents have them." Her face creases with concern as she watches Iris back out, too fast, too far.

We yell, "No! Stop! Stop! Stop!" knowing it's futile. Iris couldn't hear us if she were seated across us at the bridge table.

Iris plows into the car behind her with a loud scraping of metal. We rush up to her as a staff member dashes out of the building. He's waving his hands in front of her car, as she puts the car in drive and looks as if she's about to run him down.

I sprint toward Iris' car with Margaret trailing. We reach the driver's side of the car, and I knock on the window. "Stop, Iris, stop, stop, stop!"

She fumbles with the buttons on the inside of the car door and is at last able to roll down her window along with the other three.

"Cripes' sake, Iris, you smacked into the car behind you!" Margaret informs her.

"Oh, did I?" Iris presses her fingertips to her mouth. "Oops, I thought I heard something."

"Are you okay?" I ask her.

"Fine, fine." She pats her hair in place, then pulls back into her parking spot and the staff member comes to her aid.

As Margaret and I walk away, I whisper, "I thought I heard something."

"Yeah, finally."

We share a good laugh. "Let's go someplace," I blurt.

"Okay. Where?"

"Uh…"

"For a frozen yogurt?"

"I'm still full from lunch."

"Oh. Then where?"

Escape is on my mind, any escape at all. I'm desperate to get out of Shady Meadow, but can't think of any place to go. "We could go for a drive."

"A drive?" Margaret's mouth hangs open.

I feel ridiculous for suggesting it. Creeping along in traffic for no reason, with the price of gas. "How about the mall?"

"Sure, let's go!" Margaret is delighted to have an excuse to stop walking.

As soon as we arrive, I remember I don't like the mall. The vast, open corridors are nearly void of customers. Half the store fronts are empty. Companies moving into town build massive new stores, leaving the mall a hollowed-out shell. I usually order what I want on Amazon. It's great for gifts. Let someone else hassle with the packaging and the sending. These days people rarely bother to thank you or even acknowledge receipt of a gift, but with shopping online I can at least track a package on my computer to know it's been delivered.

As we pass the Hallmark store, decked out in red and pink for Valentine's Day, Margaret asks, "Need a card?"

"Nope." I rarely buy greeting cards now. They want five, six, seven dollars for a piece of cardboard people don't know what to do with after they've read it once. I use free cards sent to me from charities I don't contribute to, blotting out the Scripture quotes with stickers sent to me from another charity I don't contribute to. Except for the local food pantry and state parks, I've all but given up sending money to charities. If I donate fifty bucks, they'll spend it all begging me for more.

Margaret and I go into Mayfair, a store where I've shopped all my life. "I just remembered. I don't have anything to buy,"

"Oh, you do, too." Margaret shakes her finger at me. "Don't be one of those old people who don't need anything."

"But I am."

"No, you aren't. Old people think they have enough clothes to last them the rest of their lives. What they don't know, or don't notice, is their old clothes are shiny with age, coming apart at the seams, sagging in the butt, stained where they fed their fronts. You don't want to be one of those old people, Colette. Now, go buy something, for cripes' sake."

I have to admit, Margaret has a point. While she wanders into the shoe department, I linger at a table of sweaters on sale. Brooke talked me into giving away all the clothes I haven't worn in over a year because that's what an article on the Internet says to do, and if the Internet says to do it, Brooke does, but now I find I need more variety in my wardrobe living at Shady Meadow.

I hold a sweater up against my front, and it looks like it will fit, but it's tan and I would prefer it in blue. I look around for a sales clerk, but don't see one. I roam through the store and find three young clerks in a huddle, one guy and two girls. The guy is arguing with one girl and the other girl is bent over her phone. All of them look like they slept in the gutter and haven't bothered to brush themselves off before coming to work. Who would have thought the ravaged-by-wild-animals look would be in vogue for two decades? There was a time when styles changed every year, and you would be embarrassed to wear last year's fashions. There was a time when sales clerks had to look presentable. When I had a part-time job in a department store during college, I was expected to dress up and do my hair and makeup. One of the other girls I got friendly with came to work without pantyhose and her bare legs got her fired on the spot.

"I covered for Ron the last time he didn't show for a shift," says the girl minus the phone.

"I'm not staying in this shit hole another shift," says the guy.

"Excuse me," I say, "do you have this sweater in blue?"

"What?" says the guy. He and the girl he's been arguing with look put out that I interrupted them. The girl on the phone lifts her head, glassy-eyed.

"Would you please look in the back to see if you have this sweater in blue?" I ask.

"All we have is out," says phone girl.

"Could you just check?"

The clerks look at each other. "It's on sale," says the guy. "That's all we have."

"Thanks, anyway." I decide to get the sweater in tan because it will go with my brown pants and the sale price is good. I wander further in the store and find a clerk at a register in housewares.

I have strategies for not looking like an old lady fumbling around at the checkout, holding up the line. Before I approach the counter, I check how much cash I have, the bills arranged according to denomination, from ones to twenties. My Visa card is always in the same slot, but I check for it anyway. I rarely save coupons anymore, but I check the fine print and expiration date before I try to use one. I know approximately how much my purchase will cost including tax. That's my prep. What could go wrong?

When the clerk rings up the sweater, she asks me for forty-four dollars and twenty-six cents.

"It's on sale for twenty-five," I say. "There's a big sign on the table where I got it."

The clerk calls on a phone for another clerk to check the price. It takes several minutes. A line is forming behind me. The second clerk is the girl I saw on the phone. "You gotta use your Mayfair credit card to get the sale price," she says.

"The sign doesn't say that." My armpits are getting clammy. The line behind me grows. I hear a deep exhaling of breath behind me.

"I can sign you up for a credit card," says the first clerk.

"I have a Mayfair credit card, but I don't like to get bills in the mail."

"But you need to use it—"

"Never mind," I snap. "I'll pay full price. I don't have to shop here anymore."

"I'll give you the sale price," the clerk says meekly.

"Thank you." Usually I like to offer exact change, but I don't want to appear to be a fumbling old lady counting out coins, even though I already have sounded old and crotchety by haggling over the price and refusing to use my Mayfair credit card. I hand over a ten and a twenty. The clerk stuffs my change into my hand without comment. It's a lost art for a clerk to count back change from the cost of the item to the amount rendered. If the cash register didn't show the change due, the clerk probably wouldn't know how much to return. This is a fact of the modern world. I shouldn't let it irk me, but it does.

I step away from the register with my purchase before counting my change, then place the coins in my coin purse and the bills in correct order in my wallet. I check to see all my credit cards are in place, even though I didn't remove any. I think wearing the new sweater will remind me of this stressful shopping experience.

On the way home, I tell Margaret all about buying the sweater, while she nods her head and says, "Uh-huh, uh-huh," throughout my whole story, which only frustrates me further. I did escape Shady Meadow for a couple of hours, I'll say that.

10

After several days of rain, Margaret and I go out walking during a break in the storms. The sky is an angry mass of puffy bruises, variegated grays, blues, purples, with splotches of white peeking through. High winds have caused large branches, whole trees, power lines to come down. Margaret and I pick our way between puddles. She's shuffling in oversized rainboots and yacking about her kids and grandkids when she abruptly asks me about my divorce.

I take a deep breath and exhale warm air into the chill. She side-glances me. "You don't wanna talk about it?"

"No, no. I don't mind." My divorce seems like ancient history, a previous lifetime. It's been a good while since I've recounted it to anyone. I'd like to be as brief as possible and avoid the grisly details. "Well, for one thing, I didn't see it coming. I thought Al and I were fine. No more sparks, but it was an old marriage. Our daughter was away at college. We got along, we enjoyed our routine, cooking dinners for each other, talking over——"

"He cooked? Murray couldn't boil water. If I left for a couple of days to see the kids, I'd have to pack the freezer with casseroles. Once, you know what he did? He left the freeze open and all the food thawed and spoiled."

"On purpose?" I ask incredulously.

"No, no, not on purpose."

"How do you know for sure? Maybe he was trying to get back at you for leaving him alone."

"No, no, Murray wasn't like that. Unless—" Margaret presses her fingertips against her lower lip. "I never thought of that—unless it was one of those Freudian slip thingies, accidently on purpose." She shuffles headlong into a puddle and splashes muddy water onto my pant leg without noticing. "No, no, he just wouldn't. Never mind. You were saying about Al?"

"Losing the man isn't the half of divorce. It's half of everything—the house, the bank account. Thank God I could afford to keep the house, buy him out."

"I always warned Murray. I always told him, 'You run off with a young girl and I'll chase after you and snip off your balls!'" She straightens two fingers and snaps them together like scissors.

"Tabby was twenty-two years younger than Al." Fierce, old resentments rise up in me like bile, feelings I've put to rest years ago. I didn't expect to be affected like this. Is that what making a new friend means? "Tabby was a real glamour girl, caked on the makeup, false eyelashes, the works. Cleavage like the Grand Canyon!"

Margaret's eyes drop to my bustline. "You have very nice boobs."

I have to laugh. "That's what I think! I just don't let them flap in the wind. No one wants to see that. And Tabby's so dumb! I don't know how Al could have a conversation with her."

"So it was bigger boobs that got him?"

I shrug. "Maybe, partly. I suppose I was too independent. If I was upset about a parent-teacher conference, I'd leave my hurt feelings at school. If Brooke was freaking out over a single pimple, I took her to the dermatologist without mentioning it to him. I thought I was doing him a favor. He claimed I had shut him out. Tabby *needed* him. He was her psychiatrist. She had all these problems Al could rush in and fix."

"Do you see him at all, anymore, like at family functions?"

"Oh, no. He's dead. Died three years after he married Tabby."

Margaret halts, looking stricken. "Cancer?"

"Accident."

"Car accident?"

"Skiing." I press her shoulder to get her moving again. "Tabby *needed* him to learn to ski so he could take her. He smacked into a tree during his second lesson."

Margaret throws back her head in one of her braying guffaws, the gold in her molars glinting, a reaction I'm not expecting. "A regular Sonny Bono."

"What? Oh, yeah, that. Going skiing was so out of Al's character. After the funeral, everything he had went to her."

"Nothing for your daughter?"

"Technically, yes. In reality, no. Tabby is the executrix of Al's estate, which is set up to support her until she dies. She's supposed to submit an annual state-of-finances report to Brooke, but she hasn't filed a single one in like thirty years. Brooke will probably never see a single penny." Now I'm mad, my heart racing. "The bitch will go through all Al's money, and when she dies, her three daughters will sell the house she and Al owned together, take the money, and run. That gold brick never worked a day in her life! Doesn't have a clue what the real world is."

Margaret responds with shuffle, shuffle, sandpaper on wood. "Pick up your feet," I want to say. What's the point of rehashing all this now? It does me absolutely no good. I scramble for another topic of discussion. "Any news on the Sam front? Any sightings? Conversations?"

Margaret is silent, her mouth working. She blurts, "She raised three kids. That's work."

"Who? Oh, you mean Tabby. Sure, I raised just one daughter and that was tons of work. I just mean I was in the classroom, years and years, down in the trenches doing hard, hard work, and then Tabby swoops down with her inch-long red nails and snatches away half my pension."

Margaret's feet freeze in place. "After Betty Friedan and *Ms.* Gloria Steinem, we homemakers get no respect at all." I can't tell if she's being sarcastic or not, our friendship is too new. Tense, bumpy wrinkles appear on her brow. "I think I'll turn around here." She about-faces, her shoulders up around her ears, and stomps off, the clasps on her rainboots rattling.

"Margaret, wait!" I call after her. When she ignores me, I jog after her. "Did I offend you? I didn't mean to. I thought we were talking about Tabby. Please, let's finish our walk." When I try to take her arm, she shrugs me off.

"You go on! You're the champion walker, the big career woman." Her retreating shuffle grows faster, causing her to pant. There's nothing to be done now. I let her go.

11

I was watering the brown spots in the lawn one evening after dinner when Al came up behind me and announced, "I'm seeing someone." I looked over my shoulder and noted he wore his constipated expression. That usually meant he didn't think I would go along with what he wanted.

"About what? A contractor for the back bathroom?"

"No, no, a patient." The tension in his withered face didn't go away. He was seventy-one and had grown a little stooped over.

"And he's so screwed up you can't think of a way to treat him?"

"Not he. *She.*" Al crossed his arms, spread his legs in a stance that emphasized his bowed legs. "I'm going to move in with her. I want a divorce."

"Oh. Oh." The first thing I thought: *Now I can read after dinner instead of watch some dumb show with him.* The second thing: *I thought I was the one hanging in there in this marriage.* I had been disappointed that we had stopped having sex about a decade previously, when I was only fifty. Once, when we were in a motel room that had two twin beds pushed together, he dropped his bag on the carpet and, with a scowl, pulled them apart. Toward the beginning of our platonic phase, I tried making a few overtures, but they all fell flat. I suggested a marriage counselor, but Al pooh-poohed the idea. He was a therapist who didn't believe in therapy for himself. He just said he didn't feel like having sex—that's what I get for marrying someone thirteen years my senior—and that was the end of it. This led me to thought number three: "Are you having sex with her?"

"What a question!" Al actually blushed, squirming like a worm on a hook. I rather enjoyed that.

"I'm just curious because you haven't been interested in sex for years. Are you using Viagra?"

"That doesn't concern you."

"It kinda does. Let me guess: She's a youngster in her late forties." Al didn't respond to that. Later, I learned Tabby was forty-one. "Does she think you have money?"

He showed his back to me and stalked away. I turned the hose on him, watching the light blue of his shirt turn navy.

After that, there was the usual drama. One day while I was at school Al came to the house and took his clothes and stuff, including the one good iron skillet we had. I bought a new one. Brooke was in her freshman year at UCLA. She arrived home in a rage, stormed into Al's office, and in front of a patient, chewed him out. She went to Tabby's house and chewed her out. She made Tabby cry. She made Tabby's daughters cry. Brooke said to the kids, "Do you know your mom is a homewrecker? A bitch? A whore?" The little one, Cammy, was only eleven at the time. I don't think she understood those words, but that's how Brooke is. If she thinks someone needs to be told off, she takes care of it.

Once things settled down, my life didn't change that much. I was busy with school, I liked that I had less housework, no meal planning, and little cooking. A bowl of Cheerios and a banana was fine for dinner if I felt like it. My main challenge was filling the hours between dinner and bedtime. The house was too quiet. I grew melancholy. Negative thoughts crowded into my mind, and I couldn't shake them. I turned on the TV just for company, and I don't even like TV that much. I solved the problem by shifting my walks from after school to early in the morning. I started getting up earlier and earlier, which meant bedtime got earlier, too.

I walked alone in the dark. Brooke urged me to carry my cell phone, but I would turn it off while I was teaching and forget to turn it back on. "Mom, you're so bad with your phone," she'd say. They were new enough then that I still thought of them as an intrusion rather than a help. I enjoyed my lonely walks, just me, the black sky, the stars, the moon, an occasional car passing, a dog barking. It was peaceful. I thought of the Frost poem, "Acquainted with the Night." It felt like that, but early in the morning and not at all sad.

Surprisingly, Al and I remained friends. He called every week or so to ask how I was doing, if I needed anything. He'd come by the house if it needed repairs, either fix it himself or call someone in. He kept my car maintenance up-to-date. He'd sit with me sometimes when he came over, and we talked together just like we always had. Once, he started complaining about Tabby. I said, "Oh, no, you don't get to do that." Once, Tabby called, waking me up in the middle of the night, I thought, but then I realized nine o'clock wasn't the middle of the night for most people. When she started complaining about Al, I set the receiver in its cradle, but gently.

I miss Al to this day. I still talk to him and imagine what he would say back. Al wouldn't have stood for me moving into Shady Meadow against my will. He would have found a way for me to remain in my home, I'm certain of it.

12

I have shut the blinds and lie back in my recliner, eyes closed against throbbing pain. Migraine? I don't know; I've never been diagnosed. I've never admitted to migraine. I used to get atrocious headaches rushing around, doing too many errands, trying to finish too much school work, squeezing in too many household chores in a few hours. Now I rush toward nothing and my head hurts anyway.

My mind rakes over and over my last conversation with Margaret. Maybe that's what's giving me this fierce headache. There's been no sign of her these past three days. I don't know if she's avoiding me, or I'm just not in a position to run into her. I could call her, I have her cell number, but she is the one who is mad at me. If she decides to forgive me, she is the one who will call. I wonder if I've lost her for good. I try to tell myself it's just as well. We are too different to be friends. She talks her head off, she repeats her stories, she walks too slow. But my afternoons weigh on me, long and empty. God, I miss her. I'm surprised how dependent I've become on our friendship.

I once had a walking friend named Cheryl. We were both teachers, but in different grades, different school districts. For a couple of years, we walked together nearly every Saturday morning, a long way, six to eight miles. Her daughter Megan went off to med school at the same time Brooke began law school. These daughters of ours are very smart; they appeared strong and capable to everyone around them, but actually they were quaking inside. They reserved their meltdowns for long phone conversations with their moms. Cheryl and I talked and talked to each other about our daughters, and when we confided in each other, our daughters' problems lifted off us like helium-filled balloons. We stopped worrying so much about them and found the humor in their complaints. We laughed and laughed. We said we were each other's psychiatrist, taking the talking, walking therapy.

Like Margaret, Cheryl is a devout Catholic. She uses expressions like, "I've prayed about it," "God is watching over Megan," "Everything is part of God's plan," "God only sends us what we can handle," I suppose, like civil war and earthquakes that kill sixty thousand people at once. I don't pray. I don't talk about God. I'm sure Cheryl noticed this. God might have been the reason she dumped me.

At first, our walks became irregular. I would email her asking if she wanted to walk the following Saturday, and she would have some excuse, and finally she said she didn't have time to go anywhere with me. She had gotten a personal trainer whom she met with three times a week and she had school, and that was all she had time for. I spotted her walking with other women, talking and laughing like we used to. I felt jealous and hurt. Once, out-of-the-blue, she invited me to lunch. She asked me over for a glass of wine for my birthday. She stopped by an open house I hosted around the holidays. Our friendship limped along. It was a friendship that no longer felt like a friendship. Now, all we do is like each other's stuff on Facebook. Really, that's no friendship at all.

I have wondered, I still wonder: What did I do to offended Cheryl? My sharp tongue probably delivered too many barbs. Once she was excited about a new Catholic Church being built in a small town in the Central Valley, Visalia, which cost twenty-three million dollars and would seat three thousand people. I said, "Oh, I didn't realize there were three thousand Catholics left in this world." She replied, "The Church is growing all the time, especially in Africa and Latin America," and while I should have shut up at that point, I couldn't resist countering, "Oh, the places in the world where there's already a lot of superstition." She just looked at me.

I think Cheryl distanced herself from me because the faithful are uncomfortable around the unfaithful, as if a loss of faith can rub off on them. Or maybe it's this: The faithful don't believe the unfaithful completely understand them and so therefore they can't fully relate to them.

I wonder if it's the same with the Women's Movement. Margaret can't be my friend because she doesn't believe the Women's Movement respects her as a homemaker. I wish I could convince her that without the Women's Movement, there's no respect for women at all.

I know I have my own prejudices. When I encounter a Trumper, I see red! How could anyone support such an ignorant, lying criminal? I find I can't stand it! I find myself fantasizing heated, angry conversations with Trump supporters or defacing their lawn signs and getting arrested for it. It's the same with COVID-19 anti-vaxers, especially those in the medical profession who should know better. Worse are the anti-vaxers against all vaccines. Thank you very much, Robert F. Kennedy, Jr. We had all but eradicated polio, and now it's back. Even if I like—love in the instance of my grandson Carter—a Trumper or an anti-vaxer, I can't help but resent them, and therefore only have casual conversations with them or avoid them completely. I wish I were a bigger person than this, but it happens that I'm not.

There's a soft knock on the door. Marisol is due. I've gotten to know her a little. She has told me about her three small children, her gratitude for their being admitted into the U.S. after Typhoon Rai hit Siargao and left her house a pile of sticks. I love to hear her soft, sweet singing voice. But right now any sound at all will exacerbate my misery.

My door creaks open. I peer through fluttering lashes, pinpoints of light exploding before my eyes, waves of crushing pain like the sea against the craggy shore. I manage to speak in a croaking whisper, "Not now, Marisol. Please." I close my eyes again, press my fingertips against my pulsing temples. My heavy arms flop into my lap. My head lolls to one side.

Silence. Darkness. Pain.

Someone is removing my moccasins with the touch of a feather. Have I passed out? Have I been moved to an infirmary? Hospital?

Strong, firm hands grasp my feet. Thumbs press into the flesh of my big toes, draw circles. Pause. Draw circles. Pause. Draw circles. The pounding in my head weakens, recedes. Someone has come to my rescue. Someone is taking care of me.

I lift my heavy lids and peer through slits. It is Marisol, clutching my foot, miraculously massaging away the pain in my head. I recall the first time she came into my room. With rumors of a killer whirling about, I was actually wary of her. Marisol is no "snuffer-outer," to use Margaret's terminology; she is my healer.

13

By morning my headache has vanished, but I'm listless and lack energy. I rise out of bed, use the bathroom, and wash the sleep out of my eyes, then plop down in my recliner to think what I want to wear to the dining room. Getting dressed and looking presentable just for a cup of coffee—such a bother. Before I can make any decisions, Margaret arrives at my door dressed in her fuchsia Lululemons, an exposed, doughy muffin top between her bottoms and crop top, which can only mean one thing. "Come on, girl, get dressed! Time for class."

"Yoga class?" I groan, but I'm thrilled to see my friend. First things first, I feel the need to clear the air between us. "I'm sorry if I said anything to offend you on our walk the other day. I just meant—"

"Come on, come on, get dressed." She pushes her way into my room and waits, hands on hips. "We can't be late. You know little it-ty-bitty Athena just hates that, claims we'll hurt ourselves if we don't warm up properly."

I rifle through my drawer for clean leggings and a stretchy top. "I don't believe that's her real name, do you?"

"It's Jenna. Jenna Smith."

I catch Margaret's eyes in my mirror and grin. "How do you know this stuff?"

"I have my ways." Margaret guffaws so exuberantly that she farts. "Oops. Didn't feel that one coming."

"I have that problem, too," I admit. "Farts just sneak up and out when I least expect them."

Walking down the hall toward the workout rooms, Margaret takes my arm and tucks it under her elbow. I'm a little embarrassed to touch her bare skin, but appreciative of the affection. How I have missed her!

"You'll never guess," she gushes. "Sam and I went on a date, well sort of a date."

"Sort of?"

"Well, yeah. He and the guys were playing pickleball doubles, and I was just hanging around the courts hoping to get a chance to talk to him, running after stray balls, handing out towels, refilling water bottles, you know, making myself useful, and when the guys were done playing, Sam asked me to come along with them to the patio bar for a beer."

"Just you and Sam and three other guys?"

"Well, yeah." Margaret looks up at me, blinking hard. "You're saying it doesn't really count as a date?"

"Sure, it does! Much better than you, Sam, and three other girls." I raise my eyebrows and open my eyes wide. "This Sam better watch out. One of those other guys will grab you up."

Margaret shakes her head. "Don't want any of 'em. One guy can barely walk, another one can't see, and the other one can't remember one minute to the next. He was looking all over for his cap, and it was on his head."

I'm tempted to ask if the guy who can't see is Harry, but for some reason I hold back.

Margaret leans into me so that I can smell her Warm Vanilla Sugar body lotion. "News flash: we have a celebrity among us," she announces in a hushed tone.

"Oh?" I'm not readily impressed. Some of Margaret's Shady Meadow gossip is hearsay and hyperbole. "An actress?"

"Susan Hartley."

"The author Susan Hartley? It can't be! Must be a different Susan Hartley."

"Nope, nope. I recognized her at dinner last night. She's aged some since her Wiki photo, but it's her alright."

"No kidding!" I wave my splayed fingers in excitement. "She's one of my favorites!"

"Me, too."

"I must've read a dozen of her novels."

"Me, too."

That's one thing Margaret and I do have in common: we're both readers. Susan Hartley writes quiet novels about ordinary people just trying to get by, encased in astounding prose. I used to be thrilled every time a new Hartley novel was released, couldn't wait to read it. "I can't remember the last novel of hers I've read. It's been a while. I suppose she stopped writing years ago."

"Nope. She has a new novel this year."

"She does? What's the title?"

"Feathers something. Can't remember exactly, but it's on my Goodreads Want-to-Read list."

"I'll look it up on Amazon." We've arrived at Studio B, the yoga class just beginning, which puts an end to our conversation. I still can't believe a Pulitzer-prize-winning author lives among us at Shady Meadow. I'd be thrilled to meet her.

$$14$$

A man is out in the rose garden hunched over a bush, a giant among the plaster gnomes. He's not one of the gardeners. He almost looks like…. I lean forward, nearly bumping my nose against the glass. It's Harry! He's picking the roses? Is that allowed? If it were, then all the roses would be in vases in the residents' rooms and none on the bushes. It's probably *not* allowed. Oh no, I don't want Harry to get into trouble.

I stick my arms into the sleeves of my new tan sweater I have draped over my shoulders and exit through the French doors leading to the patio. As I cross the lawn, the morning dew soaks my penny loafers. Up close, I see that Harry is snipping off dead, withered blooms with pruning shears. He looks up as I approach.

"I thought you were picking the roses."

"These tiny buds? No, just deadheading. It seems the gardeners never get around to it. Poor roses."

When I was a girl, my dad gave me that same chore. I would let the spent blooms fall on the ground, but Harry is collecting them in a paper bag. "Deadheading—I didn't know it had a name."

"Yep. Same as following The Grateful Dead around the country." He straightens to smile at me. "Pretty day, isn't it?"

"Yes." The grass and shrubbery are emerald green from the recent rains. The white blossoms of nearby almond trees drift in the gentle breeze like falling snow. "I never got too excited about The

Dead," I admit. "Too disorganized. Their songs seem to go on and on without going anywhere."

Harry chuckles. "Too much weed. They did enjoy themselves performing. It was infectious. I saw them a few times at the Filmore back in the day." He snips a deadhead and it plops into his paper bag. "Beatles or Stones?"

"Beatles, of course."

"Why of course?" Harry hooks an eyebrow at me beneath his houndstooth driving cap. His stare is so penetrating it makes me slightly uncomfortable. I realize I don't know how much he *can* see. I've seen photos of how some people with AMD have to peer around black, quarter-sized splotches before their eyes. His glasses have turned dark in the sunlight so I can't read his expression, but dark glasses makes an old person look younger. I'd like to take the shears to that wiry white hair spilling out of his shirt. I realize I've been staring while he's waiting for me to reply.

"The Beatles had better songs. They were better singers."

"Remember their first appearance on the *Ed Sullivan Show*? They looked like prep school boys in need of a barber. The Stones were sexy."

I raise my upper lip. "Mick Jager prancing around stage looked like a rooster."

Harry laughs with a quick shake of his head. "Joni or Judy?"

"Oh, that one's harder. Judy has the better voice, but Joni has better songs."

"Which Judy got rich on."

"Yes. 'Both Sides Now' and 'Circle Game.' I read that Joni resented that."

"Judy became quite the songwriter herself late in life."

"Oh? I didn't know that."

Harry gives me another long gaze. "Remember our conversation about dementia? Later that day I got to thinking you should hear Judy's song 'In the Twilight,' about her mother's Alzheimer's."

He's been thinking about me? I've been thinking about him. "I'll have to look for it on YouTube."

"I own the CD. Would you like to hear it?"

I cross my arms and hug myself against the breeze that has picked up, or is it a gesture of self-defense? I rock back on my heels. "Sure, when?"

"No time better than the present."

"What about the roses?"

"The deadheads will always be with us." He extends his hand. "Harry, by the way."

"Colette." When we shake hands, he gently squeezes my fingers, and I feel a tiny charge.

"Pretty name."

"Is it? My mother was French. I felt the odd girl out, the only Colette among all the Kathys and Lindas."

"I was Harry among all the Mikes and Johnnies. Named after some great uncle I never knew and got teased a lot." We walk toward a wing of the main building I've never been to. He leads me down a hall and unlocks a door. He extends an arm to invite me to pass ahead of him.

I stand at the entrance and look around. "Wow, oh wow." Harry has a whole apartment. His living room holds two recliners, a sofa, a Yamaha Clavinova digital piano, and a music cabinet, just like mine only in ebony. There's a full kitchen and small dining area. Light floods in from a sliding glass door leading to a tiny private patio. I peer around an open door to find a spacious bedroom and bath.

"This is really living," I exclaim. "I just have one room."

"Oh, you're over in assisted living." He rolls his eyes upward. "Dottie's neighbor, I remember you telling me."

"Right." I'm embarrassed by the term, as if I'm a helpless invalid. Harry invites me to sit on the sofa and hands me the jewel case of *Bohemian*. He peers at the CD through his magnifying glass to find the right track. Judy Collins begins to sing about her mother, who barely knows her name in the twilight of her life. She drank Chardonnay and once met Rachmaninoff. She danced with her blind husband and voted for Obama. The song transports me to a soft, dreamy place.

"That was lovely. Thank you for sharing." I nod toward his instrument. "How is your Bach fugue coming?"

"I'll show you what I've got so far." He sits at his Clavinova. It has weighed keys and sounds close to a piano, but it isn't quite the real thing. I would never have one, but I suppose it's good if you have to live in a place with shared walls. Harry leans forward, his face up against the music. He plays in fits and starts, sometimes pausing to study the notes before playing a few more measures. He's quite musical if he could just recognize the notes fast enough to play them in time. He makes it haltingly to the end, twists on his bench, and looks toward me for an opinion.

I don't know what to say. I don't think he can possibly have it ready for the talent show only a few months away, but I want to be encouraging. "You're getting the notes."

"Yes, it's coming along, but I've got a lot more work to do."

"You're doing better than me." I hold up my hands, the fingers gnarled and bent, joints bulging with bone spurs. I try to curl my hand closed. "I can't even make a fist."

"Arthritis? That shouldn't stop you from playing."

"Are you kidding? My fingers are as agile as dried twigs."

"All the more reason to play. Motion is lotion. The exercise will limber things up."

"You think so?" I open and close my hand, grasping air.

He dips his head and chuckles, "But, I'm afraid your guitar-playing days are over."

The comment startles me. How does he know my ardent wish as a teen was to be the next Joan Baez?

"You could take up the trumpet," he suggests playfully.

"I already tried that! In middle school! Blowing into a piece of metal pressed hard against my mouth didn't do much for me.

I much prefer producing sound by touch." I let my hands flutter, playing air piano.

"You seem to know a lot about music."

"I was a piano major. Loved it! Alas, talent skipped a generation in my family. My mother was a composer and my daughter was a wonderful violinist until the day she announced, 'Mom, music is your and Grandmere's thing.' She went on to become a corporate lawyer. Were you a music major in college?"

He removes his highly magnified reading glasses and looks at me with crystal blue eyes with dark irises. "There were five boys in my family and no money for college. I took a few years of piano lessons as a kid from a kind, old church lady who didn't know much herself. As an adult, I had a terrific teacher who taught part-time at City College."

"What did you do for a living?"

"Worked in ag. Water controller."

"Did you like it?"

"Never thought to like or dislike it. It was a job. Back in the day, you just felt lucky to have a job." He jumps up from his instrument and claps his hands. "Are you hungry, Colette? I can whip up some lunch."

He's full of surprises. I glance over at the kitchen and back at him. "Well, sure. If it isn't too much trouble."

"No trouble at all." He seems happy to have me around. He offers his hand to help pull me up from the sofa. "Come keep me company."

I sit on a stool at his counter to watch him work. He takes out a pot, fills it with water, and sets it on the stove. From the refrigerator he removes an armful of salad fixings and a jar of pesto sauce. He pulls out linguini from an upper cupboard. He moves about his kitchen seemingly with no hindrance due to his poor vision.

"No glasses?" I note.

"I don't wear them much in the house. They're tinted now from wearing them outdoors, so for close-up I can see better without them. Distance and detail are what I can't see. Wine?"

I know wine in the middle of the day will cause me to nap in the afternoon, but what else do I have to do? "Sure, if you're having some."

"Why not? At our age, every day is a celebration is what I say." From a small wine rack on the counter, he selects a bottle of red and uncorks it with a satisfying pop. He tears lettuce leaves and sets them in a colander, then washes and dices a tomato.

"You look like you know what you're doing."

"I like to cook. My wife did all the cooking when our three boys were growing up. She insisted on the four food groups every meal, the family eating together at the table every night, the whole nine yards. But when the kids were gone, she threw up her hands and gave it all up. She wanted to go out to eat or take in fast food. I went along with it for a while, but I started gaining weight and just didn't feel good. I let her have her fast food and started cooking for myself."

"My ex-husband did the grilling, and he made fabulous coffee. Ground his own beans. The smell of it got me out of bed in the morning."

Harry sets the table and serves the meal. It's lovely to dine in such peaceful surroundings, without the din and confusion and certain unwanted company in the dining room. Here I am eating food prepared by a man in his private apartment. Drinking wine at lunch! When Harry raises the bottle over my glass a second time and hooks an eyebrow at me, I nod in acquiescence.

"Harry, why are you here? Is it your vision?"

"Oh, no." He right shoulder tenses. "My wife wanted to live here. She picked out this apartment. She said she was done with keeping house, even though by then I did most of the cleaning."

I pan the room, searching for evidence of a woman. "Your wife?"

He shakes his head, looking down at his plate. "Gone."

"Oh, Harry, I'm sorry!"

"Don't be." He looks in the distance out the sliding glass door and then back at me. "We hadn't been getting along for years. When we lived at the house, we could avoid each other, but this here is pretty close quarters. She'd go on rants, start swinging her fists." He mimics at high-pitched voice, "I hate you, I hate you, I can't stand to live with you!"

"How awful. Was it dementia?"

"Oh, no. She was quite clear-headed."

We laugh together about what isn't funny. The wine makes me bold. "What did you do to make her so mad?"

He raises his shoulders and lets them drop. "Exist, as far as I could tell."

"Did you cheat?"

"God, no." He takes a swig of wine. "Too complicated. Too messy. I am not a good liar. What you see is what you get."

I nod. I have every reason to believe him, but there's always two sides to every story. "I know how rough marriage can be over the long haul. After twenty-five years, my husband up and left me."

Harry looks intently at me from across the small table, his blue eyes probing. "He must have been crazy."

The obvious gesture of flirting causes a flood of emotions within me. Embarrassment and pleasure, wariness and appreciation. My cardigan is suddenly too warm. I can't hold his gaze. I turn to look out at his patio and change the subject. "You've got such a nice place. I can't even tell you live in an old folks' home."

He laughs. "It's like a resort, a forever vacation!"

"That's how my friend Margaret feels. Oh, you know Margaret Walsh?"

He grins. "Everyone around here knows Margaret."

"Well, I came here kicking and screaming. I'd planned to die in the privacy of my own home, but then my daughter and my doctor ganged up on me, and here I am."

"Give yourself a chance to get settled in. Maybe the place will grow on you, lots to do, friendly people." He reaches across the table and pats my arm. I feel another charge of electricity. I barely know this guy. Why should he have such an effect on me? It can't just be about Bach.

A few minutes later, I make my exit. "I must be going. Thank you for lunch."

"Thank you for the lovely company. I'll get to work on the Bach so I'll have more to show you next time."

Next time. I avert his inviting gaze. He walks me to the door, and places a broad hand against my shoulder blade. It is warm and strong and awakens my old, tired body.

15

I thought when I got back to my room, I'd lie on my bed and sleep off the wine, but no, I'm too excited to sleep. I'm aroused. I have to admit, at least to myself—definitely not to Margaret or anyone else—that I have a romantic interest, when I didn't go looking for one nor expect to ever have one again.

When Al left, I tried the dating scene. A lot of guys I met just wanted to whine about how their ex-wives had wronged them. I was curious to see what sex would be like again, but soon found out if I'm not emotionally involved, there's not much satisfaction in it. I began making excuses when friends tried to set me up, and I scoffed at online dating. I realized I'd rather stay home with a good book.

Sheridan was different. He was the manager of a small but capable community orchestra in the Bay Area. He called me out of the blue with an interest in programming one of my mother's four symphonies. By then, she had been dead over twenty years. He wanted my opinion on which would be the best choice and my permission to perform it. "Next time you're in the city," he said, "let's have lunch."

This was the jolt I needed to get out of the house and into the car heading down Highway 80 to San Francisco. Sheridan had a wide face with a closely-cropped reddish grey beard and crinkly eyes. He had a teddy bear physique and wore a blocky navy suit and a polka-dot tie, which I found nerdy, but looking across the table at him for over an hour, he became appealing, even handsome. After lunch—Dutch treat, him explaining that he didn't have an expense account—we went for a walk in Golden Gate Park. We talked and talked. He knew a lot about my mother's music, more than I did, asking me questions I didn't have answers to. I was only six or seven when she was at the peak of her career. I didn't understand what a Pulitzer Prize was nor what the excitement was all about.

Long story short, we hit it off. Sheridan came up to Sacramento to visit me; I went down to the Bay Area to visit him. He lived in a tiny rented bungalow behind a mansion in Atherton, which I never stepped foot in. He claimed it was a bachelor's pad, and he was embarrassed by its disarray. It crossed my mind he could have a wife hidden away in there. No kids, though. It was too small. He told me he was divorced and had two grown sons.

It wasn't long before he was spending weekends at my house. He was a fabulous cook. He would dictate a shopping list to me over the phone for the following weekend. We would cook together, drink wine, and listen and listen to music, mostly on LPs from the vast collection I had inherited from my mother. Sex with Sheridan didn't send up fireworks; it was more like getting wrapped in a patchwork quilt a grandma made. Cozy, comforting, what I needed at the time.

Together, Sheridan and I poured over my mother's manuscripts, many of them in her own hand, still unpublished. I confessed to him I suffered the burden of guilt that my mother's music would be forgotten and it was all my fault because I had done nothing to promote it.

He batted the air and said, "Don't worry your dear head about it. Your mother can rely on her own genius. Even Bach was forgotten for a good hundred years before Mendelssohn revived him. Florence Price died in fifty-three, and it's only now she's making a comeback."

"Who?" I asked, leaning into him.

"Florence Price. The first African-American woman to compose a symphony performed by a major orchestra. In the coming years, she'll be huge. She'll be performed all over the world," he predicted correctly.

I can't say I was in love with Sheridan, but his presence in my life buoyed me up. I was happy. I found myself thinking less and less of Al. I can even say I was glad he had divorced me. Sheridan and I agreed to share expenses on a trip to Europe. I hadn't been since I was a mere girl of twenty-one, and although I begged Al to take me on a European tour several times over the years, he had always refused me. Sheridan said we could meet with various musical directors and encourage them to program my mother's music, making the trip a tax write-off for us both. I contacted a travel agent as was customary in those days, and before long she returned my call with an itinerary of plane, train, hotel, and restaurant reservations, and I made the necessary deposits. When I reported this to Sheridan, he assured me he had some money coming in and would pay me back soon. Besides the small orchestra, he managed several classical musicians: a semi-famous string quartet, a soprano, and several pianists.

As time went on, I began to mistrust Sheridan and my own judge of character. He seemed too good to be true. What was he hiding in that little bungalow I never gained entry to? He name-dropped so profusely I began to suspect he was a phony. This was before you could simply Google a name, but I did do a little investigating. I was a member of Friends of the Sacramento Symphony, and at one of our functions, I asked a guest conductor from the Vienna Philharmonic if he had heard of him.

"Oh, yes, I know him. Quite the talent agent and music promoter, very well-connected." The conductor leaned into me so that I could smell his cologne, laced with perspiration. "Just make sure your credit card is well-secured when he comes around."

We laughed together. I assumed the conductor meant Sheridan was always trying to raise funds for his orchestra. I assumed wrong. When the next payment was due to the travel agent, I mentioned it to Sheridan over dinner. He patted his mouth with her napkin and said, "Colette dear, this is so embarrassing, but those funds I've been expecting haven't come in. Could you possibly loan me the money for my share of the trip, and I'll pay you back in the coming weeks?"

I had the money, plenty to go around. I was still teaching school, the house was paid for, and Al was putting Brooke through college. What else was there for me to spend my money on? I was so excited about our European adventure, I didn't want to cancel just because Sheridan was having a bit of a cash flow problem. "Of course," I replied, forcing graciousness into my tone.

"Thank you, my darling. Cheers." He clinked my glass with his, containing wine I had paid for.

I tried not to let Sheridan's financial problems bother me. After all, managing Classical musicians was a hit or miss way of making a living, and what a service he was doing for the musical world. But supposing he was never able to pay me back? I confided in my best college friend Karen. She replied, "Sure, go for it. You've got the money, and you've been dying to get back to Europe. Do what makes you happy."

For a while I thought that was what I'd do. One night, however, I lurched awake and bolted upright in my bed. "Oh, hell no!" I shouted in the dark.

I called Sheridan and told him the trip was off. I lied, saying I couldn't afford to pay for us both.

He acted very understanding, even apologetic about his finances. Our relationship limped along, but we got together less frequently. It began to irk me that I paid for all the food and wine we consumed. He never took me anywhere unless he had complimentary tickets. Mooch, freeloader, gigolo, kept man—all these terms swirled in my mind, and what did that make me? A fool, a victim, a desperate middle-aged woman who had to pay for a man's attention?

Plans for his orchestra to perform my mother's third symphony fell through, as these things often do. What of it? Mother was dead and wouldn't know if her music survived her or not. Was it my responsibility to promote it? Maybe. I've suffered guilt over this, and

I still do. I wondered if Sheridan took my mother off the program because I wasn't willing to pay his way to Europe. Did he know all along he wouldn't be able to afford the trip and had allowed me to make all the arrangements thinking I would pay his way because I wanted to go so badly? I had no way of knowing, but I began to resent him, to hate him even. The last time he called, I simply replaced the receiver in its cradle without a word. I didn't learn of his death until three years after the fact.

That was that. My last big fling. Now Harry arrives on my doorstep. Spending time with him today was quite pleasant, but when I look up at the ceiling, there's a stop sign looming. Don't get your hopes up, don't get involved. You know counting on a man usually leads to messy circumstances, disappointment, regret. Who needs a Santa Claus hanging around? Certainly, not me.

16

I round the corner to the sunroom, and there she is, sitting on a flowered cushion looking out at the lawn like any other Shady Meadow resident. I recognize her because I saw Susan Hartley read at Black Oak Books in Berkeley decades ago. I was so moved by the reading I nearly drove off the freeway on my way back to San Jose. The author is tall and big—not fat, big—with a broad jaw. Her rusty-red hair has turned pink with age or dye.

I hesitate. I nearly panic, almost turn and scurry away. Maybe I should wait and meet her with Margaret, who most certainly would keep the conversation going. A fan-celebrity relationship is so awkward. I recall my meeting with the author at her reading. When it was my turn in the long line to have my book signed, I babbled, "I buy your novels for birthday presents," and she replied, "Well, then, let's hope there are lots of birthdays." I felt really dumb. Now I still don't know what to say. I won't resort to the weather, that's for sure.

The author swivels her head on a seemingly stiff neck and smiles at me. "I could look at the budding branches all day."

"Spring is on its way, but it's still plenty cool in the morning, isn't it?" I chirp. Timidly, I slide into an adjacent chair. "I'm Colette."

She doesn't exactly ignore my extended hand; she doesn't seem to notice it. "I'm Susie Beck."

Is that a maiden name? A married name? A name she uses in her private life? She doesn't look like a Susie to me. I forge ahead. "I just love your books!"

Her eyebrows rise above her glasses. She seems delighted to be recognized. "Do you? What's your favorite?"

For a moment, my mind goes blank. I can't recall a single Susan Hartley title. "*Breathing Lessons*," I blurt.

Her mouth presses into a thin line, the corners slightly turned up in a wry expression. "That is a lovely book. Not her best, but I suppose the Pulitzer is sometimes handed out as a sort of lifetime achievement. *Accidental Tourist, Saint Maybe, A Spool of Blue Thread*—those are my favorites."

A slow burn rises from my nape making my sweater too warm. "Oh! I'm so sorry!"

"No worries. I've often been confused with Anne Tyler. Jane Smiley, too. Good company."

I'm racking my brain. Oh, why didn't I do my homework on the Internet for such a chance meeting? Snow, something about snow, foot prints, no, footsteps. "I loved *Footsteps in the Snow*." I can't recall any of the characters' names. "The choice the young man has to make at the end, such a moral dilemma."

Susan shakes her head tersely and looks at the carpet. "Not my best really."

I manage to drag a few more titles out of my memory. "The homeless guy in *Rambling Summer*—your characters are so sympathetic, so…uh…complex!"

The author looks at me hard as if I have said something to upset her. "Vagabond, I like to think of him."

"Oh, okay, the vagabond, and the mom in *The Remodel Disaster*. I like how you find the humor in the tragic."

"Near misses, both." She contemplates her hands, laden with rings, silver and gold bands of various widths. Her right ring finger has a diamond set in a gold heart, her right pinky bears a blue stone and insignia that looks like an age-worn class ring, a large opal in an antique gold setting is looped over her left thumb, a bright square emerald sets on her left forefinger, all in need of a serious cleaning. She murmurs, seemingly more to herself than to me, "I set my sights on writing the great American novel and fell short."

"Oh, I disagree!" I exclaim, slapping my lap.

Susan stares into the yard again, seemingly lost in the moment, as if she's forgotten my presence. Her tone is distant and forlorn. "I was fearless in the beginning, certain I was a great talent. I thought I'd set the literary world on its ear." She looks back at me, draws in a deep breath so that I see her chest heave. "Now I don't matter at all."

"That's not true! Your books are wonderful!"

Susan bends over to rummage in the large bag decorated with needlepoint kittens resting at her feet. She withdraws a spiral-bound notebook and a pen. "That's a rather good line. I might be able to use it." She writes in a large loopy hand, "Now, I don't matter at all."

"Oh! You still write?"

Her head snaps up, her wide eyes boring into me. "What else would I do? By the way, I'm Susan Hartley."

I'm confused. Could it be that she uses Susie Beck to go incognito, and Susan Hartley to her devoted readers? Abruptly, she stands and starts to leave.

"Oh, your bag!" I call after her. "You forgot your bag!"

Susan looks back, her brow furrowed. "That isn't mine."

"Yes, it is. You put your notebook into it."

"I did?" She smiles broadly. "My mind is elsewhere. My husband always said that about me." She picks up her kitty bag and saunters off.

As I walk back to my room, I bump the heel of my hand against my brow. I can't believe how I blew it! I had the chance to tell Susan Hartley how much I love her novels, and all I could come up with was an Anne Tyler title! I open my laptop for a Google search. Hartley has written twenty-four novels, one published last fall, many

I haven't heard of. When did I stop reading her? Wikipedia says her first husband was named Beck. She's had two more husbands since, divorced now. No children. I navigate to Amazon and order her latest novel, *The Thing with Feathers.*

17

Out to lunch with Brooke the following Saturday, I wonder how I can express myself with an original statement, but decide to quote Margaret instead. "We have a celebrity among us."

"Hmm?" Brooke is pecking away at her phone, and I'm sure my comment hasn't registered. The restaurant is crowded and noisy. We had to wait forty-five minutes to get seated. I suggested we go someplace else, but this place serves her favorite pumpkin soup.

"Susan Hartley!" I blurt. I bite into a sweet potato fry, a treat I wouldn't get at Shady Meadow.

Brooke looks up, her eyes unfocused, like she is still looking at what's on her phone. "Sorry. What's that, Mom?"

"Susan Hartley lives at Shady Meadow. I met her." Brooke crushes her eyebrows together, and I exclaim, "The author!"

Brooke's face blooms into a broad smile. "Oh! I just loved *A Thousand Acres.*"

"That's Jane Smiley. Here's Susan's latest." I hold up my shiny new hardcover copy of *The Thing with Feathers.*

"That's hope. That's Emily Dickinson." Brooke tastes a spoonful of her pumpkin soup. "Damn, this soup is lukewarm. I like hot food." She puts down her spoon to scroll through her phone some more.

"It was hot when it was served," I say, allowing my frustration to harden my tone. "You've been on your phone ten minutes!"

"You're exaggerating, Mom. You always exaggerate." Reluctantly, she clicks her phone closed and takes up her spoon again. I'm certain she has lost interest in our topic of conversation, but then she says, "Don't you think it's cheating to use someone else's poetry as a title?"

"Oh, I don't know. You can't top *I Know Why the Caged Bird Sings.*"

"Right. The book is more famous than the poem. Maya Angelou is more famous than the poet."

"Do you know the original poem? Who wrote it?"

Brooke plunges into her phone to Google the information while I imagine discussing Susan's new novel with her, an exclusive book club of two, just me and the author, but I realize I better ask Margaret along. She was the one who had to remind me that Dwayne, the elderly man in *A Thing with Feathers*, is the baby abandoned in a McDonald's ball pit by the homeless guy—the vagabond Teddy—in *Rambling Summer,* who was raised by Fay in *Remodel Disaster,* the same Dwayne in *Footsteps in the Snow* who enjoys a notorious law career in which he gets off a celebrity chef guilty of poisoning a series of restaurant reviewers. I was in awe of Margaret's memory for detail and told her so. She tapped her temple with her forefinger and said a bit boastfully, "Like a steel trap." In the opening of *A Thing with Feathers,* Dwayne suffers a crisis of conscience, gives away all his wealth, and becomes homeless—a vagabond—like Teddy, who may or may not be his biological father; this is never clear. I notice my bookmark close to the beginning of the novel. I've had it for a few days, but when I try to read it my mind wanders or I doze off. Either Susan Hartley doesn't write as well as she used to or I can no longer comprehend profound literature.

Brooke lifts her head from her phone. "'Sympathy.' Paul Laurence Dunbar."

"Oh, that's a Florence Price song, too. What do you hear from Carter?"

She frowns. "Nothing unless I call him."

"When I call him, he doesn't pick up. When I text, he returns with a thumbs up or American flag emoji. The most I can get out of him is 'Hi, Gram.' What happened to our boy?"

Brooke raises her eyes to the ceiling. "Q happened. Q and Trump."

"Is he still in D.C. working for that Patriots for Freedom thing?"

Brooke pushes away her soup bowl and lifts her fork to stab her salad. "More like volunteering. How could he get a job with the shit degree he has?"

"It's not a shit degree. A BA in Digital Game Design is highly marketable."

"Oh? Is that why he's never gotten a decent-paying job?"

"He went to college to pursue his passion." I think of my degree in music which I never used and add, "I believe college is the one chance you get in life to be completely absorbed in the subject you're most passionate about."

"Oh?" Brooke flips her long hair over her shoulder in irritation. "I think it's to find a way to make a living."

"I've always wondered, Brooke. What is your greatest passion? Certainly not the law."

She shrugs with one shoulder. "It's worked out for me, for the both of us," referring to her husband Jonathan, the least passionate person I know.

I feel the need to further defend my grandson's choice of study. "Carter learned to code, to create software. That's useful for any number of occupations."

"Yep, and then he logged on to a computer and fell into a deep, black hole. He's lucky he's not in prison, doing time like all those other insurrectionists."

"He's not stupid. He was sensible enough not to spew selfies all over the Internet of breaking and entering the Capitol."

Brooke rolls her eyes up at me. "The last time we spoke, he told me the White House is harvesting children for their adrenochrome to rejuvenate Biden. How sensible is that?"

I lean in on my elbows. "If that's the case, then it's not working."

We laugh together, even though none of this is funny. Our dear, smart, funny boy is lost to us. Only humans and whales go through menopause. The survival of these species depend on the grannies to help the young moms raise the kids. Now that Carter has drifted far from the pod, I can't think of a single way to grandmother him back.

After our meal, I prepare to leave by checking the table for my belongings and discover my reading glasses and phone are already tucked away in my purse. I stash my paper napkin in the outside pocket.

"Mom! Don't tell me you've started hoarding used napkins."

"It isn't used. It's perfectly clean. You never know when you might have to wipe up a spill or have a good blow." I look pointedly across the table at my daughter. "I could spit on it and dab the pumpkin soup off your face."

Her eyes grow wide as she swipes at the right corner of her mouth.

"Other side."

She scrubs some more.

I cock my head and look upward. "Now it's gone up your nostril."

With shaking fingers, she extracts a compact mirror from her purse and inspects her perfectly clean face. "Mom!"

I offer up a faux sweet smile.

I'm trying to read *The Thing with Feathers* in the large community room referred to as the library. It's a pleasant room with a fireplace, two overstuffed sofas facing each other, and a coffee table, which always bears a large arrangement of fresh cut flowers. Two whole walls are lined with shelves filled with a mishmash of books. Residents are encouraged to leave books or take them. I love the idea. I enjoy strolling along the shelves reading titles on spines, even though many of them bear the names of authors I don't read—Danielle Steel, Nora Roberts, James Paterson, Nicholas Sparks—and topics I don't read about—Self Help, Dieting, Religion, Money. One day, I'd like to come in here and organize the books, fiction arranged by author in alphabetical order and nonfiction by topic.

I'm distracted by a man and his teen visitor. The girl's thumbs fly over her phone, and she shows him a video with annoying, mechanical music. She shrieks with delight and he opens his mouth in a braying laugh, which I recognize erupting from the bar, if I happen to be passing it the hour before dinner. He has long incisors and big jug ears, reminding me of the bad boys in *Pinocchio* as they are about to turn into donkeys. I've seen the guy around, but don't know his name.

I read the same sentence three times. I mouth the words, then speak them aloud in a low, murmuring whisper. Another loud video comes on. The girl shrieks, throws back her head, and straightens her legs. Her jeans are of the attacked-by-wild-animals style. She has pink strands of hair, a nose ring, and checkmarks at the ends of her eyeliner like Barbra Streisand's in the sixties.

I could retreat to a quieter reading space, but I'm drawn to the girl for the same reason I watch women's college basketball. All that beautiful hair caught up in ponytails and braids, the flash of lean, muscular legs, the vibrancy of the players running up and down the court. I miss being around young people. I like listening to this girl's high-pitched voice and bubbly chatter. I admire her smooth, firm skin, her skinny little body, such gifts of nature, while most young women can only beat themselves up over self-perceived flaws. After a time, the girl kisses the man's grizzled jowl and departs with a flutter of fingers and a grin.

"Bye, Jennifer," he calls after her.

I look up from my book to comment, "Sweet girl. You're lucky your granddaughter comes to visit you."

"You mean *daughter.* Got two of them, 'cept the oldest is off the deep end."

My surprise is easy to read. She's so young, he's so old. He doesn't sport a Santa beard and he even has hair, obviously doused with black Grecian formula, growing haphazardly down his nape like a werewolf in transition. He has thick, hairy forearms and a faded, topless mermaid tattoo on his right upper arm. Now that his bicep has turn to flab, the little mermaid's boobs sag, too.

He leans forward, presses together the tips of his sausage fingers. "It's called entrapment."

"What do you mean?" My pulse quickens, my face flushes.

"Two different women, two different times in my life, got knocked up just so they could drag me to the altar. Got me two divorces to show for it. One of the wives married a nice fella, the other is just a mess like her kid."

"Do you tell your daughters you were entrapped?"

"Oh, they know it."

"So, they know you never wanted them?"

"Don't twist my words, lady." His smile slides off his face and his eyes narrow. He looks mean, like he could do bodily harm. It never occurred to me until now that the snuffer—if there really is a snuffer—could be a resident. He smooths down his T-shirt which almost covers his beer belly. "I'm just not the settling-down type, is all."

"Oh, okay," I say, when it really isn't. I spring to my feet, my finger stuck in my book, not even bothering with the bookmark, so eager to get away from this oaf.

19

Some of the Shady Meadow residents are gathered in the large living room, waiting for the dining room to open. Pandora is all dressed up in a purple floral dress, her silver-gray hair done in tight curls like a cap.

I tell her, "You look nice."

"I've been to the funeral of an old friend. Memorial service, I should say. No body in sight these days, like it doesn't exist."

"Fine with me," says Judy Flann. She is a big woman whose chin and throat blend together so you can't tell where one begins and the other ends. Her dark, penciled-in eyebrows slash upward at the ends, making her appear angry all the time. "I don't want anyone gawking at my sorry dead carcass, makeup caked on my face. And the expense of all that casket and plot business! I'd rather leave the money to the kids."

"I gave my Murray the works," says Margaret. "Open casket at the rosary, Requiem Mass, graveside service, a big lunch in the parish hall. I knew if I didn't, he'd be looking down from heaven, shaking his finger at me, calling me a cheapskate."

"I'm having my Cioppino recipe etched on my gravestone," announces Lucia Rossi. She has thick, white hair flowing to her waist. It's not all white. There're some areas of gray and creamy yellow, the heavy weight of it, swishing around all the time. Some old women just can't give up their long hair.

"Your Cioppino recipe? Are you joking?" asks Mei Lu.

"No, really," says Lucia. "Some women etch their signature recipe on their gravestones. I read an article about it. Cookies, fudge, pot roast. I'm doing my Cioppino."

"Do you make your own sauce from scratch?" asks Margaret.

"Of course," Lucia says, her chin in the air. "It takes all afternoon."

Margaret throws back her head and brays her loud signature guffaw, the back of her mouth flashing gold. Lucia squints in her direction. No one likes to be laughed at, especially so raucously. "That's too many ingredients," says Margaret. "Is your gravestone going to be as tall as the Washington Monument?"

Everyone laughs at that, even Lucia. Death is so funny.

Pandora waves her arms, crossing them before her. "I don't want any kind of service. All those people getting up there and saying embarrassing things about you. They get their stories all wrong, and you can't even defend yourself."

"They're all looking over at the buffet table, wondering what they get to eat," says Mei.

"Yes," agrees Pandora. "And when it's all over they go about their business. Poor, dear Ruth. We were once girls, playing jacks and hopscotch. Where did the time go?" She takes a Kleenex out of the sleeve of her dress and blows her nose.

"*Tanchumin.*" Esther Goldfarb pats Iris's knee, her left ring finger still bearing her thick gold wedding ring, even though she's been a widow for decades.

I touch Pandora's shoulder. "Are you all right?"

"Yes, yes. It's just so humiliating to die."

"Such an interruption," says Margaret. "You're right in the middle of knitting a sweater or planning a dinner party, trying to decide between wings or meatballs—then smack." She slams her palms together with a thunderous clap. "Not a thing matters. The kids have to drop everything and make arrangements. And the ones that can't make the service feel guilty about it. Such a bother."

"I think about my things after I'm gone," says Judy. "The coins in my change purse, the jewelry in my case, all the junk in my closet. People will paw through my *things.*"

"Yeah, and then they fight over your money. That's when some sibs make enemies for life," says Edith. "I got a friend whose two girls don't speak to each other on account of who got what."

"Everybody dies," I comment. "Then why is one's own death so inconceivable?"

Blessed-day Man raises his palm and looks in the distance. "Death is just passing through a door from this life to God's mansion. But only if you have accepted Jesus Christ as your Savior."

He means well, of course. I don't know why I find him so irritating. I understand faith is a consolation to some people, that praying makes them feel like they are doing something helpful in a hopeless situation, but this guy is so damn smug with his big jeweled cross swinging from its silver chain.

I turn to him. "I've always wondered: Do you wear clothes in heaven?"

Blessed-day Man chuckles, his long pale face flushing. "Of course."

"So if you wear clothes, you have to buy them and launder them. You have to have a job to pay for the clothes."

Blessed-day Man presses his fingertips together to form a steeple. "The Lord provides everything in heaven."

"If you have a body, you have to clean it," I continue. "Are there showers in heaven?"

Judy laughs. "Only when it rains."

Blessed-day Man creases his brow. "You have a spiritual body in heaven."

"Either you're spirit or flesh," I argue. I feel the tip of Margaret's foot nudging my ankle, but I persist. "Which is it? You can't have it both ways. Clearly you haven't thought this through."

Esther flutters her hand, her gold ring flashing. "Jews don't believe in an afterlife. We live in the memories of others. My mother still appears in my dreams and she's been dead fifty years."

"Spirits are very real," Edith puts in. "You can feel them around you, especially in a place where someone has just passed. I felt my Paul around the house for several days after his death. I even saw him once. He was standing before the record player choosing an LP to play, but I know his body wasn't really there. It was just my imagination because the presence of his spirit was so strong."

"What exactly do these spirits in heaven do?" I ask.

"Look down and watch over you," says Margaret.

"That's only good for a generation or two," I counter. "Then all the people you're looking down on are dead, too. Now what are ya gonna do for the rest of eternity?"

Blessed-day Man's face glows from within. "It's a mystery, but the Bible assures us that the spirit is united with the body on Judgement Day."

"Oh, the Bible." I roll my eyes. "That's just a bunch of made-up stories stitched together from all sorts of civilizations that existed long before the Hebrews."

Blessed-day Man grips his cross with white knuckles. "The Bible is the word of God."

Margaret's swinging foot takes aim at my ankle again, but I shift out of reach in the nick of time as I continue the debate. "The Bible is the word of man, used to keep women and the masses down."

Pandora shakes her finger at me. "No life everlasting for you, Colette." I can't tell if she's being facetious or not.

One guy points to the ceiling. "Just so my dog is up there with me."

"Sorry to say, but dogs don't have souls," says Blessed-day Man.

"Humans! They think they're better than dogs!" Judy laughs, clearly enjoying the debate.

"Dogs are definitely better than people," argues Edith.

"Cats rule," I exclaim.

"Elephants are the best. And whales," pipes up Clem Learner, a wizened man who slumps in a wheelchair most the day and rarely speaks.

The dining room doors open. The residents rise out of their seats, some more quickly than others.

I'm not done yet. I lean into Blessed-day Man who is trying to heave himself off a sofa, but doesn't seem to be making much upward progress. "If you have a body, you have to eat, and if you eat, you have to poop. Is there poop in heaven?"

There's a rumble and a stench. It's hard to know where it's coming from. It's hard to know if it's flatulence or feces. Everyone eyes everyone else suspiciously, except Clem, who stares at the carpet. He doesn't seem to give a damn if his Depends are loaded or not.

20

It's not a date. Still, I don't mention it to Margaret. She would tease me to death. Harry has asked me to go to the Rose and Garden Show. We both enjoy flowers and it's a chance to get the hell out of Shady Meadow. I'm excited, more than I should be. I put on my black pant suit, but the pants are uncomfortable, too tight at the waist. I look over my burgundy dress, but I don't wear dresses anymore. I don't know why I've kept any, except for funerals and memorial services, not so occasional. I remember my mother-in-law saying the sad thing about longevity is missing all the people who go before you. Now, when I think of a friend or relative, I have to recall if they're still alive. I settle on the jeans I wear nearly every day and a dressy purple blouse with embroidered flowers and paisleys at the neckline and down the front. I realize that the clothes I'm most attracted to are similar to those I wore as a girl, back in the hippie days. I fling my new tan cardigan over my arm. It doesn't match my outfit, but at least it's new.

I use the curling iron. I flick on mascara, choose a darker shade of lipstick than my usual, and ply my cheekbones with blush which I haven't bothered with since pre-mask wearing. Am I trying too hard? Who am I trying to be? What the hell, it's a special occasion that's not a special occasion, a date that's not a date.

Harry is waiting for me in the lobby. He's a bit more dressed up than me, rare for a man. Slacks, a knit shirt, his signature driver's cap, and a sport coat. Do you even say "sport coat" anymore? I haven't heard the term in ages. As soon as we walk outside, I spot a problem. I'm embarrassed for him, but I want to ignore it. Then I think it will distract me all day so I decide to take care of it right away.

I lay my hand lightly on his arm. "Have you ever noticed some knit shirts look about the same inside out as right-side out?"

"What?" He looks confused a moment, then follows my gaze to his shirt. "Oh, damn it to hell. I'll be right back."

He hustles back into the building and returns a couple of minutes later, problem solved. "Thanks for letting me know."

"It can happen to anyone."

"You're just being nice. You look lovely, by the way. I like that blouse."

"Thanks."

As we step off the curb, he takes my arm and tucks it under his. I can feel the bulge of his bicep. His gait is spry. I know that he lifts weights, jogs several times a week, and plays pickleball. I like that he's fit. He guides me to a teal-colored Prius and, as we approach, the doors unlock with a click.

I stop short, pulling my arm free. I had expected we'd take an Uber or Lyft. "You're driving?"

Harry laughs. "I can see cars. I can see people crossing the street. I just can't read their T-shirts."

I don't budge.

"Ah, Colette, I have a current driver's license. Wanna see?" He reaches into his back pocket.

"Old people and driver's licenses! Did you hear about the guy who mowed down five people on a Florida sidewalk, and then when he went up for trial he didn't remember doing it? The DMV just keeps renewing licenses in the mail."

"Not for me. I have to take a behind-the-wheel test every two years." He looks directly into my face. His glasses have transitioned to dark shades so I can't see his eyes. "Trust me?"

I don't. I've been looking forward to this outing, but I don't want to get into a car with a blind man at the wheel. He opens the passenger door for me, gallantly old-fashioned. He waits. I slide into the seat.

Harry isn't a horrible driver. I've seen worse. He drives below the speed limit, and his reaction time is slow. A couple of times I press my foot to the floor where there is no brake. As we approach a green light, he slows.

"The light is green," I comment.

He speeds up. "Oh, I see it now. There's a glare behind it. I just had to be a few feet closer."

At a red light, he slows at the proper time.

"How did you see that one so far away?"

"I didn't. The cars moving perpendicular through the intersection tipped me off."

I glance at him sideways with a wry smile. "I guess that works."

He laughs. "Lots of times, I take cues from what the other cars around me are doing."

"I guess that's fair. A lot of drivers don't even notice there are other cars on the road."

The exhibition hall is filled with roses, people, talk, echoes, and fragrance. I breathe in the intoxicating scent, reminding me of my father's roses on a fresh spring day. There're garden roses, wild roses, climbing roses, and miniature roses. Pink, yellow, white, deep red. Some bear award-winning ribbons: blue, red, white, and green. How would the judges know which is best when they are all so beautiful? There's an Elizabeth Taylor rose and a Nancy Reagan and a Princess Diana. The Princess is in full bloom, long stemmed, light pink with curling petals.

Harry cups it in his hand and I recite, "'There is simply the rose; it is perfect in every moment of its existence. Before a leaf-bud has burst, its whole life acts; in full-bloom flowers, there is no more.'"

"Lovely."

"It's Emerson. Some people meditate on the Bible; I prefer Emerson's essays. He's as long-winded about roses as he is about a lot of things. I forget the middle part, but he ends with 'Man postpones, or remembers; he does not live in the present.'"

"I do."

"Lucky you. If only I had something to fill my time. I taught third grade for thirty-six years, always wishing for a free moment to myself. Now all I do is sit around wondering what it was all for."

"Third grade? I imagine you taught hundreds of kids to read."

"Oh, anyone can do that."

"I don't think so. You've done the world a great service."

Flattery embarrasses me. I can't help feeling he's really pouring it on. "All I can think of is my past mistakes, and that I don't have much time left."

He unexpectantly laughs, which irks me because it feels like he's laughing at me. He looks kindly into my face. "Then stop it." He takes my hand, and as we continue our stroll down the long isles of roses, he doesn't let go. I like his sure grip, but I also like to swing my arms freely. I'd like to hold on and let go at the same time. I look around, self-conscious, wondering if people notice an old couple holding hands like teenagers.

We talk and talk. When I mention Brooke, he asks, "Are you close?"

"At times we are the best of friends. At other times…" I shrug and roll my eyes to the high ceiling.

"I wish I had a girl. Nothing but boys in our family. Three sons, five grandsons, two of them step-grandsons."

"I wanted a boy, but after Brooke, my husband wasn't interested in having more children. When Brooke had her son Carter, I thought of him as my boy, but a while back we lost him."

His face crumples with sympathy. "Oh, that's tragic. When did he pass?"

"I don't mean he's dead. He's into QAnon."

Harry shakes his head. "What's QAnon?"

I rear back. "You don't know?"

"I've heard of it. What's it about?"

"It's complicated, but basically a group of far-right conspirators believe the government and the media are secretly run by Satan worshippers involved in child sex trafficking and cannibalism."

His laugh erupts like a short hoot. "Seriously?"

"Very seriously. We can't understand how Carter has been lured into the fold. Not his parents, not me. He was raised in a middle-class home. College degree from UC Santa Cruz. How could it happen? There's no discussing it. There's no reaching him."

Harry walks a few steps, seemingly lost in thought. "Couldn't you just get together with him and *not* discuss it? Talk about something else?"

His comment has caught me off guard so I come up sputtering. "No, you—no, you don't understand. He's been brainwashed. It's like a cult, only worse. He knows we don't believe what he—so we…" I pull my hand free of his, throw up my arms and let them slap against my thighs. My chest is heaving. How did we get into this?

After a moment, Harry says quietly, "I've upset you."

"Not you. The situation. It's impossible." I take a deep breath, pull myself together. "What about you? Are you close to your sons and grandsons?"

"Oh, there's an ebb and flow to that. You know, shared interests. The baby, Marty—he came much later than the older two boys— he and I did a lot of camping and fishing together. The wife hated the great outdoors, so we went off alone. Then he got a girlfriend he rather spend time with, then he became a drunk, recovered, fell off the wagon, back and forth a few times. He struggles more than most people. I try to be sympathetic, but his mother babied him too much. What he needs is a swift kick in the ass." He shakes his head, chuckling. "Old school philosophy, I suppose."

"My grandson Carter truly loved his piano. Took lessons for ten years, but, like most teens, he got too busy to practice so he quit. Then he discovered Minecraft. Played that up to six hours a day, sometimes into the night. I once suggested to my daughter that she limit his gaming time and she jumped all over me."

"My kids' kids call the shots these days. If they misbehave they can't help it because they have some diagnosed syndrome or disorder, and they have to go to therapy. I know some kids are really hurting and need help, but all of them? It's a different world we live in."

"Well, you know. Social media, COVID isolation, too much information on the Internet, all that bad stuff." It's soothing to discuss such things with someone who empathizes. I take his hand, and his frim, warm fingers curl around mine. "Brooke wasn't all that easy to raise either. She was a stellar violinist, nearly a prodigy, in youth orchestra at eight. But then, in high school, she wanted to be a cheerleader and cheer practice was the same time as orchestra, so that was that. She was no good at tumbling, sat on the bench as an alternate, but she didn't seem to mind. It was all about playing the role of a cheerleader, wearing the outfit. On game days, she'd wear it to school, her skirt up to her ass, much too short for the dress code the other girls had to adhere to. She was assigned a football player and directed to interrupt a class to walk in and hand him a bag of candy. How subservient is that? Didn't we have a Woman's Movement? It really burned me up." I raise my shoulders and let them drop with a sigh. "My daughter and I are pretty good now. We went to lunch just the other day."

"My sons visit me occasionally, but I'm not sure they enjoy it much. They spend most the time looking at their phones. Their wives are looking at their watches. I'm happy to see them come and happy to see them go: There, another visit done with."

"Does it make you sad?"

"I wish there was more there between us, but then I have my own life. I like it very much." Abruptly, he leans down and kisses my cheek. Startled, I peer into his face. So this *is* a date. "I wanted to get that out of the way," he confesses, almost apologetically. "I was a little nervous about it."

I brazenly kiss him back, on the mouth, dry and perfunctory, but I get the job done.

21

Harry got me thinking. Yes, I was a good teacher. I worked extra hard with the reluctant readers, at recess, at lunch, after school. I thought they would hate me for keeping them in, but it turned out they caught on that I cared. Over the years, I've seen my grown students around town. They might be checking out my groceries, drawing blood from me at the clinic, having a beer at a pub. "Hey, Mrs. C.!" someone shouts out, and I have no clue who they are. An eight-year-old looks different at eighteen, thirty, pushing fifty.

But when Bobby Feemster poked his head out of the drive-through window at Starbucks, there was no mistaking his goofy grin. On favorite character day, he dressed up as Dorothy from *The Wizard of Oz*, blue gingham dress and a pigtail wig, and when the other boys tried to tease him for being gay, he wasn't bothered in the least. Handing me my coffee he said, "Hey, Mrs. C.! We're pregnant!"

An expression I loathe. Last time I checked, it's the woman who carries the child. It's the woman who suffers vomiting, crowded organs, swollen ankles, a bladder used as a trampoline, internal kicks, and heartburn over nine miserable months. It's the woman who bears the pains of childbirth, the late night and early morning feedings, the cracked nipples. The guy offers a satisfying little squirt and that's it. There's no "we" about it.

"My girlfriend is due in August," said Bobby.

Girlfriend, of course. Wife, hardly ever. "Congratulations," I replied, "I bet you'll be a good dad," although I had no proof of that.

"Gee thanks, Mrs. C. I'll read to her, I promise." This coming from a kid who ranted, "I hate reading. I hate books." Maybe he was just telling me what I wanted to hear, but maybe not.

22

I'm abruptly roused out of a deep sleep by shouting from next door.

Dottie is ranting, "I didn't take anything! I got nothing to take."

"Oh? What was in this pill container? This bottle of cough medicine is almost gone," says a low, male voice. I think it's one of her sons, but then I recognize it as belonging to a staffer, Juan.

"Mind your own damn business," says Dottie.

"It is my business, ma'am. We've had complaints. People around here are trying to sleep. Who have you been yelling at? Were you on the phone or are you imagining someone is here with you?"

"None of your goddamn—hey, stay out of there. That's my own private stuff."

"Where did you get this bottle—this jug—of wine?"

"It's not mine. Someone left it here. Give it here. Hey, you fucker, let go." There's the tinkling of broken glass. "See what you did? I'm calling the police."

"We've called the police," Juan says in a calm voice.

It feels like the middle of the night, but I see it's only a little after ten. As the ruckus continues, there are footsteps and voices up and down the hall. It's none of my business, but the impulse to be nosey is strong. It's usually Margaret who comes up with the juicy gossip. Now, I'll have a story for her. I climb out of bed, slip on my robe, and crack my door. A young, white cop treads by my room, his heavy belt creaking with equipment, bouncing on his hips. From behind, the tops of his ears are pink. Someone's baby boy.

"What the fuck do you want?" rants Dottie. "You're trespassing. Get out of my room."

"She's high as a kite," says Juan. "There's no calming her down."

"We just want to be sure you're safe," says the cop. "Your caregivers here are concerned about you. How many pills did you take? What were they?"

"I didn't take nothin'. Get out of my goddamn room or I'll bust your head with a frying pan."

There's a low chuckle. "Ma'am, you don't really want to hit a police officer with a frying pan."

Why would Dottie have a frying pan? She doesn't even have a kitchen.

"Oh, oh, she's out!" exclaims the cop. "Good catch! Here, let's lift her onto the bed."

A few minutes later, medics arrive to wheel Dottie out on a gurney. As she passes my door, I expect her to be unconscious, but her glassy eyes, rolling in their sockets, abruptly land on me. I'm startled and embarrassed to be caught snooping. Her flailing arms flutter and weaken. She closes her eyes and goes limp. The kid cop follows behind the gurney, a frying pan dangling loosely from his thumb and forefinger.

23

Margaret and I arrive in the dining room at seven to beat the crowd. We get a table to ourselves apart from a few other early risers. I relate to her the events of the previous night, and she laughs when I get to the frying pan part. "Once she threw a bowl of soup across the dining room."

I nod. "Harry told me."

She hooks an eyebrow at me, making me wish I hadn't mentioned him, but then she goes on about Dottie. "She's addicted to OxyContin, but she's not allowed to take it on her own. They only give her a small dose, but then she gets a lot of other people to buy her over-the-counter stuff—Nyquil, Allegra, Nicorette Gum."

"Like who?"

"Anybody she can con—her sons, grandkids, her poor sister, even visitors of other residents she doesn't know. She's resourceful. She steals. Once she swiped a bottle of gummy laxatives from someone's room, thinking they were gummy something-else. Boy, that was a mess."

I wince and grin at the same time.

"She hides the stuff around her room, takes it all at once, and goes crazy. They have to raid her room, clear it out every once in a while."

"They should kick her out."

"They've threatened to." Margaret shrugs. "Maybe this will be it."

I stir Sweet 'N Low into my coffee. These days there's all types of sweeteners—the blue packet, the green one, the yellow, but I stick to pink because that's what I've used since college, so that none of the others taste right to me, not even sugar. "What do you think a water controller does?" I ask.

Margaret shrugs. "Controls water? Why do you ask?"

"No reason."

She looks at me out of the tops of her eyes. "You sweet on Harry?"

"Naw." I give my head a vigorous shake. "I like him as a friend."

Margaret hoots raucously, embarrassing me. "That's what we used to say in junior high, 'member? That and I like him, I don't like-like him. 'Member? It looks to me like you like-like Harry. Where did you guys go yesterday afternoon?"

I narrow my eyes and feign annoyance. "Are you spying on me? We went to the Rose and Garden Show at Cal Expo. We both like flowers. So?"

"So you gotta like-like him if you're willing to get in a car with him in the driver's seat."

I have to smile. "He's not that bad of a driver, actually."

"And he wined and dined you in his apartment."

I feel myself blush. "Shit! Where do you get your information?"

Margaret wriggles her bottom. "Word gets around."

"We share an interest in music. That poor man, fumbling around on the piano and he can't even see the notes."

"You're sweet on him."

I wrinkle my nose. "All that gross chest hair oozing out of his shirt."

"Go on! You're attracted to his youthful physique."

"I find his optimism refreshing."

"Call it what you like. Good for you, robbing the cradle."

I straighten and squint at Margaret. How does she know how old he is? How does she know how old I am? Now, I'm curious. "How old is he?"

"Sixty-seven."

That isn't so young, I muse. Only seven years younger than me. At our age, what's the difference?

"Harry is a real nice guy." Margaret jabs me with her elbow. "I'd say go for it, but just let me warn you, you're asking for trouble."

"What do you mean?"

Margaret holds up a palm. "I'll say no more. It's not my business."

"When has that ever stopped you?"

"I'll say no more."

"Fine. How are things with your Sam?"

"He took me to movie night."

"That's nice. Any hanky-panky?"

Now it's Margaret's turn to blush. "He invited me to his apartment for a night cap, and we fooled around a little on the sofa."

"And?"

Her eyelashes flutter. She looks over her shoulder and leans into me. "He asked me to sleep with him."

"And?"

"I left."

"Why? I thought you wanted to know what it would be like with another man."

"Shhh!" She scans the room and whispers, "Not like that. I'm not cheap. What if it turned out to be just a one-night stand? Word would get around. I couldn't hold my head up in this place. I saw him with Bonnie at Bingo the night before."

So it's not Margaret who's cheap, it's this Sam guy. Neither one of his "dates" cost him a nickel, but I don't say so.

"I just don't know what to think, Col. Maybe he's a guy who likes to play the field. Or maybe Bonnie saw him first and I should bow out."

"If she did, she certainly doesn't remember it," I comment, which gets a chuckle out of Margaret. "When am I going to meet this amazing man, Sam?"

"Oh, you will. I'm surprised you haven't already. He's very popular, always the life of the party. Why would he want little ole me?"

Margaret looks down in the dumps. She leans on both elbows to slurp her coffee.

"If he really means something to you, don't give up so easily. Follow your heart."

"Follow your heart. Listen to you. A regular Hallmark greeting card." Margaret has bounced back to her cheerful self. "A frying pan—that's a hoot."

24

I've rehearsed this, thought up a number of topics to discuss about *The Thing with Feathers* with its author, but as I babble on, Susan Hartley stares out into the yard, her face as still as stone. Am I boring her? Saying something offensive? She doesn't even seem to be listening.

Marisol pushes her cart along the large picture window of the sunroom, spraying the glass as she goes, rubbing it spotless.

I wave enthusiastically. "Good morning, Marisol!"

"Good morning, Mrs. Colette." As she smiles, her broad nose flattens and a dimple appears in her fleshy cheek.

"She's just wonderful." I tell Susan about Marisol's miracle foot massage that cured my headache.

The author turns to me and snaps, "She steals."

My spine stiffens in alarm. I whisper, "What? Marisol? That can't be!"

Susan shakes her head like an angry bull, her chin a knot of tense bumps. "That sweater she's wearing is mine. She took it from my room!"

Marisol, who has moved out of earshot, is wearing a baby blue cardigan that I've never seen before over her polo.

Susan presents her hands to me, wrists bent. "See? Gone! She stole my rings while I was sleeping."

I see that her fingers are bare, bands of white flesh marking where her rings had been. "Are you sure you didn't take them off before bed?"

She creases her brow in frustration. Her pinkish hair is unkempt and a greasy spot in the back is flattened to her skull, revealing white roots. She points after Marisol's departing figure. "A thief! She's a thief! She stole from me!"

"Are you sure it was she?"

"Of course! She's the only one who comes into my room!"

I'm shocked. Marisol's cheerful chatter, her singing, the massage. Was it all to win my confidence, put me off guard so she could steal from me? She's even been in my room unattended. I'll have to take inventory of my things, my jewelry case, cash in my wallet. "Have you informed the management?"

"What? What for?" She looks around in a confused state.

"About your missing things."

"Oh, that. Why bother? They wouldn't do a damn thing about it."

Iris and Pandora enter the room, and I greet them and introduce them to Susan. They settle on the opposite sofa. Iris begins to talk loud enough to hear herself and drown out everyone else. In a moment, Susan shuffles off without another word.

$$25$$

I'm reading *A Thing with Feathers* in the library when that Pinocchio donkey-boy man enters with another visitor. It's not the giggly teen girl I saw him with previously, but a young man, late twenties-early thirties, tattoos from shoulders to wrists, a ginger, scruffy beard he can't quite grow.

"Hi there," I greet them.

"Hey." The man hooks a thumb toward the young man. "This here's my oldest daughter, Phyllis."

With a huff, the young man throws himself onto the sofa opposite me. I notice now the nicely-sculpted muscles in the muscle shirt are on the small size, the neck delicate like a flower's stem. I smile at him encouragingly and say, "I didn't quite catch your name."

"Philip." His voice is high-pitched even though he seems to make an effort to lower it, clearing his throat and angling down his chin.

"Phyllis," the man insists, falling into the cushions next to him and man-spreading in baggy gray sweatpants. "My daughter. I was there when she was born."

Phillip looks askance at his dad and backhands his thigh. "No, you weren't. You were shacked up with Bernice."

The man chortles. "So I was. Well, I came back to your mother, didn't I? I did the right thing by your mother."

"Yep. When Grandpa died and she came into some money. After you tore through that—"

"You act like I spent it on myself. I invested that money for the family."

Philip snickers. "In a racing dog? A *lame* racing dog? Who does that?"

The man laughs along with his son, although he doesn't seem to be enjoying the topic of conversation. The two are at odds, but also seem to share a genuine affection. "See here, Phyllis. You're leaving out some of the story. Bambi won some races. You can ask Jennifer."

"I forgot that part. When Mom's money ran out, you divorced her and married Jen's mom."

"I did the right thing. Jennifer needed a legal father. Both my daughters needed a legal father."

I can't believe I'm privy to this painfully personal conversation between a man I don't know but know I don't like and his trans son. I slide toward the edge of the sofa to make my exit.

Philip crosses his arms and scowls. "Why don't you get used to it, Dad? You have a daughter and a son."

"Not according to my Bible. Little girls grow into women and little boys grow into men, plain and simple."

"Your Bible is wrong," I blurt, even though it's none of my business. My blood is boiling even though these are strangers and this isn't my battle.

Philip slowly shakes his head. "Never mind, ma'am. I'm used to this."

Their conversation shifts to football, a mutual interest. I bend my head over my book, pretending to read, and when the young man says his goodbyes, I follow him out of the room.

Out in the hall, I call after him. "Hey, Philip! He's just terrible! Why do you even bother visiting?"

He smiles a sweet smile and shrugs. "I got to. He's my dad."

"Are you sure that's a good enough reason?"

He turns and walks backwards, touching his forefinger to his brow, in a salute of farewell. "Sometimes I wonder."

26

I've thought long and hard and have decided it's for the best to go to admin about Marisol. When I approach the front desk, I see a greeting card splayed out on the counter, which a number of staff members have already signed. This means only one thing at Shady Meadow. I wonder if I know the deceased.

Latrice, the assistant manager, is tapping away at her computer keyboard, her gold, scarlet, black, jeweled nails flashing. I've always marveled how women with such long nails can type; piano playing would be virtually impossible. She's a young Black woman who is highly efficient and always seems to have too much work to do. I stand at the counter, patiently waiting for her to notice me. "Can I help you?" she asks, without looking up.

An attendant walking by notices the sympathy card and stops to sign it.

Latrice glances up at me from beneath her tousled, copper-high-lighted, tight curls. "Yes, ma'am?"

I don't want to be overheard. I roll my eyes toward the attendant. "Who died?"

His eyebrows shoot up. "Uh…I don't know."

"Maryanne Bullard," says Latrice.

"Oh, she's in yoga," I exclaim. "I didn't know she was ill."

Latrice sighs. "Passed quietly in her sleep last night."

She just stopped breathing, I want to ask, my heart beating quicker, as if a pillow was pressed over her face? The attendant wraps up

103

his kind remembrances and strolls off. I lean over the counter and half-whisper, "I'd like to report a theft."

Latrice resumes her typing. "I'm sorry to hear that. What appears to be missing?"

Not what is missing, but what *appears* to be missing. "Some very valuable rings and a blue sweater. Marisol was wearing it."

Latrice's chin snaps upward, her coaster-sized hoop earrings swinging. "Marisol was wearing *your* sweater? You sure?"

I take satisfaction in finally gaining her full attention. "Not my sweater, a friend's. She spotted Marisol wearing it and her rings are gone so naturally she suspects—"

"Who's your friend?" she interrupts curtly.

"Susan Hartley."

Latrice's eyes narrow. "Oh. Her."

Has Susan caused some difficulty with the administration? Perhaps she's a chronic complainer. I'm compelled to stick up for her. "She's a famous author, a Pulitzer-Prize-winning author."

"So I've heard." Latrice doesn't sound the least bit impressed. There are so few readers these days.

"Susan said it wouldn't do any good to report the theft, but I knew you'd want to know."

Latrice eyebrows ram together. "Have you told anyone else about this?"

I hold up my palms and shake my head. "No, no, I came to you first."

"Thank you for that. And you'll keep this in confidence while we look into it?"

"Yes, of course." I promise, even though I'm dying to tell Margaret.

"You realize that the sweater Marisol was wearing could have been her own. It's possible Ms. Hartley stowed away her rings and forgot where she put them. I'll send someone over to help her look for them. Theft is a serious allegation, and Marisol is a highly regarded employee."

I feel my face flush, suddenly realizing Susan might have been mistaken about the sweater. "Oh, yes, I appreciate Marisol, too, but…"

"So you'll keep this little matter hush-hush? It's only fair." There's a chill in her tone. She obviously annoyed, not at Marisol, but at me. I should have left an anonymous tip in the suggestion box, but then I've always enjoyed taking credit for setting things right. "I thought you'd like to know," I repeat lamely.

Latrice does not respond, but resumes her typing, this time with savage jabs at the keyboard.

27

I'm reading and dozing in the afternoon when I hear someone knocking. I expect it's Margaret, even though we haven't arranged anything. When I open my door I'm surprised to see a short woman with a puffy face, whom I recognize as my next-door-neighbor. She's clear-eyed today, as innocent-looking as a child. Her soiled house-coat is replaced by a blouse with one of the shoulders cut out, trendy a few years ago, and flowered Capris. Apparently, she has her good days. She is holding a big bowl of fresh popcorn.

"Hi, I'm your neighbor, Dottie."

I know. Dotty is right. Soup thrower, frying pan swinger, Harry hater. "Uh…hi. I'm Colette."

"I know. Do you have *Wheel of Fortune* on?"

"Uh, no." My first impulse is to get rid of her. But the delightful aroma of freshly popped corn is making my mouth water. Maybe I can find out what she has against Harry. I swing the door wider. "I can turn it on."

Dottie scooches into my recliner, making herself comfortable. I have no choice but to sit on the foot of the bed. I really ought to get another chair, but the room seems crowded as it is. Dottie offers me the popcorn, and I take a handful. It's warm and salty and delicious.

She leans forward, glommed onto the TV screen. Her head draws little circles as she follows the spinning of the wheel. I've al-ways thought *Wheel of Fortune* is for dummies. Now, take *Jeopardy!* You really have to know something to be good on that show, and fast! I always think of the answers about ten seconds too late.

"V!" Dottie chides the contestant, a tiny man with a mustache and sweater vest. "There is one, but that's dumb luck. T and S are much better guesses. D? Stupid dipshit!"

"He got one," I counter.

"Dumb luck."

"I would like to buy a vowel," says the man. "A."

"Ass wipe! Obviously, if a vowel stands alone it's an A. He should have bought an E."

The second contestant, a woman with big hair in a frilly pink blouse, does buy an E.

"There you go, six of them," says Dottie. "Women are a lot better at this game. The show always puts two women and one man on. My husband thinks it's cuz women like to see other women win, but it's really cuz women are smarter."

My ears perk up at the word husband. "Where's your husband?"

"Oh, he's got a place of his own."

He parked Dottie at Shady Meadow when she went dotty? "Does he visit you?"

Dottie's fist full of popcorn stops midway between the bowl and her mouth. Her head rotates with the wheel. I think she hasn't heard me, but then she replies, "Sometimes. When the boys come around." Many of the letters on the game board are still unknown when Dottie bursts out, "'Revenge is a dish best served cold.'" She throws her handful of popcorn into the air in celebration. It lands in her lap, on the carpet, and back in the bowl. "Whoopee, I got it! But it's bullshit. I like my revenge fucking hot!"

"How do you know Harry?" I venture to ask during the commercial.

She smirks, one side of her mouth raised. "From Kindergarten. We were both raised in Elk Grove when it was a dinky little one-horse town. Do you know to set your alarm for tomorrow?"

"For what?"

"You don't know? Around five a.m. Mercury will be its maximum angle of twenty-three degrees west of the sun, about thirty-eight percent illuminated. It's gonna align with Venus below and Saturn above. Just spectacular."

"Oh. No, I haven't heard. I don't know much about astronomy."

"I just love it! I really got interested in space when I worked at JPL."

"What is—"

"Sh! They're starting."

When the program is over, Dottie swings her legs to the side and jumps to her feet. "Thanks for watching with me. Want me to leave the rest of the popcorn?"

Actually, I do, but I resist the offer. As soon as I shut the door behind her, I open my laptop and Google JPL. Jet Propulsion Lab at NASA. Really? I would think even their clerical help would have to be educated and well-mannered. Not someone who threatens a cop with a frying pan and watches *Wheel of Fortune*. Hard to believe.

28

One morning I wake up happy, looking forward to the day. I have to admit my change in mood has to do with Harry. I find myself spending more and more time at his place, just hanging out. We talk and listen to music. We watch shows on Netflix, cuddling on the sofa. I enjoy the affection, the human contact, but I'm not used to pressing against another body, so sometimes I have to push away. I use the bathroom as an excuse to get up and return to sit a bit farther from him. Other times I can't wait to feel his arms around me. I like to watch his face light up when he sees me at his door. Someone really wants me. I like the feeling of sharing space with him, breathing the same air. Sometimes I just sit around reading while he's on his computer or puttering in the kitchen.

Other days I slip back into my anhedonia. I sit alone in my room and feel sorry for myself. I don't feel like seeing Harry, I don't feel like walking, I don't feel like doing anything. I miss my home, my cat. When I was younger and felt like this, I could console myself with chocolate or cookies or chips, but as I age I seem to have fewer food cravings. I air-stroke Willie Whiskers, I take out my cat figurines, gaze into their eyes, wipe the dust from them on my T-shirt.

Eventually, I'm done with moping around. I'm back to knocking on Harry's door. I play bridge with the girls, endure yoga class, and walk with Margaret. She teases me about Harry, tries to get me to talk about my feelings for him, but I don't quite understand them myself. My relationship with him feels so tentative I fear it will dissolve into thin air if I dare discuss it. I want to cling to him until I can't. It's easy to shift the conversation toward Sam, Margaret's favorite subject.

It's an unspoken agreement between Harry and me that we don't display any affection in public. Sometimes we eat together in the dining room or go to Bingo or movie night, but we don't touch. Probably we're not fooling anyone. Probably the Shady Meadow residents see there's something between us, just by the way we look at each other.

One afternoon I'm sitting on his sofa reading *The Thing with Feathers* when Harry goes to his instrument and slides on his earphones.

"You don't have to use those," I tell him.

"Aren't you trying to read?"

"Your playing won't bother me. I want to hear your progress on the Bach."

His brow furrows and his tone grows harsh. "My wife hated my music."

"How could you marry someone who hated music?"

"Not all music. Just my playing. At first, she seemed to like it, then she merely tolerated it, then she told me to give it up. She said my lessons were a waste of money, when we had plenty of money." Harry's cheeks bloom pink above his white beard. "She told me I sucked."

"How mean!" I exclaim.

"She could be mean. But she had chronic back pain and sometimes I think it was the pain talking. Other times I'd think it was my fault. We were just kids when we married, and you know, life is long. Over the years, I disappointed her somehow and she got resentful. I've tried to think how I'd failed her. I guess I didn't pay enough attention to her. We both worked and devoted our time off to the boys. By the time they were out of the house, she had developed her own interests, shopping for antiques mostly, and I had the piano and the great outdoors. She was a talker and sometimes I'd just switch her off in my head. She'd make a simple request like taking her out for ice cream after dinner, and I would refuse her, maybe make some crack about her weight. I could've been a better husband." He sighs and looks down at his hands. The room fills up with silence.

I've often wondered what I did to send Al running into the arms of Tabby. It's all over now, there's no going back for me or Harry. "Play, Harry," I say quietly. "I want to hear your Bach." I sit back and listen. He has nearly all of the first page in hand. When he refers to the score, he weaves his head from side to side. He has told me that he does that to find a space to see the notes between the dots in his eyes. As he ponders the next phrase, my gaze falls upon his music cabinet. "May I see what music you have?"

"Of course. Help yourself."

As he continues to practice, I open the top drawer and see that he has organized his music by era. There's Bach and Scarlatti—Baroque. The next two drawers contain the Classical period—Clementi, Haydn, Mozart, and Beethoven.

Harry pauses in his practicing to ask, "Are you finding what you're looking for?"

"Oh, I'm not looking for anything special. I just want to see what you have. I often think if I were on a desert island with a piano and could have only one volume of music, I'd choose Beethoven's sonatas."

"That would be two volumes."

I laugh. "I know, I'm just saying. The sonatas span really three eras, Classical and Romantic, of course, but some of the stuff in the late sonatas is really out there, very modern."

"Yes, and the fugue in the Hammerklavier harks back to Bach."

"So all four eras then."

Harry's copies of Beethoven look almost new, while mine are ragged and falling apart. They hold the precious markings of my college professor in his neat, nearly feminine, cursive. "Connect." "Ritard." "Same tempo." I sometimes think: Really? He had to tell me that and that and that? Didn't I know anything? Studying piano with Dr. Grimes was a revelation.

Harry's next two drawers are a jumble of Romantic music—Chopin and Brahms, Schumann and Tchaikovsky. The last two drawers are contemporary—Bartok, Copland, Kabalevsky. I gasp, hold in air.

Harry peers over at me. "What did you find?"

"*Big Sur Suite.*"

"Ah! Emmeline Le Roux. Have you played her?"

"She's my mother."

"Oh!" Harry comes over to sit next to me as I turn the pages of the score: "Crashing Waves," "Winding Road," "Soaring Egrets."

"What was it like, having such a famous composer for a mother?"

"Lonely. The house had to be very quiet while she worked. No TV, no friends over. And then she was traveling much of the time. It was usually just my dad and me. He would tell me my mother was a great composer and conductor and I should be proud and happy for her, and I would think: what about me?"

"So you were closer to your dad?"

"Not really. He…" I've lost my train of thought, distracted by the way Harry is looking into my face, like everything I say matters, that I matter in such a way as I haven't mattered to a man in a very long time, maybe never.

He takes my hand, runs his smooth fingers over my bumpy joints, still looking intently into my eyes. A smile flickers on the corners of his mouth. "You don't have to tell me if it's too hard."

"No, no, it's not that." I gently squeeze his fingers, and he squeezes back. "My dad was just innocuous. He was a businessman, quiet, formal. He really didn't know what to do with a kid. He seemed relieved when a friend invited me over or when my mother returned. Then she would try to make her absences up to me. And that was just…embarrassing."

"Embarrassing?"

"When I was in the fourth grade she came as a guest to my school to conduct the orchestra for a youth symphony she'd written. I was so proud. All the kids would pay attention to me. They would see how important I was because I had a famous composer for a mother. But then, if you ever saw videos of my mother conducting, you'd know she could be quite animated and passionate. Well, at recess I saw the three most popular girls in my class playing what I thought was horses, but then to my horror, I realized they were mocking my mother's conducting, throwing back their heads and pawing the air. They couldn't comprehend the kind of prestige she had so they made fun of her. I was the daughter of a weirdo. Whenever she suggested another school visit, I made excuses to avoid it. She was a disappointment to me, and I was a disappointment to her. She expected me to be a concert pianist, and I failed to get into Juilliard. Nothing I did was ever good enough for her." I flip to the end of the *Big Sur Suite* score and close it.

Harry places his hand on my knee and asks gently, "Not good enough for her or not good enough for yourself?"

"Fair question. At her funeral, so many people came up to me to say how proud she was of me. It seemed too little, too late. I regret I wasn't better to her. I could have been a more compassionate daughter." Strong feelings well up inside me. I avoid Harry's searching eyes by returning my mother's music to its place and opening the bottom drawer of his music cabinet. Duets. When I take the pile onto my lap, Harry sorts through it and pulls out a beginner's collection.

"Come on, let's try these." He takes my arm and tries to pull me toward his instrument.

I protest by leaning back and trying to squirm out of his grip. "Oh, Harry, no! I haven't touched the piano in years."

"You will today." He sits me down to his right to play the Primo part while he takes Secondo. He slides the music rack as close as it will go and leans forward. He opens to the first piece.

"Can you see well enough to sight read this?" I ask.

"I can read notes this big. Why do little kids get the big notes? It's we older folks that need them. Now, I'll count us in. One, two, ready, play."

My hands remain in my lap. He places them on the keys.

"One, two—"

"Hold on." I look ahead in the music, play it in my head. It's easy. I can do this. "Okay, here goes."

"One, two, ready, play."

We are playing. I am playing, after so many years. My stiff fingers creak and protest but I will them to move. I miss a rhythm, Harry misses a note. We laugh and try again. This time it goes more smoothly. Harry turns the page. We play the next piece. He turns the page. We make it all the way through the book.

"Let's do it again." Harry flips the music back to the first piece. "We'll be better the second time through."

Such fun! I can't believe I'm playing again.

29

My mother. She told me repeatedly that the only thing which made the sexes equal is a wire hanger. She would go on rants about the lack of legal abortion. She said I was a lucky, lucky girl when birth control pills came on the market. She had me taking them at sixteen, a good two years before I became sexually active. She told me I'd never know when passion overtook me and I must be prepared, I must protect myself. Passion—hooey. That's just an excuse. I've always believed having sex is a rational decision, except in the case of rape, drugs, or too much alcohol.

My mother devoted her life to what was nearly impossible for a woman to do. Clara Schumann had composed, but she was married to Robert. Fanny Mendelssohn had done it, but she was Felix's sister. There were a handful of other women composers. Being a woman composer is hard, but being a woman conductor is out of the question. What self-respecting man would bend to the will of a woman's direction? Female musicians were not allowed to play in major orchestras, except for the harpist, because men didn't play the harp. The female harpist's name was left off the program, and in televised performances, only her hands were visible. Since men deemed woman to be inferior musicians, the rational thing to do was to deny her existence if an orchestra needed one. All this changed when orchestras began to hold auditions behind screens.

My mother's teenage years were shattered by the Nazis occupying France. After the war, she immigrated to the U.S. with her cousin Simone, as an undernourished, scared young woman of eighteen. In a photograph of her embarking from Ellis Island, the biggest thing on her are her hungry eyes, peering out from raggedy, shorn hair and an oversized beret. Her exceptional musical talent was evident, but Julliard didn't know what to do with her because she couldn't play an instrument at a virtuosic level. She transferred to Bard College where women were allowed to study composition and orchestration.

I didn't know my father wasn't my father, not my biological father, until I figured it out at sixteen. My mother's lifelong confidant was her cousin Simone who had settled in Quebec. They talked on the phone at least once a week. When my mother didn't want me to know what she was talking about, she switched to French. She never tried to teach it to me. In her view, speaking a language other than English in America was a stigma. I was a C student in high school French, another way of failing her. It never occurred to me that language classes were meant to actually learn a language. You repeated dialogue you heard on LP records, you did the written exercises in your workbook, and you took tests based on the content of the exercises. But after three years of this, I began to pick up the language.

Also, I could count. My father gave my mother red roses—a dozen, supposedly—on their wedding anniversary every year. At age fifteen, sitting on the couch staring at the roses on the coffee table, I noticed there were thirteen. When I mentioned this to my mother, she said, "Oh, chere, you've heard of a baker's dozen." The following year, when I heard her laugh and mention my name to Simone over the phone, followed by the words *quatorze* rosés, my ears perked up. I went into the living room and counted the roses for myself. A light came on: one rose for each year of marriage.

Of course, I didn't mention my discovery to anyone. Such things were not discussed. In the following days, I stared and stared at my father, so that once he asked, "What is it, Colette?" I shook my head.

"Nothing." The realization didn't bother me. He was the only father I knew, the only one who took care of me, a true father for all practical purposes. The other guy didn't matter to me. The term "biological father" wasn't tossed around then. I lacked curiosity. By talking about it, I knew I would be doing something wrong. It would be insulting to my mother and father both.

Like many teen girls, I butted heads with my mother. What really set her off was my boyfriend Mike. One Saturday night, she forbid me to go to the movies with him because I hadn't practiced the piano that day. I sneaked out of the house and went on my date anyway.

The following morning she ranted, "He is no good. He will get you pregnant and there will be no recourse for you but a wire hanger. You will have to drop out of school. You will amount to nothing. You will shame me and your father."

Insolently, I glared into her face, which had purpled with rage. The center of my being felt as cold as steel. "You know, Mother, you should have gone the wire hanger route yourself. A lot of woman have survived it. Think how much happier you would be if you never had me."

Her eyes grew wide with disbelief. "What are you saying?"

"You've been shaking the wire hanger into my face my entire life."

"That doesn't mean I didn't want you! You are the greatest joy of my life!"

Really? I thought her Pulitzer Prize was her greatest joy, but I had the grace not to throw it up at her. "I am nothing but a disappointment to you, a failure. You always say so."

She collapsed to her knees before me and gripped me tightly around the waist, sobbing in anguish, her snot bubbling out of her nose onto my skirt. I was embarrassed for her. I tried to pry her arms away from me and hoist her to her feet, but she would not let me go until I said I was wrong in thinking she didn't want me.

"Then who is my father?" I blurted. "He is not who you pretend him to be."

She didn't deny it. We sat at the kitchen table drinking tea with honey and lemon as we calmly discussed the matter. It was a typical story. He was an attractive, much older man of influence and power in the musical world who was able to open doors for her, the husband of a woman his own age and the father of three nearly-grown children. Mother refused to tell me his name. He was eminent in the musical world, and such scandal would hurt his reputation.

"I had no intentions of having an affair with him," she said, "but it happened. He was clear from the beginning that he would never leave his family for me. I didn't desire it. We parted ways before I discovered I was going to have a baby. He never knew about you." My mother further explained that she went to live with Simone and her family through her pregnancy and my birth. I was about eighteen months old when she took a position on the faculty of the San Francisco Conservatory of Music and soon afterward she met the man who would become the only father I would ever know.

That morning, Mother and I reached a stalemate. I agreed to go on birth control pills, and she never mentioned the wire hanger again. Again she said I was a lucky, lucky girl when Roe v. Wade was decided. (Guess what, Mom.) I didn't learn the identity of my biological father until decades later after both of my parents had died, when a much older half-sister contacted me via 23 and Me. It was rather a letdown. I had never heard of my biological father. He doesn't even have a Wiki page. I had always imagined him to be someone really famous, like Leonard Bernstein.

30

I'm reading *A Thing with Feathers* in the sunroom when a shadow crosses me. I look up and am startled to see Susan Hartley looming over me. She wrenches the book out of my hands and plops down on the sofa across from me. She runs her fingers over the white wings of the dove on the dust jacket, which are slightly raised and outlined in gold. "Pretty."

"I think so, too."

"What's it called?"

What does she mean? The title of her own novel? Is she joking? I feign a chuckle. "It's your book."

Susan's thick eyebrows ram together. "Did you steal it?"

I'm shocked by her confusion. Does a medication she's on make her a bit looney? I have noticed she's had a few slips in memory, but nothing like this. I gently slide the book off her lap, hold it up, and underline her name with my finger. "This is you. See? You're the author of this book."

"You always took my things, Mary. You always went into my closet and took…oh!" Susan's lips try to form the words she is looking for. "…you know what I mean, the things I put on my body."

I notice then that her shirt is inside out. That isn't so crazy; I think of Harry in the same situation, but hers is buttoned wrong, too.

"My clothes! You spilled spaghetti sauce on my good blue sweater and it never…never went away." She grabs the book away from me again, shouting, "Mine!" She raises it high over her head, and slams it down on the back of my hands.

The pain in my knuckles brings tears to my eyes. I pan the area for a staff member, but not a single person is around. "I've got to go, now." I try to remain calm, but I hear a quiver in my voice. I rise to my feet and begin walking swiftly toward my room, scanning the hallways for assistance.

Susan follows close behind me, so close she barks my heels several times, seemingly on purpose. Fear rises in my chest. Can she really do me serious harm? I speed up, thinking I'll be safe in my own locked room where I can call for help. At my door, I fumble for my key. My fingers tremble as I try to fit it into the lock. "Goodbye," I call over my shoulder. I try to shut the door behind me, but Susan pushes against it and barges in, her strength alarming me. She strides over to my dresser, opens the top drawer and begins rifling through my underwear and socks.

I concentrate on keeping my tone steady. "What are you looking for, Susan?"

"Mine! Mine!" She tries to push the drawer shut, but since some of the articles are hanging out, it won't close. She releases a cry of frustration, pulls the drawer out of the dresser and lets it drop to the floor with a crack of the wood. She opens the second drawer.

I try not to panic. Maybe if she finds something she thinks she's looking for, she will take it and go. A realization flashes through my brain. Marisol! Sweet, dear, innocent Marisol! I betrayed her! Such a righteous fool I am!

Susan whirls around and spots my shadowbox of cat figurines. She stomps over to it and grabs one of my favorites, the gray tabby with the wide eyes and Elizabethan ruff, and hurls it into her knitting bag. She sweeps her arm across an entire shelf, and my little cats fall into her bag, with a dismaying clink and clatter, no doubt getting chipped or broken. They are just cheap ceramics mostly, mere objects of sentimental value, yet a source of delight as I've collected them over the years.

The front of Susan's tan pants turns brown, pee trickling down her legs. She doesn't seem to notice or care. I'm outraged, not because her urine is pooling on my floor, but because a Pulitzer-prize-winning author—any human being at all—has to withstand this indignity, this cruelty. I reach for my phone and call administration.

Getting Susan out of my room isn't pretty. She struggles against two caregivers, one male and one female. "My room! My pretty things! Mine!" The renowned author bares her teeth and sinks them into the man's wrist, drawing blood.

31

The following day Brooke and I go to lunch. She chooses Estella's Garden of Delights, a vegan restaurant I'm not crazy about. She orders the kale salad, and I make the mistake of ordering pizza. The crust is like cardboard and the so-called cheese tastes like sour soybeans. I tell the whole, sad Marisol-Susan story. In my telling I find my behavior not so terrible, a mistake anyone could make. It's a relief to confess it to my daughter. She listens quietly, dipping the tines of her fork into the dressing on the side, before stabbing a leaf of kale.

I finish with, "My kitty-cats are all right, just a few nicks here and there and one severed paw. It's Marisol I feel just awful about. I went to admin immediately to apologize for my false accusation, but I haven't seen her around and I'm afraid they've already let her go."

Brooke shoves aside a sliver of walnut, because, heaven forbid, it could cost her another five calories. "Well, Mom, you've always been racist."

"*What?*"

"It's just like you to side with a privileged white woman against a poor woman of color trapped in servitude."

My stomach flops over; my throat goes dry. I take a sip of iced tea as I formulate my defense. "It's true I put Susan Hartley up on a pedestal, an author I've admired all my life, who surprisingly turned up at Shady Meadow and become an acquaintance, if not an actual friend. I don't believe race has anything to do with it."

122

"I'm afraid it does, Mom. Racism is systemic."

"If it's systemic, then that includes you."

Brooke shakes her head, her long mane hanging on either side of her gaunt face. I believe women of her age and beyond begin to look haggard when they are overly thin, but, of course, I'd never tell her so. "It's your generation that can't adapt to a diverse society. I stood by and watched your racism come out in your teaching."

"My teaching! I was fair to all my students!"

"I remember your complaining how your third-graders lost ground in the summer when they only spoke Spanish at home."

"I never said speaking Spanish was bad. Bilingualism is a good thing! I just wanted a summer school program to keep their English from back-sliding. What is racist about wishing my students academic success?"

Brooke shrugs. "You can fix this, Mom. It's not too late for you. You can go into therapy, learn to be mindful of others."

I'm struck numb. I stare at my plate, tears prickling at the corners of my eyes.

"Are you even listening to me, Mom?"

I can't find the words to convince Brooke that she's misjudged me. This isn't the first tongue-lashing I've taken from her. There's no convincing her of anything. She is right and I am wrong. Always. It has been a while since she verbally attacked me like this, and I thought that maybe we've moved on, that my daughter no longer feels the need to beat me up. I throw down the piece of pizza I'm holding.

"Something wrong with your food, Mom?" she asks, seemingly oblivious to my crushed feelings.

"They forgot the pepperoni."

"Mom, this is a vegan…oh, I get it. Very funny." She changes the subject to her husband Jonathan making plans for a getaway golfing weekend with another couple from their country club whom she doesn't particularly like. Jonathan is also a lawyer, a decent man, although a little self-important, a little finicky, a snob, really. Al and I belonged to a country club, and the country club always gave me a pain in the ass. For decades country clubs banned people of color and Jews. Not even women could hold memberships; widows, divorcees had to relinquish memberships for the sake of the members' wives, of course; the *wives* wouldn't want unattached women running around the country club luring their husbands away from them. It was nothing about the country club being a man's domain.

I can't eat another bite. I ask for the check and pay for both of us. I always pay. I have paid for Brooke's upbringing and helped with Carter's too. I have paid for hours of therapy for her during her adolescence and college, her dermatologist, her podiatrist, her two nose jobs. I have paid and paid and still somehow my daughter can't muster enough gratitude to spare my feelings, to treat me with the respect I deserve.

When she drops me off at Shady Meadow and reaches across the seat to hug me goodbye, I turn away, slide out of the car, and slam the door.

32

On my walk with Margaret that afternoon, I relay my conversation with Brooke. She utters her litany of "Uh-huh, uh-huh, uh-huh," as I speak, making me wish she'd just shut up so I could get one word in edgewise between a uh and a huh. I lose my train of through several times and my temple begins to pulse. I finish with "I just don't understand it. The person I raised, the person I've given so much to. I taught her morals, how to be kind and caring. How can she think I'm a piece of shit?"

"Yep," replies Margaret. "You think you're a good person and lots of people say so, but just have a daughter, and she'll take you down. My oldest Mary Fran has been my biggest critic. I would get dressed to go out and she'd look me up and down and say, 'No, Mom, no. Not that blouse with that skirt.' I guess she didn't realize my two other good blouses were sopping with breast milk, and after seven babies in twelve years, it was the only skirt I could squeeze into. She didn't notice if I had a few extra bucks, I'd spend it on a new outfit for her or one of her sisters instead of myself."

"How'd you do it? Take care of the emotional needs of seven kids?"

Margaret shrugs. "Oh, I couldn't. I wiped their tears, I cleaned out their scrapes and cuts. When Tommy the baby was about four he fell out of a tree and scraped up an elbow and a knee pretty bad. He was more scared than anything and was crying so hard I gave him two cookies. 'Here, this will make you feel better.' He put one cookie on his elbow and one on his knee and said, 'I don't feel no better, Mama.'" Margaret tosses her head and guffaws.

I cross my arms and hug myself. "Adult children are harder to deal with than little kids."

"Ah, hell, I figure they're on their own. Peter is homeless, a drunk, nothing I can do about it. Billy is stationed in Japan. He's gay, but he doesn't think I know it, thinks I won't accept him, haven't seen him in years. I got into it with Joey's wife a while back and he was estranged for a few years, but we've patched things up since. My kids who want to be in my life make the effort, the others, no. I live my life, they live theirs. I'm closest to Patsy—Patricia, she goes by now—second to the youngest, but she can hurt my feelings, too. It blows over. We go on."

"I have just the one child. I've got to hold on to her. The trouble with Brooke is I just never know what I'll be getting. I have hoped that she would outgrow her attacks on me, but now I don't see it happening. Once I decided I wasn't going to take it anymore. I tried to stick up for myself in one of our arguments and she doubled down, said the meanest things to me."

"That's a shame."

"It is a shame. I'm ashamed of myself for how she humiliates me, and I'm ashamed of her for her behavior." I press my thumbs into my temples, the throbbing intensifying. I think of Marisol and a wave of remorse and sadness washes over me. "Hey, Margaret, do you mind if we turn back early?"

A big grin stretches across her face. "Suits me! You're the one who always wants to go farther."

"Not today. I'd like to lie down before dinner."

"Look, we can cut through the pool area."

As I open the waist-high gate, a whiff of chlorine stings the lining of my nostrils. I belch and taste sour soybean bile. There's a group of four men shooting the breeze, their baggy sweats drenched in sweat, no doubt from a heated game of pickleball. I scan the group for Harry, and find the brute with the trans son instead. He holds a pile of fast food wrappers, which he pushes off his lap as he rises to his feet.

As he begins to walk away, I call after him, "Wait! Wait!" I charge up to him, pick up his garbage and hand it to him. "You dropped this."

"We've got custodial services around here, lady."

My sudden sprint has caused my head to pound harder. "That doesn't mean you have to be a slob. Pick up after yourself."

He glares at me as I narrow my eyes at him, daring him to drop his trash again. His friends hoot and jab each other with their elbows, delighting in the stand-off.

"I got it!" Margaret dashes to my side, takes the trash from the man's hands, and walks two steps to dispose of it in a receptacle. "No problem, Sam."

Sam? This is her Sam? I reel on unsteady feet. My head feels as if it's about to explode. I squeeze my eyes shut and see stars.

33

The worst fight Brooke and I ever had was over Carter, when he was thirteen, a surly eighth-grader. His grades were in the toilet, and he had discovered the F-word, which he wielded against both parents. We were out having lunch and as usual, she was complaining about him.

"He plays this online computer game Warcraft at all hours of the day and night. I thought he was playing with his friends, but it turns out some of the players are strangers, grown men."

"God, that's a major concern. You need to do something about this. You should limit his time on the computer."

Brooke went bug-eyed, her lips aquiver. "What would you know about it? When I was growing up, you ignored me every day of my life. I wasn't one of your students so I didn't count for shit. You wonder why Daddy left? You only care about yourself. I'm surprised he stayed married to you as long as he did. You wonder why your third-graders can't read? They have you for a teacher." She stormed off, I assumed, to the ladies' room.

I sat there in shock, as if I had been drenched by a tsunami, my hair and clothes dripping, freezing to death because I couldn't move. Time went by, ten minutes, fifteen. I already had paid the bill. I went looking for her, prepared to apologize for butting in, ready to smooth things over so we could move on. She wasn't in the bathroom. Her car wasn't in the parking lot. She had left me stranded. I felt frightened, panicked. How would I get home?

I could have called a friend to come pick me, but I felt too humiliated. I could have called a taxi, but I didn't feel like it. I have always been a walker so I walked. It was about six miles; I felt I could walk sixty. The dress flats I was wearing pinched my feet, so I took them off and walked in my stockings. It was November, and the chill of the sidewalk traveled up from my soles to my core. It didn't make it to my head, however. My head was steaming.

Eventually, Brooke came by in her car. She stopped in the middle of the road, rolled down the passenger window, and yelled, "Mom, I've been looking all over for you."

I kept walking, my eyes focused straight ahead.

"Mom, get in the car, please."

Another car rolled up behind her and honked. She was forced to move on, drive around the block. She passed alongside me again, shouted out her window, "Mom! Don't make a scene. Why does everything have to be about you?"

Fuck you. That's what I felt about my own daughter, my only child. By then, my knee-high stockings were shredded. I bent over, yanked them off, and flicked them into somebody's hedge.

On her third pass, Brooke parked the car and physically headed me off, her hands gripping my forearms. "I'm sorry, Mom. I didn't mean what I said."

"I know it," I said in a cold, even tone. "Thank you for apologizing."

"It's just that I'm under so much pressure at work, and Carter has been such a shit. You're right. Jonathan and I do need to do something about his behavior. It's just that I don't want you telling me how to raise my son."

"Understood."

She hugged me. I did not hug her back. I felt like stone. "Will you get in the car now?"

"You know how much I enjoy walking." I stepped around her and continued on.

"Then you haven't forgiven me."

"I have," I called over my shoulder. And meant it. I love her as much as ever, my only child. But that day, something inside me shifted, changed. I imagined a dial deep inside me that I turned down a few notches. I would no longer trust her with my well-being. I don't understand it exactly, but she has some deep-rooted resentment toward me that wasn't going away. That day, when she left me stranded in the restaurant, I quietly quit Brooke, like some workers quietly quit during COVID. They kept coming to their jobs, drawing their paycheck; they just didn't give it their all anymore, knock themselves out. Before that day, when Brooke called, I would drop everything and answer my phone. Afterward, if I'm busy with something, out with friends, or engrossed in a book, I don't answer. If she wants me to go someplace with her and I don't feel like it, I say no. That's what I mean about quietly quitting.

When it was decided that I could no longer live alone, Brooke asked me to come live with her and Jonathan. They already have a mother-in-law wing in their house, complete with kitchen, living area, bed and bath, where Jonathan's mother stayed before she died. One perk was I could keep Willy Whiskers, but to tell you the truth, I wanted to laugh in Brooke's face. I thought, I imagined, if I went to live with her, one day, out of the blue, she would get angry with me about something or other, pack up my stuff in boxes and set them on her front porch, along with me. Willy Whiskers would be in my arms, struggling to get away because he was cold, and I was cold because a blizzard was raging, which is ridiculous because it doesn't snow in Sacramento, but my humiliation and fear would be real as I stood there shivering, not knowing what to do or where to go.

So here I am at Shady Meadow. I don't get to have my cat, but I'm not at my daughter's mercy either.

$$34$$

I can't bring myself to tell Harry about the whole Susan Hartley-Marisol fiasco. I'm ashamed of callously reporting Marisol. Every time I think of Brooke calling me "racist" and "unmindful," I feel the heat rise to my face, and I shake with indignation, embarrassment, humiliation. How can I disclose such feelings to Harry? On the other hand, if indeed I do have a meaningful relationship with him, or at least am developing one, shouldn't I be able to confide in him?

I want him to think of me as independent and strong, but am I presenting myself to him in an unrealistic way? Why can't I just be myself? Way back when Cameron dumped me, he said, "You don't know yourself. You're not the person you think you are." It was the worst insult I had ever received from a man. I wanted to fire back, no, *you* don't me, you big phony! Why wouldn't you tell me how many siblings you had and where you were from? Ordinary, commonplace information I deserved to have? He was all wrong for me, as I've said. Harry might be right. Still, how involved do I want to be with him? How involved does he want to be with me? Too soon to tell.

I carry around *The Thing with Feathers* as it has always been my habit to have a book with me, but my bookmark is only sixty pages in, and as the days go by, it doesn't budge. I'm tired of looking at it. On my way into the dining room one evening, I slip into the library and park *The Thing with Feathers* between Danielle Steel and Nicholas Sparks. I leave the room feeling lighter. It's okay to not finish a book. It's about time I figured that out.

I sit with Margaret, Iris, and Pandora at the bridge table in the sunroom. Outside, it's nearly as black as night in midafternoon, lightning and thunder in the distance. At any moment, we're sure to get a deluge.

As Margaret deals, I think of Marisol and yet another wave of remorse ripples through me. "Me and my big mouth! I still feel just horrible about Marisol."

Iris leans into me, cocking her ear. "Your parasol? You lost it? Where do you think you left it?"

Margaret and Pandora laugh, and I don't feel like broadcasting my shortcomings at the top of my lungs. It would help if Iris wore her hearing aids, but she's too vain for that. "I'm afraid I got her fired," I say.

Pandora sorts her cards and blurts, "Naw, she quit."

Iris turns to Pandora. "Who's having a fit, about what?"

"How do you know?" I ask Pandora.

"A friend of a friend hired her. Cushy job in a private home as a personal caregiver. Better pay, less work. Shady Meadow can't keep a jewel like Marisol."

This relieves my guilt somewhat, but I still feel terrible. I'm not too old to learn a lesson here: don't be too quick to believe what you hear, don't be too quick to act. "Poor Susan Hartley! Can you believe such a brilliant mind can just turn to mush?"

Margaret peers over her fan of cards. "Off to memory care she goes."

"Snow?" says Iris. "Oh, I doubt it. It never snows here. Tahoe might get some."

35

Harry and I work through all his big-note duet books. It's lots of fun, but I crave more challenging music. I dip into my music cabinet and come up with Brahms' *Waltzes* Op. 39, Faure's *Dolly* Suite, and Debussy's *Petite Suite.* Leafing through the volumes, the familiar music plays in my mind. Some of the selections are difficult, but some are at an intermediate level which I'm certain Harry and I can play, if only he could see the notes. At least, we would have fun trying. I'm so glad Brooke wasn't able to talk me into giving away all my music.

I almost run to Harry's place to show him my find.

He eagerly takes the music from me and thumbs through it. His face crumples into a wince. "Hmm. These are great pieces, but the print is pretty small. It will take me a while to recognize the notes."

"Then let's play something slow. Here." I open to Debussy's "En bateau."

Harry bends closer to the music, lifts his chin, and looks through the very bottoms of his eyes. "I might be able to handle the Secondo part."

"Super! Let's try it."

We take our seats at Harry's Clavinova, and he studies his part before we began. We manage a few measures before he fumbles through a barrage of wrong notes. He scrutinizes the faulty measure through his magnifying glass, and we began again.

More breakdowns. It's just impossible. I regret bringing the music to him. It only supports what I already knew: Harry can't recognize notes fast enough to play in time. After a few more attempts at Debussy, he suggests, "Want to go back to my big-notes?"

Not after Debussy. "Not right now. Why don't you work on your Bach?"

As Harry practices, I sink into one of his recliners with a magazine. I read a whole paragraph of an article before I realize the meaning isn't registering. I'm busy thinking how I could make the music big enough for Harry to see. Suddenly, I leap up and stride up behind Harry, startling him as I snatch my duet books off the Clavinova.

"Gotta go." I hug him from behind and gave him a quick peck on the cheek.

"Where's the fire?"

"I'll be back."

When I sheepishly approach the front desk and ask to use the photocopier, Latrice replies with a smile and a nod, apparently not holding any grudges against me. I set the machine to magnify twenty-five per cent larger and discover that it's difficult to get all the notes on the page. After several ruined copies, I realize I have to set the pages sideways and copy first the top, then the bottom of the pages. There's overlap, so I have to pencil-out repetitious lines. I copy not only the Debussy's "En Bateau" but Brahms' slow waltz in D minor, and Faure's "Berceuse." In my room, I cut and glue the pages together, top to bottom, then front to back, checking the original scores to prevent mistakes. The process is time-consuming, and my finished product stands eighteen inches high and looks a little weird, but I'm pretty sure Harry will be able to read it.

When I present it to him, he's obviously delighted that I've gone to all the trouble. He studies the music several minutes, and then we begin to play. We make it through the first page of the Debussy, but then, when I turn the page, Harry stumbles and quits.

"Aren't the notes big enough?"

"They're big enough when I look straight ahead and down, but when I look up at the top of page, the notes are too fuzzy to decipher."

"Oh! Oh!" I think a moment, then spring from the bench to grab scissors off his desk. I cut a page of my tall score through the middle and set the two halves, top and bottom, side by side, like a child's primer. "Now try."

Success! Harry can read the music. I clap in delight. I jump up and gather up my tall scores. "Back to the drawing board."

He laughs. "You know there's going to be twice as many page turns."

"I know it's a pain, but we can decide which part is the least busy and assign each page turn."

He shakes his head, chuckling. "You're quite determined, aren't you?"

"Absolutely."

Over the next several weeks, we make good progress on the duets. Harry still has some problems recognizing the notes, the frequent page turns are annoying, but the primer-sized editions I have handcrafted do work. Harry has a great sense of rhythm, and I am easily caught up in his flow. I especially enjoy this because my sense of rhythm is not innate. I had to teach it to my body with hours and hours of metronome work over many years, and still it is not reliable. With Harry, it's smooth sailing.

One afternoon after a satisfying session with the Debussy, Harry exclaims, "We ought to program our duets on the talent show!"

"What? Oh, no, no, no." I lean back on the bench and cross my arms.

Harry is surprised by my reaction. "Why not?"

"I've suffered from stage fright since I was twelve."

"But sweetie, I'm not talking Carnegie Hall. Most of the folks in the audience don't know one note from the other. It would be loads of fun."

I shake my head. "It was my ardent wish to be a performer, but my body will not cooperate. My heart pounds, my fingers shake. The waiting is the worst. I used to have diarrhea for weeks before a recital. Once I started a performance, actually once I made my first mistake, I was okay, not great, but okay. Usually. Usually it wasn't a disaster, but sometimes it was. Memory slips, mostly, finger slips, a loss of concentration for just an instant, but that's all it takes to really mess up. In college, I took up open water swimming. I thought I could confront my fears by swimming across a lake. I was wrong. I wasn't a bit afraid of the water, but my stage fright continued."

"You can swim across a lake? I would drown. Playing the piano isn't life-threatening. And don't worry about memory slips. We'll use the music for our duets."

"No, no, no. I can never be comfortable performing because I can never convince myself I'm any good. I've got the soul of a musician, but none of the equipment that goes along with it: fast fingers, a good ear, a solid sense of rhythm."

"But you are good. You're classically trained. You're very musical."

"Thanks for that." I bump shoulders with Harry, such a dear, sweet man.

36

In the Sunday brunch buffet line, Margaret picks up a muffin, turns it around in her hand, sniffs it, and sets it back in its basket.

"Margaret!"

"Well, I couldn't tell what kind it is. Banana nut. I hate bananas. Oh, look, we have a celebrity among us."

I wince. The Susan Hartley-Marisol episode is still a fresh wound. I thought Susan was long gone. I look where Margaret is pointing and see a tiny woman in a wheelchair, deeply wrinkled and liver-spotted. She's wearing an orangish-pink tracksuit and her head is thrown back in laughter.

"That's Coral Broome. She's a hundred-and-five."

I scoop a big spoonful of fresh fruit onto my plate. "So that's her claim to fame? Her age?"

"Oh, no. She's a world cycling champion."

"Oh? What year was that?"

"Last year. She rode the farthest distance in one hour of women, age one hundred to one-hundred-and-four."

I give Coral a second look. "How many women were in her age group?"

"Just one. She's planning to set another world record this year because she's moved up an age category."

I'm mildly surprised someone that old has any plans at all. "Are you sure she can still get on a bike?"

"You'll see. She trains right outside our place. She's just in a wheel-chair to rest her legs when she's not riding. She's strong, though. Cycling is very good for the legs. Murray knew a guy who had both knees replaced, and he could ride two hundred miles in one day."

I'm certain she's exaggerating, but I let it go. She reaches for another muffin. I click my tongue. "If you touch it, you have to take it."

Margaret's hand pauses in the air. "What kind do you think it is?"

I point. "Blueberry. You can see them."

"Oh, yeah." Margaret withdraws her hand. "I hate blueberry."

"What kind do you like?"

"I like oat bran with raisins. You know that joke about oat bran muffins?" I shake my head and she continues. "An old guy and his wife die within a couple of months of each other and reunite in heaven. It's gorgeous, with green fields and streets paved in gold, and lots of their friends who had passed before them are there. 'This is wonderful,' gushed the wife. 'Why didn't we get here sooner?' The husband says, 'We would've if it weren't for your damn oat bran muffins.'" Margaret emits her signature bray, and I laugh along with her, not so much because of the joke, but because of her delight in telling it. "Gotta keep stuffing down those bran muffins if I'm gonna make it to a hundred."

I roll my eyes. "God forbid."

"Why? How long do you want to live?"

"I don't know."

"Come on, pick a number."

I wave her suggestion away. "Just so my body goes before my mind."

"A number."

"Oh, all right! Eighty-five or ninety. Ninety-five tops."

"But not a hundred?"

She got me! We laugh some more. There's no oat bran muffins in sight, so Margaret chooses plain wheat bread and pops it in the toaster. She nudges me with the back of her wrist, nods toward the door. "Get a load of that outfit."

Dottie enters donned in the blouse with a cut-out shoulder and ripped jeans.

"The attack-by-wild-animals style looks especially bad on the elderly."

Margaret lightly slaps my arm. "Shame on you for calling us 'the elderly.'"

"You're the one who's talking about living to a hundred." I sneak a few more glances at Dottie, not wanting to stare. "She looks pretty good though. You know, not high."

Margaret nods. "Yep. She has her good days."

When we settle at a table, Margaret wiggles her bottom and says, "I talked Sam into doing the ballroom dance classes with me. He's got two left feet and just sort of stumbles around stomping on my toes. What a hoot!"

Lying on my tongue, ready to fly from my mouth, is my opinion of Sam. I want to say he refers to his marriages as entrapments. He's such a slob that he doesn't know how to use a wastebasket. The urge to talk trash about Sam is powerful, but the older I get, the stronger my filter is. Margaret is totally gaga over him. She may even think less of me for dumping on him.

"You and Harry should take the dance classes with us. We'd have a blast. And your toes would be safer than mine. Harry is a smooth dancer." She sways as if she is waltzing in a man's arms.

I shrug. "I don't know. I don't think so. I don't want us pegged as a couple, not yet anyway."

I wait as Margaret gulps down a big swig of coffee. I expect her to counter my reservation, but she says, "I don't blame you. It's complicated."

What's complicated? I want to ask, but she's back to Sam. "His girls came to visit him, both of them in one week.".

I stir my coffee, thinking girl and *boy*.

"They're quite far apart in age, you know. Two different marriages, you know. Jennifer is the little one, his favorite. Phyllis is quite a bit older."

Philip.

37

There's this wedding we're invited to, Brooke, Jonathan, and me—all of us. It's a girl Brooke grew up with, Mallory Martin. I never liked her; she was kind of snotty, and she wasn't very nice to Brooke. Didn't her parents know "Mal" means bad? Plus the alliteration of her name sounds dumb, although who knows what last name she goes by now. This is her third marriage, so really what's the point? I thought nowadays after people have a couple of failed marriages, they just shack up. I told Brooke I don't want to go to the wedding. It's in Santa Barbara which will require the expense of a hotel and a gift—that girl has a three-hundred-dollar pot on her registry, no takers yet—plus there's the long hours in the car, listening to finicky Jonathan pick everything apart.

But Brooke won't take no for an answer. She calls and texts. "Come on, Mom, it will be good for you to get out."

For once, I don't want to get out. I'm settled in my routine, my walks, yukking it up with Margaret, bridge with the girls, yoga even, and best of all, I'll have to admit, hanging out with Harry. During one phone call I say to Brooke, "I don't know why you even want to go. I don't remember you and Mallory being that good of friends."

"It's true we were in different groups in high school, but Mom, we grew up together. T-ball, dance, 4-H, all that shit."

"Remember, you got the idea to rent a limo with her to go to Sadie's freshman year, and she invited two other couples and crowded you and your date out, so your dad ended up driving you?"

There's a pause. "That's not how it happened, Mom."

I don't bother with a rebuttal. Brooke and I frequently have conflicting memories. It's sometimes hard to tell we've had shared lives. "I'll pass."

"Come on, Mommy. It will be fun. We can leave Jonathan at home. Just us girls. I'll get the hotel and the gift."

Something is going on here that I can't quite figure out. Probably Jonathan doesn't want to go and Brooke doesn't want to go alone. Or maybe she really does want to treat me to a getaway weekend, play nice. She knows she hurt my feelings at our last lunch, calling me racist and unmindful. She can sense I don't pick up her calls readily or return her texts always, giving her the lukewarm shoulder.

The thing is Brooke can be fun. She's my favorite traveling companion. That long-ago planned European trip with moocher Sheridan—I called my travel agent and asked her to change the name Sheridan Lark to Brooke Corbyn on all the travel documents and reservations. That summer Brooke had just graduated from college and I gave her the trip as a graduation present. She was the same age that I was on my first trip to Europe.

My daughter loves gross, weird things: the Disgusting Food Museum in Malmö; St. Teresa's five-hundred-year-old black severed finger bearing a tarnished jeweled ring in a glass case in Avila, a sacred relic; the Paris Ossuary with its walls of stacked tibias and skulls of seven million dead people; *La Specola* in Florence, the Eighteenth-Century anatomical wax museum with Venus-like young women, their exposed guts in violent purples and reds. After some of these sights, I had a hard time eating lunch. I got a kick out of Brooke's reaction to the abundance of exposed male genitalia in European statuary and paintings. Apparently, she hadn't taken art appreciation for GE credit. Copies of Michelangelo's *David* abound in Europe. There's Caravaggio's *Cupid*, Rodin's *Thinker*, the Barberini *Faun*, the little *Manneken Pis* in Brussels, and so many butt-naked ancient Greeks. It got so when Brooke was confronted with yet another set of exposed male privates, she turned around, stamped a foot, and burst into peals of laughter that sent rivulets of tears streaming down her face. Such hilarity is infectious, and I got to laughing, too. To this day, I can't see a depiction of *David* without a memory and a smile.

"So, Mom? Please? What do you say?"

38

On the drive down Highway 101 my phone doesn't stop pinging. First, it's Margaret texting, then some spam, but mostly Harry.

"Who keeps texting you?" Brooke asks.

"A friend."

"Margaret?"

"Yes and another friend."

"I'm so glad you're making new friends. See? Better than moping around that big old house of yours all by yourself."

"I did not mope. I loved my home. And my cat."

Another ping.

"What does she want?"

"He wants to know about dinner plans for tomorrow night."

"*He?*" Brooke taps her perfectly-manicured, blue nails on her leather-padded steering wheel and looks askance at me. "What's his name? Do dinner plans mean walking into the dining room together?"

I gaze nonchalantly out the passenger window. "Not really."

"Then what?" She elbows me to get my attention, and when I turn to her, her eyes are wide with excitement.

"Watch the road!"

"I've got self-driving."

"There's plenty of accidents with that."

She peers out the windshield again, grinning ear-to-ear. "Tell me, Mom. Are you going out to eat?"

"No, he wants to cook dinner for me in his apartment. Wants to know what time I'll get in."

"Apartment? Is it at Shady Meadow?"

"Yes, a beautiful unit. Just like in real life."

"So you're visiting a guy in his apartment? Do you sleep over?"

"Brooke, no!" I exclaim in mock indignation. I wriggle my shoulders. "Not yet."

My daughter emits a cascade of giggles. "What's his name?"

"Harry. He's a pretty good pianist. He's learning a Bach fugue for the talent show. We play duets together."

"This guy Harry has got you playing again? That's huge! For the talent show? Can I come?"

"*He's* playing in the talent show."

"Mama's got a boyfriend," she chants.

I'm forced to smile. "Stop!"

"You're smart to go slow. I remember when you fell madly in love with that Sheridan guy."

"I was never in love with Sheridan."

"You were devastated when he backed out of that European trip."

I don't try to correct her. I never told her the real reason that trip fell through. I guess admitting I had a potential gigolo on my hands hurt my pride. "Lucky for you."

"Damn right! That was the best vacation I ever had."

Happiness explodes in my chest. "I never knew you felt that way about it."

"I know I was sulky some of the time. I had just started dating Jonathan, and I was in a hurry to get home, afraid he would forget about me. But reflecting as I've gotten older, I realize some of things I was in a hurry to get through or skip over were the best times of my life."

I have known this about my daughter since she was four, but I don't say so. "Now you're talking like an old person."

"I am old, Mom! I'm pushing fifty."

"Fifty! At fifty you're a mere child."

The wedding is only entertaining because we make fun of it with each other. Mallory Martin was just a twig as a girl, but she's gotten really fat, maybe fatter after she bought her wedding gown, because she's oozing out of it, especially in the back. Why do women feel such diabolical glee when skinny women get fat?

"Fat back is the worst," comments Brooke, picking apart the sushi on her plate. She accuses me of being judgmental when, in fact, she is the most judgmental person I know. It could be the wine talking. We've had more than our share.

The groom is sweating profusely. His jet black, greasy hair is obviously dyed. "A powder blue tux and frilly shirt?" I mutter in Brooke's ear. "Is this the sixties?"

Brooke's wine glass pauses midway between the table and her mouth as she gazes at the newlyweds waltzing—yes, waltzing—to *The Fiddler on the Roof* song "Sunrise, Sunset."

"They look happy."

"They do. You know what they say, 'Third time is a charm.'"

"Mom, that's mean!" Sure enough, I get dinged for being mean when Brooke is way meaner.

One reason Brooke wanted to attend this wedding is that she thought she'd see some of the kids she grew up with, but she doesn't recognize a soul and neither do I.

When we say our goodbyes, Mallory hugs Brooke hard. The bride's gardenias are wilted, her elaborate hairdo is sticking out in all directions, her makeup is running down her cheeks, but her face is glowing. She grasps Brooke's hand and my hand, and sincerely gushes, "I'm so happy you came. It means so much to me. Thank you, Brooke; you, too Mrs. Corbyn. Remember when we shared a limo for Sadie Hawkins? That was such a blast!"

Brooke and I had planned to go out to dinner, but we are both so stuffed with hors d'oeuvres, wine, and cake, that we skip it. Later, when we get hungry, we sprawl on our beds in comfy lounging clothes and munch M&Ms from the candy machine and share a bottle of wine from the mini bar.

"She really thought you and she split a limo ride, when, in fact, she booted you out," I comment.

"That's not how it happened, Mom."

The wine puts me in an argumentative mood. "Honey, I know for a fact Daddy drove you and your date. You wept bitter tears over that whole episode. At one point, you even threatened to cancel on—what was that kid's name? You had the biggest crush on him. Benny Somebody."

"Yeah, Benny Garrett. What a douche."

I pour more wine into our plastic cups. Both of us prefer wine glasses, but what can we do? This hotel charges wine glass prices and delivers plastic cup services.

"The cutest boy in your class, kind of a bad boy."

"You can say that again. He was the one that caused all the limo drama."

"What? How?"

Brooke blows out air, causing her lips to vibrate. "Oh, Benny refused to ride with Mallory's date, Gerald Cushman. He and Mallory were in the God squad—you know, the Campus Crusade kids. Gerry helped get Benny busted for dealing pot out of his trombone case."

"He played trombone? That's a lot dope to be carrying around."

"The case wasn't completely full, Mom. He needed room for his instrument." She laughs as she's trying to pour us more wine so that it splashes on her white satin sleeve. She doesn't seem to notice or maybe she doesn't care. "Anyway, word got around about some kid dealing weed at school so the campus cop started calling kids into the office to ask them questions. Gerry told the truth."

"Wow! How come I'm just finding this out now?"

"Because I was afraid you wouldn't let me go to the dance with Benny if you knew."

"I think I was more open-minded than that. "

"Anyway, Benny was awful to me that night. He danced the whole night with Ashley Grove and left me stranded."

"So that's why you never picked up your Sadie Hawkins photos, even though we'd paid for them. You kept telling me you forgot to do it."

"Yeah, I didn't want you to know what a shitty time I had. You were always so set on me being happy."

"All mothers want their kids to be happy."

"Not as much as you, Mom. I felt a lot of pressure. Sometimes, it was just easier to pretend to be happy. But there's more to the story. When Benny left me stranded, I drifted over to sit with Mallory's group. Gerry danced with me a couple of times and so did this other guy. Mallory talked me into ditching Benny and going home with them in the limo. We didn't go straight home. We went to the batting cages and then to Denny's."

"The batting cages? In your formals?"

Brooke hoots to the ceiling.

"How did Benny get home?"

"How the fuck would I know? In a couple of days he was gone. The cops made a deal with his parents. They could keep him out of juvie by getting him the hell out of town. He went to go live with an aunt in Phoenix." Brooke tips the wine bottle over my cup, but only a dribble comes out. "End of story."

The next morning, Brooke suggests we spend another night away, in Pismo Beach. She entices me with clam chowder bread bowls, salt water taffy, and a barefooted walk on the beach. I leave my phone back at the motel, thinking the ping, ping, ping would detract from the placid crash of waves against the rocks. Brooke's toe nails are blue to match her fingers. The sand is cool and fine under my feet, the sky is wide and gray, the surfers in their black wetsuits bob in the water like seals, and I feel fantastic.

I grin at Brooke. "Good idea."

"I thought you'd like it. Can I ask you something about your divorce?" I nod and wait. "I never understood how you felt about it. Was it mutual?"

"God, no. I was a death-do-us-parter. If Daddy hadn't left me for Tabby, he'd be alive today, taking care of me. That's what old married people do for each other. I wouldn't have to live at Shady Meadow."

"I really didn't know what was going on. I hid out at college. I should have been there for you, Mom."

"No, honey, you had your own life to live."

"I could have come home more. Were you lonely?"

"At first. But once I got past all the upheaval and anger, I saw that the divorce had its advantages."

"Really? Like what advantages?"

"Your dad wasn't around."

"Then what were the disadvantages?"

"Your dad wasn't around."

I get a laugh out of her. "Did you feel—maybe I shouldn't be asking you this."

"Ask me anything."

"Did you feel replaced by Tabby?"

"That lightweight? Hell, no. I came to understand your dad wasn't happy. We'd had this long, shared life, we'd raised you. That didn't go away, but your dad needed something more. So, yeah, Tabby."

"Well, I felt replaced." Brooke folds her arms and hugs herself. "Daddy's family became Tabby's three little girls. He was complacent to forget about me."

"Honey, no."

"I hardly saw him."

"You were away at college."

"Yeah, and I'd think: I'm not contacting him, I'm going to wait for him to contact me, but months would go by and I wouldn't hear from him. I'd break down and call him to plan something."

"He was always so happy when you did. He told me so."

"Yeah? So why didn't he contact me?"

"You were pretty hard on him, if you remember. He figured things would go smoother between the two of you if getting together was your idea."

"Yeah?" Brooke's eyebrows lift hopefully.

"Yeah. He was always afraid of confrontation, of rejection. He was a big chicken. Brack! Brack!" I put my hand in my armpit and flap my elbow in emphasis.

She laughs. "I was kind of a bully to Dad. Jonathan never let me get away with that with him, one of the reasons I married him." She lifts her arms overhead for a stretch. "I wonder what happened to Tabby's girls."

"All grown up now. Time marches on. I got an invitation to the middle one's wedding last June."

Brooke looks wide-eyed. "You never told me that. Did you go?"

"Fuck, no."

We laugh some more.

Back at the motel, I check my phone and find six messages from Harry. I forgot to tell him I was staying away a second night. I text him my apologies, promising to let him know when I return to Shady Meadow, but by then I am so exhausted, all I want to do is fall into bed.

39

When it's time to get up, I roll over and go back to sleep. When it's time for breakfast, I decide to skip it, still feeling full from so much extra eating this weekend. Finally, I drag myself out of bed, shower, and wash my hair. I'm ready for coffee, but instead of leaving my room, I sink into my recliner to reflect on my conversations with Brooke. That daughter of mine! We really did have a good time together.

There's a timid knock on the door. Who could it be? Probably Margaret. Maybe housekeeping. I'm not quite ready to face anybody yet. With a sigh and a grunt, I hoist myself out of my chair and open the door. A rather striking older man in fitted jeans and a pink polo unbuttoned at the neckline is standing in the hall. He has a strong, square jaw and a ring of white fluffy hair. I recognize the heavy, horn-rimmed glasses first.

"Harry? You shaved!"

"May I come in?" he asks rather formally.

"Alright, sure." But I'm not so sure. I haven't dried my hair and it's slick against my scalp. I'm wearing an old, stained sweatshirt that once belonged to Al because it's comfy. I'm flopping around in men's moccasins because women's are too narrow for me. Harry has never stepped foot into my room. He looks too big to be here, fills too much space. With the blinds drawn, it's dark and cramped compared to his airy, bright apartment. My bed is unmade and his never bares a wrinkle. My cabinet of cat figurines appears childish.

My nightstand, cluttered with a large pump bottle of moisturizing lotion, a tube of Aspercreme, a jar of Vaseline, and a slightly-used Kleenex that's good for another blow, seems old-ladyish.

He doesn't appear to notice his surroundings. He looks soberly into my face and asks, "Have I been dumped?"

"What? Harry, no!" It's a denial and an admission at the same time. No, I haven't stopped seeing him, and yes, we have something going, "in a relationship" as young people put it, "going steady" as it was phrased in our generation.

"You told me you would contact me when you got in last night!" he accuses.

"Oh! I'm sorry! I was just so tired."

"You blew off my texts."

"What? I didn't blow—"

"I haven't seen you in three days!"

I have to laugh, I can't help it. After all these years, boy time has morphed into girl time. I get the giggles which causes hiccups.

Harry looks stricken, his mouth slightly open. "What's so funny?"

"Nothing, dear man. Nothing at all! I'm so happy to see you." I stroke his clean-shaven cheek with the back of my hand. "I like this."

"Margaret said you would. She said you were turned off by the Santa Claus look."

I feel a heated blush rise up from my throat to my hairline. Harry sought counsel from Margaret about me? God knows what she could have blurted. "I didn't say 'turned off.'"

"I didn't even know I had the Santa Claus look. And here." He pats his open neckline. "She said my chest hair really grossed you out. I didn't realize—"

"Damn that Margaret! I didn't say—well, it was spilling out."

"Why didn't you tell me? My dad used to get hair hanging out of his nostrils. My mom would complain about it, and he would take the nail clippers and trim it back. It was as simple as that."

"Well, then what don't you like about me?"

I expect him to say I'm perfect, that's the sort of guy he is, but then he fires back, "Those baggy jeans you're wearing really sag in the seat!"

That penetrating look of his. I don't believe Al ever drank me up like that, nor my first boyfriend Mike, nor any man. Well, there was Tony, the guy I ran off to Europe with, but he was a moron and had me up on a pedestal, which is different. Cherished at last! That's how Harry makes me feel. I throw my arms around his neck and clasp my hands at his nape. It's clean-shaven, too. "I think you're drop-dead gorgeous."

"No, you are." He moves in for a tighter hug, our full bodies pressed together. He pulls me even closer and cups my ass in two handfuls. It's thrilling. When is the last time a man has touched me there?

40

"You chart your mucus."

"Excuse me?"

"Yeah, that's what it's called."

Margaret and I are walking around the park, when I ask her about something I've always been curious about: the rhythm method. "Explain."

She slows her gait as she always does when she's trying to walk and talk at the same time. "I sat on the toilet and before I peed I wiped myself and checked the toilet paper. If it was thick and sticky, like a raw egg-—that's the hands off, don't-come-near-me time, when you're ovulating. Other times the toilet paper is just wet and slippery or plain dry—the safe time."

"How often did you have to check it?"

"Oh, every day. Then I charted it, marked it on my private little calendar I kept under the bathroom sink behind my big ole box of sanitary napkins."

"That sounds like so much work."

"Ah, no, you get used to it, just part of your morning routine like washing your face and brushing your teeth."

"And there's a predictable pattern, I assume."

"Oh, yeah. Three or four days after your period is a real safe time. It's called the honeymoon period. Then the mucus shows up and gets really gooey by about nine days around ovulation. After that, it's okay to make love for about eleven to fourteen days until your next period."

I'm curious about during a period, but I let it go. "Thanks for the info. I always wondered."

"You're welcome."

I nudge her gently with my elbow and lower my voice. "Did you ever do it when you weren't supposed to?"

Margaret rolls her eyes to the sky, considering the question. "We tried not to. But then Murray could get mighty irritable when he was super horny. Sometimes I let him just go ahead. I encouraged him, even. I missed making love, too! And he was always so grateful after. Treated me so nice. Brought home flowers or a Snickers. He even dried the dishes once."

I nod and grin. "That is nice."

"And this is what we thought, me and Murray both thought this: a baby is a gift from God. If He wanted to send us one, it didn't matter what we did. God would send us another baby."

My lower lip juts forward. "How many times was that, may I ask, when you weren't planning for one, I mean?"

"Let me see now." She touches the tip of her right forefinger to the tip of her left one, then taps her middle finger in the same way. She pauses. Slowly she moves on to her ring finger. A longer pause. She gravitates toward her baby finger, then abruptly shifts back to her ring finger. "Three! Three out of seven ain't bad!" She guffaws her Margaret guffaw.

She stops walking. I don't realize it for a few steps and have to go back for her. She has a distant look on her face, both defiant and sheepish. "Just between you and me, after seven kids I went to the doctor and got fitted for a diaphragm. I charted like usual and all, but I used the diaphragm, too. Don't tell Murray."

"Oh, I won't."

"I think he knew. I think he thought the same way: seven kids are enough. It's considered a sin, you know, birth control, and I confessed it every time I went to confession."

"What did the priest say?"

"Say three Our Fathers and three Hail Marys." Margaret grins and resumes walking. "Your confessor isn't supposed to know who you are. That's why it's all dark in the confessional with the little screen and all, but after going to the same priest your whole life, they know who you are, for sure. Father Patrick probably thought we had enough kids, too."

41

Dottie comes knocking on my door again, looking for a *Wheel of Fortune* viewing companion. She's kind of a pain in the ass, but I like her popcorn. I haven't heard any outbursts through the wall recently, no yelling, no threats with a frying pan. She hasn't bothered Harry either, as far as I know. I see her around, in the dining room, the TV room, at Bingo. She's got her own circle of friends. The residents in old folks' homes form cliques just like high school kids.

Today Dottie is presentable in matching orange polyester knit pants and top, with a floral print, gauzy over blouse that flutters around her to mid-thigh. Her hair is done in two gray braids which ride over her shoulders like a school girl's, and her face is scrubbed clean except for a streak of red lipstick. She doesn't appear entirely sober, however. Her eyes are blood-shot, her speech is slow and slurred, and she's got the jitters. She doesn't seem all that interested in the action on the TV screen, but rather, her eyes dart around my room. Is she looking for something or is she just being nosey?

She comes to life, however, when the puzzle is about to be solved. "No matter where you go there you are," she shouts.

"You're good at this," I tell her.

"I've seen a million of these. I'll tell you why I separated from my husband. He didn't like watching the same channels as me."

"Really? Couldn't you just get two TVs?"

"Yeah, but he got to be so unattractive, just an old duffer. I couldn't stand to look at him."

"Marriage is long," I admit. "I got a divorce."

Dottie cackles. "You couldn't stand yours either."

"No, he couldn't stand me. He found someone new."

Dottie eyes widen like a taunt. "Was she prettier? Sexier?"

I'm caught in the middle of confiding in Dottie and check myself. Oh, why the hell not? "Al and I had stopped having sex," I say flatly. "She got him interested again."

"Men!" Dottie raises both hands, fingers splayed and slams them down on her knees.

"I guess after a long time, marriage is just dull, and someone new is exciting, puts a spark back into life. Al's second wife made him very happy. That is, until she got him killed."

I expect a response I don't get. "He got the bed I want."

"Excuse me?"

"My husband, he got the best bed. The boys said I got the one I said I wanted but I wanted the other one. They don't listen." She stares at my nightstand, her eyes squinting. "Do you mind if I use your powder room?"

"Go right ahead."

"I'm going to get it back."

"What?"

"The bed. The best bed."

"Oh."

She hands me the bowl of popcorn and lists and weaves toward my bathroom. Once she is inside, she locks the door as if I would invade her privacy. She's in there a long time. I hear cabinets opening, contents clinking and shuffling, which gets my dander up. It didn't occur to me until now that I shouldn't have trusted her in my bathroom. What was I supposed to say when she asked to use it? Nope, use your own? When she emerges, she announces, "I gotta go."

"But your show isn't over."

"I…I just remembered something," she says vaguely.

When I hand over her popcorn bowl, I notice her gauzy pocket is weighed down. I peer into it and see a white twist cap. Without another word, she scuttles out of my room. I don't stop her because I can't think of a gracious way to confront her about stealing my Nyquil.

42

That was the thing about Tabby: she made Al happy, something I wasn't able to do. She made him want to take her skiing. That's like— oh, I don't know—convincing a grizzly bear that roller skating would be fun. Oh, how often I have wished Tabby had smacked into that tree instead of Al! I have imagined it over and over. But then, where would her girls be without her? Al wouldn't have known what to do with them. They had a father, of course. I don't know much about him. I wonder if he ever took Tabby skiing. I don't know that either.

Al and I did golf together for a while, nine holes on Sunday afternoons. I went along with it because it was at least one thing he was willing to do with me. I liked hitting the ball; I was strong enough to drive it pretty far. The trouble was my aim was off. I often didn't know where the ball went and had to spend a lot of time looking for it. When I putted, the ball would roll by the hole in one direction and then pass it in the other. This would go on for so long I had to laugh.

"Are you doing that on purpose?" Al asked.

"What?"

"Missing the cup."

"Why would I?"

"Christ, Colette, line yourself up. At least *try* to sink it. You're pissing me off." That was one of his favorite expressions.

One time, Al got stuck in a sand trap. Here was a grown man hacking away at a little white ball with a stick that has like a little shovel on the end, spraying sand all over himself. He missed again. His third stroke appeared successful, but then the overhanging lip of the sand trap caught his ball, and it rolled back, hitting his toe. I did my best to hold in my laughter. I turned my head so he wouldn't see the tears rolling down my cheeks.

The following Sunday, when it was time to get ready to go golfing, he announced that he didn't want to play with me anymore. He said he preferred to play with people who respect the game.

"What do you mean?" I laughed.

"There you go," said scowling Al. "My point exactly." Another one of his favorite expressions.

As far as I know, Tabby never played golf with Al. I have to admit, in their short marriage, she was smarter about being his wife.

43

That afternoon, while I'm enjoying Harry's coffee and home-made oatmeal raisin cookies at his kitchen counter, I'm on the verge of telling him about Dottie stealing my Nyquil. "Hey, you'll never guess what your nemesis did this morning," is just about to roll off my tongue, when I flash on his probable reaction. He has this kind of pained expression where all his features sort of bunch up in the center of his face and ripples form on his brow. At the time of the theft, I anticipated Harry and I would have a good laugh over Dottie's antics, but now I see that it isn't funny; it's sad.

Telling Margaret about it would be a mistake, too. Then everybody would know, laughing and ridiculing Dottie behind her back. It's cruel, even to someone like Dottie who is rotten to my dear Harry. Admin is out, too. They already have me pegged as a tattletale. Every time I think of Marisol, I feel regret.

I wipe the cookie crumbs from the corners from my mouth. "Delicious. A real treat." I peck Harry on the cheek and excuse myself to use the bathroom. I notice, behind the toilet at eye level what looks like a fancy piece of graph paper. Obviously, as Harry pees, he would be staring at it.

When I return to the counter, I comment, "Interesting décor in the bathroom."

"The what?"

"The graph in the bathroom, over the toilet."

"Oh, that. That prevents me from going blind."

"Really? How?"

"I have dry AMD, but I could advance to the wet form when the retinas bleed and cause blindness. Luckily, there're shots you can get in your eyes to stop the bleeding. There's no going back, though; the damage can't be reversed. If the lines on my chart look broken or wavy, it's means an onset of wet AMD and time for me to rush over to my retina specialist to start a round of shots."

"That's good to know. I've wondered what it's like looking out of your eyes. I've seen pictures in magazine ads which show people with big black spots the size of quarters obstructing their vision."

Harry shakes his head, smiling. "I don't have that. My field of vision is as good as anybody's. I just can't see detail, what it takes to read an eye chart."

There's a knock on his door.

When Harry answers, I hear a woman's voice I immediately recognize. "Hi, Harry."

"Hi, Brooke."

"I've heard so much about you," they say in unison, a Jinx-you-owe-me-a-Coke moment.

This is how they meet. I'm mortified, like a teen girl caught in bed with her boyfriend by her mom, even though the generational thing is reversed, and I'm not doing anything but sitting at Harry's kitchen counter.

"Come in. I bet you're looking for your mom."

As Brooke appears, I stand to confront her. "What are you doing here?"

"I knocked on your door, but when there was no answer I went to the front desk, and that friendly woman Latrice told me I might find you here."

I didn't realize admin keeps tabs on which residents associate with one another. I suppose it's only a natural progression of things, but I feel my privacy has been violated by Latrice directing Brooke to Harry's place. I counterattack with "Aren't you supposed to be at work?"

"I took the afternoon off to take you to the doctor. Come on, Mom, we'll be late."

"Oh, that." I forgot all about my appointment." I fold my arms tightly across my body. "D-L-R-O-W."

Brooke's eyes widened.

"That's 'world' spelled backwards. It's what the doctor will ask me to do. And fold a paper into quarters and count backwards from a hundred by sevens. A waste of time."

"Your checkups are not a waste of time."

"Ninety-three, eighty-six, seventy-nine, seventy—"

"Mom!"

"If I have another…" I glance over at Harry, his hands in his front pockets, a blank look on his face. "…episode, I'll go to the damn doctor."

Brooke turns to Harry and beams out her winning smile. "Have you seen this side of her yet? How stubborn she can be?"

"Oh, for fuck's sake!" I stomp out of Harry's apartment. Brooke catches up to me in the hall. I'm ashamed of my own behavior, but I can't seem to help myself. "How dare you stalk me like that!"

"What? What'd I do?" She tries to take my arm, but I elbow her away. "He's cute, Mom, really cute. I like that he didn't interfere."

44

I was almost certain Blessed-day Man—whose real name is Cyrus Dennison—was on his way out, but here he is, sitting at Bingo with a bloom in his cheeks, a little meat on his bones, and his jeweled cross catching the refracted light. I've heard that he's been through chemo and radiation for colon cancer. For now, the treatments have put him in remission.

Between games, Lizzie Rutherford taps Cryus' wrist and says, "You look great."

"I feel great."

"I'm so glad to hear it." Lizzie has a lot of downy facial hair, which causes her foundation to cling and clump. "That's just amazing."

"I had a lot of people praying for me," says Cyrus.

Oh, brother. I don't know why this irks me. I should keep my mouth shut, but I blurt, "Don't you think your doctors had something to do with it?"

Edna Montes says, "Prayer is powerful."

"I don't see that it would matter to you, Edna," I counter. "Aren't you Presbyterian? Don't Presbyterians believe in predestination? Everything's been decided no matter what you do."

Edna peers at me over her half glasses. "You're wrong about that, Colette. I've never heard of any Presbyterian believing in reincarnation."

"I didn't say reincarnation. I said predestination."

Edna looks pointedly at me as if she doesn't believe me. "Oh. I better have my hearing checked."

"You know, Calvinism," I continue. "Presbyterianism is an off-shoot of the teachings of John Calvin."

"Never heard of him," Edna says, which makes me wonder how some people can join a sect without knowing its dogma. "All I know is during COVID, I missed going to church. I missed the fellowship."

"Oh, you mean the donuts afterward?" asks Margaret.

Edna has to laugh.

"I got in the habit of watching Mass on TV during COVID so when we could return to church, I just kept watching." Lizzie scratches her chin vigorously so that her face powder floats like dust particles. "Anyway, long before COVID, I was driven out of St. Philomene's by all those Asians."

I look over at Mei whose countenance remains impassive. At her age, she's heard such slurs hundreds of times, but I'm not going to let it go. "Hey, Mei, are you one of those Asians who drove Lizzie out of her church?"

"What? I...No!" Lizzie sputters and blushes, but she sticks to her guns. "I know what you're getting at, Colette. I'm not racist. I'm not talking about Mei. I'm talking about the influx of Vietnamese after the war. St. Philomene's—the parish I grew up in—became little Hanoi."

Betty Lambert looks from me to Lizzie to Mei, and tries to ease the tension by interjecting, "I believe in the power of prayer. I have a theory about it you may not want to hear, Colette."

I tilt my chin toward her. "Shoot."

"I'm a retired school teacher like yourself, and you may not agree with me at all, but I can tell you when they took God out of our classrooms, the trouble began."

I blink innocently. "God never left the schools. God is everywhere."

"But he can't do as good a job without prayer," insists Betty.

"Of course he can," I argue. "He's God."

Betty's lashes flutter as if she's confused. "That's a different perspective. I'll have to give it some reflection."

I press my knuckle against my mouth to squelch a smirk. I don't believe in anything and yet I just out-faithed the faithful.

"Don't you worry," Cyrus addresses Betty. "Our Supreme Court is going to put prayer back into our schools. How else will our children know about the salvation of our Lord Jesus Christ?"

"I don't believe there's a God," Helen Lewis says flatly. "If there was, he'd be a lot nicer. Like, he wouldn't send an earthquake to Turkey during a blizzard to kill forty thousand poor people who live in hovels to begin with."

"Yeah," says Todd Enwright, a retired aerospace engineer. "Either the earthquake *or* the blizzard. Not both at once."

"Hmm…unless the Puritans were right," interjects Helen. "God loves the rich and has already condemned the poor. Predestination, again, Colette."

"I have a question about Jesus," I say. "You know how the universe has billions of galaxies, actually two trillion is the last estimate. Does Jesus come down from heaven to each one of those civilizations and die on a cross to save sinners?"

Helen gets a kick out of that. "He must be one really busy guy."

"Each civilization is different," says Todd. "So maybe for some civilizations the cross isn't a cross. It's a circle or a rectangle. Maybe a hexagon." His eyes twinkle at Helen.

Cyrus points a forefinger upward. "'In the beginning, God created the heavens and the earth.' Genesis one."

"I think I heard that one before," says Todd.

Cyrus sits back in his chair and spreads his arms. "God has spoken. He means he made the whole universe all for us."

"*Trillions* of galaxies, stars, and planets, and God created them all for the human race?" I clarify.

Clem Learner, who is slumped in his wheelchair and appears to be asleep, opens his eyes as wide as a barn owl and announces, "What a goddamn waste."

$$45$$

The Shady Meadow pool is often deserted, but today is the annual luau, and barbequed pork, pineapple, and free Pina Coladas brings out a crowd. Sam is bouncing on the diving board. He opens his arms and sticks out his barrel chest for a rather graceful swan dive.

"Oh, that man!" Margaret gushes.

I can see how some women could be attracted to his big, burly physique, but oh, my god, what a jerk! I imagine those massive forearms could easily bear down on a pillow covering a victim's face, but I doubt if littering escalates to murder very often. "Is Sam a lot like Murray?" I ask.

Margaret cups her hands under chin and sighs. "Nothing at all. That's what makes him so attractive."

We're lolling like two beached whales on the steps in the shallow end, submerged to our shoulders in the cool, refreshing water. It's only May, but already the temperature soars over one hundred. I watch Harry swim the length of the pool, or try to. He thrashes his arms and legs and holds his head out of the water as he twists it from side-to-side, a grimace on his face. It's not a pretty sight. I'm grateful my mom insisted on swim lessons at the YMCA over several summers. I remember how proud I was as I made my way from tadpole to minnow to fish.

I assess the other women and decide I look pretty damn good in my fuchsia flowered swimsuit. I don't dare sport a two-piece, but my breasts are high and my stomach fairly flat, thanks to the crisscrossed latex in my suit. I stretch out my legs and admire how shapely they still are, thanks to all that walking. Then I chide myself for my vanity. Comparing myself to a bunch of other women at my age! Does judging ever stop?

I see that I have overlooked one woman that looks a lot better than me, Julia Bower, but she's just a baby. She and her husband Ronald are in their early fifties. Why would they want to live with a bunch of old farts? Wouldn't that make them feel old before their time? Actually, it's hard to know what Julia looks like in her swimsuit. She is seated at a corner table under a big umbrella, wrapped in a white robe and wide-legged linen pants. She wears a big, floppy hat, oversized sunglasses, and a white silk scarf up to her nose as she bends over her iPad, tapping away.

Margaret follows my gaze and remarks, "She's emailing the sun, complaining it's too hot."

I've seen Julia at dinner peel back the crust of a piece of pie and rake her fork over the contents. "This isn't cherry pie," she announces in her high-pitched, grating voice. "This is jam pie."

"It must be a living hell to be rich," I comment. "Nothing's ever good enough."

"Right. It's too cold at her Aspen condo and her Italian villa is overrun with foreigners."

"In Italy? Wouldn't that make her the foreigner?"

Margaret nudges me and snickers. Now Julia is tossing her head and yacking away at her husband, who pats her arm like he's consoling her about something.

"He's a nice enough guy," says Margaret, "a little boring, but nice enough. I wonder why he puts up with her."

"Maybe it's her money."

"Oh, no. He started one of those dot com thingies in the nineties, made a ton of money and got out before it went belly up. Retired in his thirties."

"What a long time to be retired! What do people *do* if they don't have to make money and have no kids to raise?"

"Complain. Princess Snowflake told me she never wanted kids because they would wreck her body. They would wreck her things. They would put a damper on her jet-setting lifestyle."

"Oh, Margaret, she did not say 'jet-setting lifestyle!'"

Margaret shrugs. "Sounds like a lonely, empty life to me."

Sam swims toward us, grabs Margaret's legs and yanks her underwater, sunglasses, hat, and all. I know she got her hair styled for the luau and didn't want to get it wet. Now it probably doesn't matter because Sam is paying attention to her.

At sunset, the tiki torches are lit. There's drinking, eating, dancing, and more drinking. We laugh and groan and hold our backs as we scuttle under the limbo stick, which moves lower and lower. As the crowd grows louder, so does the music. Harry and I are sharing a table with Margaret and Sam and a married couple I don't know well, the Fosters.

Bud says, "Opal is my third wife, but I liked the first one best."

Opal rolls her eyes up to her husband and simpers, "She didn't like you best."

Everyone laughs.

Margaret asks Bud, "Did she leave you for another man?"

"No," says Bud. "I left her for another woman, but I told her I'd be back, and I was."

I look over at Opal whose face bears a blank expression. Apparently, she's heard it all before, many times. She comments off-handedly, "He's been like this his whole life."

Sam rears his head back to chug the last of his beer. He has previously announced that drinks with fruit on the rim and little paper umbrellas are for "faggots." He slams his empty mug down twice on the table, indicating to Margaret that he needs a refill. This is his "please." When Margaret delivers his beer, he slaps her on the ass. This is his "thank you." She guffaws, her face aglow, the ends of her frizzy hair sticking out. I grit my teeth until my jaw aches.

The third time Sam slams his glass down and Margaret hops to her feet, I ask him stridently, "Can't you say, Margaret please get me another beer?"

Sam sucks his big yellow teeth in response, the ends of his mouth curling up.

Margaret titters behind curled fingers. "It's okay, Col. I know he appreciates it." When she returns with his drink they make a game of her swinging her hips out of the range of his swat, but he leans in with a backhand and nails her with a resounding smack, probably some pickleball maneuver.

"Now say thank you," I coach him.

He shifts narrowed eyes toward me. "Don't get hysterical."

I hate that word. I open my mouth to retaliate, but Harry grabs both my hands, exclaiming, "Hey, that's a merengue! Let's go!" He tries to pull me up out of my chair.

I shake my head, flustered. I've had a few Piña Coladas and feel a little unsteady on my feet. I don't want to make a fool of myself. I give Harry a pleading look. "I don't know the merengue."

His face is pink and beaming. "It's easy, honey! I'll show you. If you can swing your hips, you can dance the merengue."

In a few minutes, I realize Harry is right. I just follow his smooth lead. He is a much better dancer than swimmer.

When I get back to my room, I notice the Facebook icon on my phone is flagged with a notification. I open it and see that Sam has sent me a friend request. I take indignant pleasure in poking my finger in the right direction. Decline!

46

That old Greek physician Hippocrates was the first to diagnose *hysterika,* meaning "uterus." When a woman became ill or emotional; that is, when she wouldn't put up and shut up, it was caused by the uterus. It was an easy deduction because a man doesn't have one. That culprit—the uterus—wanders the body, wreaking havoc. According to the good doctor Hippocrates, if a woman screamed in protest of all the housework she had to do, her uterus was in her mouth. If she stamped her foot because her husband was screwing around, it was in her toes. This was not a religious belief like Eve enticing Adam with an apple and a lot of other things men blame women for. This was science. Hippocrates never wrote about the wandering penis, the major cause of unnecessary death and mayhem, such as war and mass shootings. Have you ever heard of someone with a uterus busting into a school or theater with an AR15 and blowing away everyone in sight?

47

I'm worried Harry's Bach isn't going to be ready in time for the talent show next month. He still has memory slips. Missing a note in a Bach fugue is like dropping a stitch knitting a sweater: the whole damn thing unravels. I lie awake at night going over the piece in my mind, as if that would help Harry play better. It was the same when Brooke was preparing for her violin competitions. Day and night, I'd catch myself mentally playing her pieces. On the big day of her performance, I'd be in the audience wringing my hands while she entered the stage, beaming. Stage fright? Not that girl. Is that what talent is? She didn't need me fretting over her at all. It's a hard lesson for parents to learn. They can't do for their children what their children must do for themselves. I knew parents who created science projects for science fairs with their child's name on them, bearing them proudly under their arms to the school gym, and perhaps never realizing that as they labored in the garage, their child was off in their room playing Mario Kart.

As Harry's practices, I hold the score and call out any note he forgets or misses. I record him on my iPhone and together we go over the results, discussing how his playing can be improved. When the hard work is done, we have fun playing our duets. Debussy, Faure, Brahms are all coming together. I'm playing the piano again and loving it.

After a rousing play-through of the Brahms waltz, Harry pats my knee. "We should play our duets on the dining room Yamaha grand.

"Oh, hell, no!" I gasp and cover my mouth with my hands.

"Why not? It wouldn't be any sort of performance, just the two of us."

Harry's Clavinova is merely a digital piano; nice, but nothing compared to a real piano. I would love to play our duets on the Yamaha, but I shake my head. The dining room is too public of a space. "Too exposed. Someone might hear us."

"No one would even notice."

I hold up my palms to fend him off. "No, thanks, Harry." He looks so disappointed, I'm compelled to give him some false hope. "Maybe someday. If I get up the nerve."

"That would be great." He kisses me on the cheek. "I'll whip us up some lunch. Are tuna sandwiches okay? "

"Tuna? A Catholic child's favorite lunch. It must be Friday."

"It's Thursday."

"Oh. Well, it's still my favorite lunch—with potato chips."

"Coming up."

"Need any help?"

"Naw. Just sit at the counter and keep me company."

Harry goes into his kitchen to start the sandwiches, and I perch on a stool checking my texts. There's just one, from on unknown number. "Want to know why you should accept my FB friend request? No, it's not because I want to see photos of your ugly face. It would be a classy way to admit you are wrong about me. It bothers me that anyone thinks negative things about me, especially a friend of Margaret's. Then you can apologize to me for calling me out at the luau. Mags gets me. You should accept that if you call yourself her friend."

I'm struck numb. Then I feel Harry's hand covering mine and gently squeezing. "Colette, what is it? Bad news?"

"It's nothing." I feel flushed and my heart is pounding.

Harry presses the back of his cool hand against my brow. "It must be something. Your face is flaming red."

"Oh, oh…never mind."

"You can tell me." His tone is pleading.

"It's that asshole Sam. He sent me a friend request, and I declined it. I didn't think he'd notice." I hand Harry my phone. He holds it close to his face, squinting as he reads Sam's text.

"This is terrible. Insulting! But it's the beer talking."

"It's that jerk talking!"

"Don't take it personally, hon. When Sam has too many beers, he gets morose. He comes up with all sorts of grudges. I've seen it before."

I snatch my phone away. "Don't take his side!"

"I'm not! I'm just saying he can be a mean drunk."

"He's a mean person! An oaf! A chauvinist pig! Probably voted for Trump."

Harry surprises me by laughing. "I voted for Trump."

"*What?*" I leap from the stool and back away. I suddenly realize how little I know about Harry. We share an interest in music, he's sweet to me, but this! "Trump! That despicable ignoramus!" I shout. "He couldn't pass an eighth-grade civics test! That swindling, corrupt criminal! He makes Nixon look like a Boy Scout!"

Harry slides his hands in his pockets, and cocks his head contritely. "I don't care for the man, in particular, but I agree with his policies, the appointment of conservative judges."

"Bigots and homophobes! A sanctimonious, lying bitch ruling against women's rights! They want to make this country into a theocracy like Iran!" I turn and scoop up my sweater lying on the sofa. "I have to go!"

"Without your tuna sandwich?"

"I lost my appetite." I can't bear to look at him. I can tell by his tone that he's crestfallen. I stalk toward the door.

He tries to stop me with his voice. "Now, Colette. Can't we discuss this reasonably?"

In answer, I slam his door behind me. I could never be with a Trumper.

The four of them arrive in unison, leaning their racing bikes against the wall of the foyer. None of them seem to have kickstands. The cyclists are all dressed alike, two men and two women, in padded black Spandex shorts that fit like second skins and orangish-pink tops that read "Team Coral" in large, black letters. As they walk toward the front desk, they click-clack like tap dancers. Coral Broome is expecting them. She is dressed just like them, only her padded Spandex sags in the rear end. Rumor has it that she wears Depends under her shorts. When she sprints, she leaks a wee bit. Perfectly understandable at age one-hundred-and-five. No wheelchair in sight now. She wheels her orangish-pink racing bike toward them.

Outside, the wide circular drive is lined with orange cones, blocking off traffic. The staff has set up lawn chairs along the sidewalk so that we Shady Meadow residents can watch Coral train. Margaret and I claim seats side-by-side along with dozens of other spectators. Out of the corners of my eyes, I glance around for Harry. Instead, I spot Sam, several chairs down.

One of Coral's team members helps her adjust and latch her orangish-pink helmet under her chin. She slowly lifts a shaking leg up and over the top bar of her bike. One of the men holds Coral by her tiny waist and sets her on the seat. Two others place her feet over the pedals. Another teammate straddles her rear wheel and clutches the back of the seat.

"Push down, Coral," says a team member.

"What are they doing to her?" I ask.

"Locking her feet into the pedals," says Margaret.

"Is that really a good idea?"

"Oh, sure. It's so she can pull up on the peals as well as push down."

Coral slowly leans forward and grips a pointy metal thing jutting out of her handlebars.

The team mate holding her seat calls out, "Ready, Coral?"

She nods. "Ready!"

"Hey, Coral!" Sam jeers, "Get an ebike."

Coral mutters something to the young men at her sides. They twist her heels out, one after the other, until they click. The guy on her right side, helps her swing her leg over her bike.

What could be wrong? Has Coral decided she's not up to a ride today?

She shuffles across the driveway, the metal things on the bottom of her shoes drawing sparks, her head listing to the left as if her big, orangish-pink helmet is too heavy for her flower-stemmed neck. It's true she has the shapeliest legs on a one-hundred-five-year old woman that I've ever seen. She stalks right up to Sam, tilts her face upward inches from his, and beats her prominent breastbone with three fingertips. "Do I look like a quitter?"

Sam rears his head and stares back at her in glassy-eyed silence.

"Answer the question."

For once, Sam is quick to back down. "No, ma'am."

"Ebikes are for quitters! I am a *competitive athlete!*" She turns on one foot, succumbs to a tiny wobble, rights herself, then with the music of a tap dancer, strides back to her bike and waiting teammates.

Margaret covers her mouth with a curved hand, sneaking little glances at Sam who's pink in the face. "My poor boy got told. That's just something you do not do: suggest to Coral that she get an ebike."

Our competitive athlete climbs back on her bike and is locked into her pedals again. It takes a while. One foot is shaking, no doubt in indignation. Finally, all the team members back away, except the one who is holding her upright by the back of her seat.

"Ready, Coral?"

"Ready."

"Five, four, three, two, one, go!" The teammate gives Coral a shove. She wobbles forward on her own, her legs slowly churning as if the cranks have a high resistance.

"Oh, my god, I can't look!" I bow my head and press my fingertips into my eyes.

Margaret snickers. "Give her time. She's just revving up."

A teammate with a long, blond ponytail hanging out of the back of her helmet mounts her own bike and follows Coral. The two cyclists disappear down the long drive exiting Shady Meadow. Time ticks by, too much time, I think.

"Have you smoothed things over with Harry?" Margaret asks.

"Kinda. But it's just not the same."

"Aw, Col, really?"

"I apologized for walking out on him just as the dear man was making me lunch."

"Harry's always doing nice things for you."

"Yeah, but *Trump*. He was the one who got all that QAnon business to be so popular. He's why we lost our Carter."

"If your grandson was susceptible to that kind of conspiracy stuff, don't you think he would've gone off the deep end anyway? It'd be Scientology or the Moonies or the ridiculous Proud Boys."

I consider this a moment. "Maybe."

"Murray voted for Trump."

"He *did?*"

"Yup. Wanna know why I voted in every single election? It was my civic duty to God and country to cancel out Murray's vote. He put a big ole Nixon sign on our lawn. I waited a few days and took it down."

"What did he do about that?"

"Never noticed. Murray was like that."

Coral appears, churning the pedals faster now. We spectators cheer, taking up the rhythmic chant, "Coral! Coral! Coral!"

Tears prickle at the backs of my eyes. You go, girl.

Around and around Coral rides, disappearing into the distance, then careering into sight. With each lap, the crowd roars in appreciation. It doesn't seem to get old, watching a very old lady disappear and reappear on her bike.

After about thirty minutes, a teammate jangles a loud cowbell.

Another teammate jogs beside her. "One more lap, Coral."

"I'm good for more," she says.

"No, no," insists the teammate, who must also be her coach. "We're not going to overdo it. Remember, we talked about this."

"Oh, shucks!" Coral shouts into the wind.

When she comes in for her final lap, all the spectators rise from their seats in an enthusiastic standing ovation. Two teammates run out to grab her bike and stop her. She swings her heels outward and her feet are released. The teammates help her off her bike, remove her helmet, and dress her like a doll in an orangish-pink velour warm-up suit. One of the girls hands her a frothy green drink.

"How'd I do?" asks Coral.

"Great!" says her coach. "Awesome."

"How'd I do?" she asks pointedly.

"Twelve-point-two miles per hour. That's just great."

"I can do better," insists Coral. "There was a goddamn headwind on the back side of the course."

Her coach laughs. "You can shatter the World Hour Record going five miles per hour."

"That isn't the point," says Coral. "The point is I can do better."

49

The next time I go over to Harry's, he greets me at the door by dangling an open letter by its corner in front of me. It's congratulating him on joining the Democratic party. He's watching my face for my reaction, but I honestly don't know what I feel.

"You didn't have to do this," I say.

"I know I didn't, but people convert to a different religion to marry. Why not to a different political party to keep the peace in a relationship?"

I force a smile. "I appreciate the gesture, but it seems disingenuous."

"Not at all." He moves to his desk, lets the letter flutter into a pile of papers and turns to face me. "My dad voted Republican, so did my grandfather. People in the ag business often do. Politics doesn't really mean much to me. It doesn't seem to matter who's president."

"Sorry, dear, I couldn't disagree with you more."

"Oh, no? Johnson escalated the Viet Nam War, then lied about it. George W. started up that whole mess in Iraq and Afghanistan. What's the difference?"

"You're anti-war?" I exclaim. "Me, too."

"Except for Ukraine. I believe Putin must be stopped."

"Oh, me, too!"

"There, you see? Common ground." He opens his arms to me and I jump in. I wonder if he really will vote Democrat. I don't ask,

179

but hug him hard. "My dad took classes about Catholicism and converted in order to marry my mother in the Church."

"And did he truly believe in it?"

"Neither of my parents practiced religion, but they sent me to parochial school and dropped me off at Mass every Sunday morning."

"And did you believe in it?"

"For a while. Not anymore. What about you?"

"When a form asks about religion, I put down Christian. It doesn't mean a lot to me."

"Okay, but do you believe in—"

He holds out a straight arm and raises his palm like a stop sign. "Enough about politics and religion!"

"Agreed." At last I realize both are dumb reasons to divide two people who care about each other, but I've been wrapped up in my feelings about both so long that it's hard to just let them go.

"Fine! We got that can of worms out of the way." He claps his hands together and rubs his palms. "Now, let's have an adventure."

"Fabulous! A grand tour of Europe?" I joke. "I've been yearning to go back."

He laughs. "I'm thinking of something more local. And shorter. I can't miss the talent show." He motions me toward his desktop computer. "Come take a look at this. I got a ten percent off coupon in my email."

I sit next to Harry, my hand resting on his shoulder, as I peer into the computer. "White water rafting? You're kidding, right?"

"It's on my list. I don't mention 'bucket' because that refers to death so I just say list." He turns his boyish grin on me, the same one he just wore when he was showing me his Democratic party letter, expecting a positive reaction.

I flat out say, "You can't swim."

"There're life jackets."

"What about hitting your head on a rock?"

"There're helmets."

I peruse the colorful photo on his massive iMac screen. It's an action shot of a six-person raft nosediving into a spray of white water. "We could get wet."

"Possibly. There're wetsuits, too."

"Oh, hell."

"Doesn't it look exciting, babe?"

"Scary, more like."

"Ah, come on. This is the American River, not the Colorado. How much white water can there be?"

The screen flashes to another photo depicting a string of rafts floating gently down the river under a wide, blue sky, towering trees all around. This is more like it. For a long time, I've been pining for a fun guy to go places with and do fun things, and now I've got one. I glance over at Harry who is starting at the flashing slideshow like a kid in a candy shop. I hate to be a killjoy. "Well, okay."

"Awesome!" He squeezes my knee in gratitude and clicks on the registration tab.

"Wait! Wait! Don't we want to give it a little more thought?"

"No time like the present." He begins to fill out the registration form. When it comes to putting in his credit card information, I say, "Let me pay half."

"Oh, no, my treat."

As soon as Harry submits the registration, he gets an email laying out the details. The starting point is farther away than I thought it would be, way up in the Sierra. The directions are complicated: set your trip odometer here, take a dirt road there. "Are you sure you can handle the drive?" I ask.

"Oh, sure. I kinda know where this is. About a two-hour drive, better give us three hours."

"What if we get lost? What if we can't make it?"

He pats my hand. "Whatever happens, it will be an adventure, right?"

I raise my eyebrows and cock my head, but I can find no words.

$$50$$

One afternoon last December I woke up on my kitchen floor. The linoleum was cold and hard against my cheek and a little gritty, even though I thought I was a pretty thorough housekeeper. I clutched the gummy spoon I had used to stir my oatmeal that morning. Hours ago. This alarmed me.

I must've fainted. The left side of my face felt numb, probably because I'd been lying on it, I reasoned. I tried to get up but my left leg wouldn't work. I took a deep breath and rested. I tried dragging my uncooperative body toward the table where I had set my phone. I didn't get far. I rested. I pulled forward with my elbows and right knee. I reached a kitchen chair, I rose just high enough to grab my phone. I called Brooke, reluctantly, knowing she would make a big fuss.

"I fainted."

"What, Mom?"

"I fainted."

"Mom, I can't understand you."

My mouth felt like it held a massive, gooey dumpling. I willed the muscles of my tongue to move around it. "I fainted, ga da it."

The emergency room doctor took one look at me and emitted me into the hospital. I don't remember how long I was there, drifting in and out of consciousness. My primary physician Dr. Zhao ordered a CAT scan and a bunch of other tests. She visited me in the hospital and told me I'd had a TIA, a transient ischemic attack, a mini-stroke. "A tiny clot blocks the blood to the brain momentarily, and there probably will be no permeant damage."

"I'm fine," I insisted. "Can I go home?"

Dr. Zhou shook her head. She is a young woman with a silky black ponytail who is as tall as my shoulder and could pass as a high school student. "There's no cure for your condition, Colette," she announced pragmatically. "After one TIA you're likely to have another, maybe even a debilitating stroke. It's no longer safe for you to live alone."

Brooke's response was swift and thorough. When I was released from the hospital, my car, my house, my cat had vanished. Hence, Shady Meadow. This is my deep, dark, shameful secret, my weakness, my vulnerability, which I can't bring myself to tell Harry.

51

As the day of the rafting trip approaches, I grow more and more anxious. I find myself thinking of ways to get out of it, but then I certainly don't want Harry following through on his own, which he very well might. I would have to talk him out of it, too.

We're cuddled on his couch trying to decide what to watch on Netflix, when I blurt, "I'm afraid."

"I am, too, a little." Harry knows exactly what I'm talking about.

"Maybe you can cancel, get your money back."

"Nope. No refunds. Look, honey, it's got to be perfectly safe or the business would've been shut down long ago. There's no experience necessary. There's a guide in each raft. What could go wrong?"

"Maybe we're too old for this."

Harry rears his head back. "You dare to use the 'o' word on us, woman?"

"My bad. Have you told anyone about this?"

"Nope."

"Not your boys, Sam and the guys?"

"Nope."

"I haven't told Margaret or any of the girls either. Certainly not Brooke." I lean into him and roll my eyes up to meet his. "Why haven't we told anyone?"

Harry shrugs "Maybe because we don't want to hear that we shouldn't be doing this."

"I don't think we should be doing this." We laugh together and then I know I've got to come clean. I pat the front of his shirt, finger the buttons. "I haven't been honest with you, about my health, I mean." In a flurry of words and a few tears, I tell him all about the stone-cold kitchen floor, the CAT scan, the TIA, Dr. Zhao's prognosis, Brooke's swift actions which landed me in assisted living. I glance up at his face expecting indignation, disgust, horror.

He wears his listening expression, passive and open. "I thought as much."

"You did?"

"I knew it had to be something. Why else would your daughter sell your house out from under you and move you in here?"

I dab at my eyes with the back of my hand. "I'm weak. My body has failed me. I have taken such good care of it all my life, and it has failed me."

"We are all vulnerable. All humans, not just folks in their sixties."

I'm in my seventies. Does he know that? Should I confess my age at this moment as well? I don't have the courage.

"We could die at any moment, any of us. That's why we gotta live like there's no tomorrow. That's why we're doing this rafting trip. Lighten up, honey. It will be fun."

"A real adventure," I comment, quoting him.

"Thrilling."

"What if we can't make it home before dark?"

"Then you can drive. You've still got a driver's license, right?"

Brooke took away my car keys and sold my car, but I still possess a driver's license. "Yes, but…I'm not supposed to drive."

"Says who?"

"Says my daughter and my doctor."

Harry dramatically rolls his head, scanning the room. "I don't see either of them. Do you?"

"What if I have another TIA? What if I pass out?"

Harry grins wide. "Then I'll reach over and grab the wheel."

52

The day of our rafting trip arrives, and all I can think is that I wish it were over. I have made a list: hats, sunscreen, snacks, drinks, towels, dry clothes. I pack everything and put it in Harry's car, which gives me a sense of security. By the time we hit the road, I feel I can relax a little. I'm getting out of Shady Meadow. My guy and I are on an adventure.

Harry is a cautious, but slow driver. When too many cars follow behind us, he pulls over to let them pass. Beyond Placerville, we turn off Highway 50. The backroads twist on and on, and so does my stomach. I'm the navigator, and at one turnoff, we have to set the trip odometer to know where to turn next. We bounce along a dirt road, make a turn at a fork that leads to a dead end. Harry carefully backs out, takes the other fork, and abruptly we see the archway to American River Expeditions.

I throw my arms around him. "We made it! We're here!"

Harry's face is rosy with glee. "That drive! It's the hardest thing I'll have to do all day."

I hope he's right. Before leaving the car, we munch a few snacks and slather ourselves with sunscreen. Already it feels like it's going to be a very warm day.

The camp is rustic and dusty. Under an awning are picnic tables where the rafting clients meet. I look around and notice all of them are twenty, maybe thirty years younger than Harry and I. One administrator comes around and has everyone sign a release. I try not to think we are signing away our lives. When that's taken care of, another young guy with dreds and a pink, peeling nose conducts the informational meeting. In a jokey manner, he goes over safety rules and commands on the raft: paddle forward, paddle back, left forward, left back, right forward, right back, stop.

I try to pay attention and absorb all the commands, but there're lots to keep straight. What if our guide tells us to do something and I just freeze up or do the wrong thing?

"High side means to lean toward a raised side of the raft to prevent flipping."

I poke Harry's ribs and mutter, "We can flip?"

He shrugs and smiles, almost apologetically.

"All in means to slide off your seat and duck into the bottom of the boat if your boat hits a rock or tree branch or you're heading into a steep drop or big wave of white water."

I elbow Harry, and he squeezes my hand.

The presenter says the course is about ten miles. Certain areas of white water are named "Donkey Tail," "Pinball," "The Funnel," "Bumpy Road," "Corkscrew," "Devil's Pit." None of them sound good to me. My bowels churn. I'm going to have to get to the restroom soon.

"You guys are like so lucky," says the presenter. "This is the last great weekend of the season. Next week the snow melt will be about done and the rapids won't be nearly as exciting."

Snow melt? We're about to be doused with snow melt? Oh, brother.

The meeting adjourns. I dash to the bathroom, which, surprisingly, has flush toilets. Afterward, I meet Harry at the venue to claim wetsuits, lifejackets, and helmets. The wetsuits are doled out according to weight, but I can't squeeze into the first wetsuit I'm handed. I trade it in for a bigger size. I get down on the ground and tug and pull at the stubborn latex. Sweat trickles down the side of my face. I hope this will be the hardest thing I'll have to do today.

When we rafters have all our gear, we board a rickety, rusty bus to drive upstream to where the rafts await us. The engine whines, the gears grind, the driver floors the gas pedal. We are riding on a narrow, dirt road, alongside a sheer drop. There's no air conditioning so the door remains open. A lithe blond guide in a bikini and wetsuit top stands at the open door, leaning her back against the rail before the front seat. The young believe death is only for the old. She chats up the driver, talking about how she will earn her living in the winter—ski instructor—and complains about her rafting clients who get the commands mixed up and are too weak to put any muscle behind their paddling. Oh, boy, what will she say about Harry and me?

An oncoming pickup truck appears. The bus pulls over, dirt clods and rocks tumbling down the embankment. I clutch Harry's arm so hard it must hurt. Hopefully the rafting won't be as harrowing as this bus ride. The road descends toward the river's edge, and the bus comes to a halt. Ten tethered blue rafts bob at the shoreline. Names are called out, six clients plus a guide assigned to each raft. I'm relieved we won't be with the skinny, complaining blond.

Harry and I wade into the chilly water, clutch our assigned raft, and climb into the center seats, Harry on the right, me on the left. They are not seats, exactly. We are instructed to sit on the bulging rim of the boat, "Crack on crack," the guide puts it. A friendly, young woman with long, brown braids draped over her shoulders, tells us she is a third-grade teacher as I once was, and clearly loves the adventure of her weekend job. One boat at a time is launched, we rafters shoving off with our paddles. Our raft is toward the back with two behind us. This is it. Here we go, floating down the river. I take a deep breath and sigh in relief.

"Left back!" instructs our guide.

Uh-oh, what does that mean? Am I on the left or the right? Oh, the left, but I'm not in the back, I'm in the middle. Is this a middle command? Oh, yeah, all three rafters on the left are supposed to be padding backward.

"Stop!"

Oh, well, I'll get the next command.

Up ahead is a wide spout of water. "Donkey Tail," announces the guide. "Forward! Dig in! Dig!"

A splash of water sprays over our raft. My spine snaps straight as I'm doused with ice water. The raft plunges nose down and begins to spin.

"Left back!"

This time I'm ready. I pull back on my paddle with all my might. In a moment the raft straightens and flattens and we are drifting on placid waters.

"Woo-who!" the rafters shout, fist-bumping the sky. We made it through our first white water. Harry turns to me, laughing, his splayed hand pressed against his chest. This is fun! Exhilarating!

"Devil's Pit!"

The raft dives and lurches through swirling white water.

"High side!" the guide commands.

My wits are about me now. I lean to the left, since I am on the higher side. I turn my head to grin at Harry, but he and the other two right-side occupants have vanished. I look out into the water and see nothing of Harry but the soles of his deck shoes, sticking up like two white flags in surrender. I open my mouth, but my scream gets stuck in my throat. Harry can't swim! My dear Harry will drown!

"Middle, slide over!" shouts the guide. "Middle, slide over! Colette, that's you!"

As if emerging from a trance, I shift over on shaky legs to the right, taking Harry's place in an effort to steady the boat. Harry's feet are gone, no sign of him at all. The raft ahead of us has flipped entirely. Hats and paddles float down the river. I recognize Harry's King's cap, his favorite. Heads bob in the water, none of them belonging to Harry.

"Harry! Harry!" I half-whine, half-shout.

Two hands emerge from the water and grasp the side of the raft in front of me. A head surfaces, a young face with a mustache. The guide commands. "Colette, grab him. Help him into the boat!"

"But he isn't Harry. This is Harry's place!"

"It doesn't matter! Everyone needs to get out of the water. It doesn't matter what boat they land in."

A hairy leg swings over the side of the raft. I clutch it and tug. The man rolls his stomach onto the rim of the raft, and I slide back to give him room. He rights himself, turns back to me, and says, "Thanks."

I cup my palm over my eyes and scan the water. Other people are being plucked out of the water and loaded into the last two rafts. And yes! One of them is Harry! He is saved! Oh, thank God!

A little way down the river, all the rafts dock on the bank to regroup. Harry staggers out of his rescue raft with a sheepish grin. Fortunately, he has thought to wear a strap for his glasses. I dash up to him and throw my arms around him. I hug him tight, trying to cover as much of his shivering body as I can.

"Oh, darling! Are you okay?" I've never called him "darling." It just rolls out naturally.

He kisses my cheek. "I'm great! Got cooled off, that's for sure."

Our guide walks up to us, grinning, addressing me with, "I bet you thought your husband was gone for good."

I don't bother correcting her. In fact, I rather like the idea of Harry and me being mistaken for an old married couple. "I just looked over and saw this!" I raise my arms and hold up both palms. "Just his feet were sticking out of the water, and then they sank, too!"

"And then I came bobbing up, like a cork," finishes Harry. "No harm done!"

"Yes, harm," I gasp. "I nearly had a heart attack, but I really didn't have time for it!"

Harry and I sit on a flat rock in the sun, sipping from our water bottles as he dries out. The warm day has grown warmer. It isn't long before his shivering stops.

"Is this yours?" The skinny blond guide approaches us with Harry's soggy King's cap in hand, so nothing is lost at all.

We rafters load ourselves back into our boats and shove off. Harry is at my side again, and I feel surprisingly at ease. The worst has already happened.

In "The Funnel," our boat spins around several times like an amusement park ride or debris circling a drain, before our guide orders, "Forward!"

At "Pinball," the commands are "Left" alternating with "Right" and "Forward" alternating with "Back" to prevent our raft from dashing against the rocks.

There are some placid moments in which no paddling is necessary at all, and our raft just drifts. The sunlight sparkles on the rolling river, and I trail my fingers in the cool water. This is it. This is living life to the fullest, but it's hard work; it takes courage.

Ten miles on the river is long, and with the business of capsizing and regrouping, the journey has taken over three hours. When the bottom of our boat scrapes the sandy beach at camp, I want to kiss the ground. Harry and I slap our palms together in double high-fives.

"We did it!" he shouts.

I weave my gnarled fingers through his straight ones and lean into him, our foreheads fused, our eyes locked. "Let's never do it again."

"Didn't you love it?" he asks, his voice still high-pitched with excitement.

"Parts of it, yes. But, let's not—"

"—not right away, at least."

Peeling off my wetsuit isn't as hard as tugging it on, but it is a challenge. We rafters are instructed to dip the wetsuits in a drum of water. How clean can they get for the next people? How clean were they when we wore them? Oh, well, it's done.

We head to the car for dry clothes. The women's room is crowded, with lines at the stalls. I'm too tired to wait for the luxury of privacy and strip off my wet shirt and bathing suit at one of the sinks. A young girl standing next to me widens her eyes, but I don't care. Let my old bare boobs and sagging ass hang out in the open. I rub myself dry with my towel and feel new again in dry clothes.

Outside, I find Harry and together we peruse the professional photographs. Harry chooses to buy one of our whole raft plunging into a spray of white water, me with a determined look on my face as I dig in my paddle, and Harry with his mouth wide with joy.

"Oh, look, here's a good one of you, Harry. I'm getting this one." The photographer has captured Harry's feet in the air sticking out of the water. "I'm framing it and hanging it in my room."

He laughs, thinking I'm being funny, but deep inside me, my feelings rage. This is the moment I thought I had lost you. I don't ever want to forget that feeling; I don't ever want to feel it again.

Back at the car, we have a quick snack of sandwiches and cookies. Both of us gobble the food as if we're starving. By the time we hit the road, the bright sun is low in the sky, and we are heading west, directly into it.

Harry flips his visor down and sometimes shields his eyes further with his hand. "It's ironic that my driver's license doesn't allow me to drive at night, when I can see so much more in the pitch dark than in this glare."

We make it over the dirt road and onto the twisting backroads, which alternates between shade and blinding glare. The speed limit is fifty, but Harry is going forty or less, and I worry we'll be rear-ended. The horn of an impatient driver behind us blares, but there is no shoulder to pull over.

"Can't you speed it up a little?" I ask.

"I can only go as fast as I can see ahead."

I muster the courage to offer, "Pull over when you can. Let me try."

We stop at the next turnout and switch places. I buckle up in a driver's seat, the first time in half a year. "Okay, here we go."

About a half hour later, I sigh. "I'm so exhausted, I don't see how we'll make it all the way home."

"Maybe we won't have to." Harry points to a billboard advertising a bed and breakfast a few miles away.

The wooden A-frame structure is so small and hidden away beneath a pine forest that we nearly miss it. A small sign in the shape of a teapot reads, "Dottie's Bed and Breakfast." When we pull into the drive, we see a horseshoe of tiny one-room cabins tucked away. We go into to the office to register. It is surprisingly pricy, but the important thing is they have a single vacancy.

"Cabin six," says the cheerful hostess. "The dining room is open until eight. I'll ring my husband to help you with your luggage."

"That won't be necessary," I say. "We haven't brought much."

53

I have wondered if this will ever happen, and then it does. We don't have a discussion. We don't have dinner. We don't have showers. We don't even turn off the light. As soon as we drop our bags to the floor and shut the door of our little cabin, we fall into each other's arms, kissing and pawing, tugging at each other clothes. I remember how it goes, even after so many years.

We fall on the high four-poster bed, now pulling at the bedspread and blankets. I wonder about protection against STDs. I wonder if Harry uses Viagra. Will I be able to lubricate? All these concerns fall away when Harry enters me. We are making love. Such an old-fashioned expression. Does anyone under the age of sixty use it?

Harry shifts position and cries out. Not in passion, but pain. Have I done something wrong? Is he having a heart attack? He rolls away from me. "Oh! Oh! I gotta…I gotta get up!" Harry swings his legs off the side of the bed. He freezes there, moaning some more, leaning over, his jaw wrenched. At last, he is able to get on his feet and, still bent over, he hobbles to his duffle bag.

"Oh, Oh!" he groans.

"Harry, what is it? Should I call for help?"

"No, no. I'm alright. I'm gonna be." He opens his duffle bag, fumbles around. He takes out a little bottle, twists off the cap and drinks. In a moment, he sighs, "Ah. That's better."

"Harry, what is that? Some medicine for a heart condition?"

"Nope! Pickle juice."

"Pickle juice?"

"For leg cramps."

"That's crazy."

"I know, but it works."

"Are you sure it's not an old wife's tale?"

"When the mouth has to pucker, the body forgets to cramp up the leg. All fixed." He drives into the bed, snuggles under the blankets, and entwines his legs with mine. "Hope you don't mind pickle juice breath."

I kiss him tentatively. He does indeed smell like dill pickles. "It's not bad."

"Excellent. Now, where were we?"

Sometime later, I creep out of bed to rummage through our provisions and return with the last of our supplies, granola bars and Gatorade. Both of us agree this will have to do for dinner. We're too comfortable where we are to venture out.

"I imagine Dottie serves a lovely breakfast," I muse.

Harry's eyes widen. "Dottie?"

"Didn't you notice the name of this place? Dottie's Bed and Breakfast."

"Oh, yeah, right." He takes a swig of luminous blue Gatorade. "Why didn't we think to pack a bottle of wine?"

"And a baguette and some brie, a chunk of dark chocolate."

"Because we didn't expect to land here," says Harry.

"I have thought about it," I admit.

"Oh, me, too, for months now. But back home, I wasn't sure how to make a move. I didn't want things to be awkward between us. I didn't want to scare you off. And to tell you the truth, I was a little shy about it. I'm out of practice."

I roll my eyes toward him. "Oh, really? With all those eligible ladies swarming the place?"

"Oh, I can't get down with just any woman. To make love, I have to be in love."

I look over at him, sporting a blue Gatorade mustache. "You're in love?"

"Of course. Aren't you?"

"Yes," I admit decisively. I fondly pat his upper lip with a Kleenex. "When I saw your feet sticking out the water today, I definitely knew it."

He laughs. "Thought I was a goner?"

"I did."

He takes another swig of Gatorade. "Who wants the first shower?"

"Me!"

I stand under the hot water a long time, thinking about the day, a glorious day, the best one in so many decades. There's no pajamas to change into, of course, so after Harry takes his shower and slides back into bed again, there is nothing between us at all.

54

As Harry and I are pulling up to Shady Meadow the next morning, I point to the park. "Let me off here."

"What for?"

"So I can get my walk in."

"I'll walk with you. Let me park the car."

"Harry, no."

"Oh, I get it." He grins boyishly. "Trying to keep up appearances. No one is paying any attention to us, honey."

"Harry, let me out," I insist, a bit more stridently than I mean to.

He is staring out the windshield with a solemn expression. "I get it. Discretion. I agree. Discretion is good." I don't know if he's being sarcastic or hurt. Something weird is going on with him that I can't figure out. When I open the car door, he grabs my arm. "It's going to happen again, right? And again and again?"

I lower my eyelashes. "I don't know. My mother taught me to keep a man guessing."

"And that generation had a bunch of screwed up game-playing."

"Only because women were powerless."

"Women were never powerless. Just ask Helen of Troy."

"Powerful in a good way." I lean over and kiss him on the cheek. "See you later, lover. Thank you for a wonderful time."

"Oh, I'm the one who should be thanking you."

I slap his forearm playfully. "I mean thank you for the rafting trip. I can't believe we actually had such a wild adventure. Thank you for not drowning. I like having you around."

I slide out of the car, and Harry drives on. I begin to circle the park. It's cool and fresh with a slight breeze, on what promises to be a very hot day. My step is lively. My shoulder is only a little stiff from all that paddling and my lower back and butt are only a bit sore from bouncing around in the raft. We did it! Our rafting trip is done. Then…we did it! I grin to myself.

"Col, oh, yoo-who, Colette!"

I turn to see Margaret galumping after me. She catches up, breathless. "Hey, I been looking for you. Where've you been?"

"Out walking."

"Brooke texted me. She's been texting you like crazy. Wanted to take you out to brunch. Didn't you check your phone?"

I pull my phone out of my back pocket. There is a pile-up of texts from both Margaret and Brooke. There was no reception at the rafting camp, and I didn't think to check my phone this morning. "There was a time when we weren't attached to these damn things like a ball and chain. I remember in the mid-nineties when car phones came out. I'd be out walking and nearly get run over by crazy drivers on the phone. I thought they were ridiculous, a hazard. What do you have to say that can't wait until you get home? When I complained about it to a friend, she said, 'You know, in the future, we will all be carrying our phones around with us.' I didn't believe her."

"I saw you and Harry leave together yesterday," says Margaret, abruptly changing the subject. "I saw you load a cooler and a bunch of bags and stuff into the car."

I narrow my eyes at her, feigning annoyance. "Have you been spying on me?"

She snickers and jabs me in the ribs with a sharp elbow. "Did you have a romantic getaway weekend?"

"Just a day trip."

"With those bags?"

"Uh-huh. A change of dry clothes. We went whitewater rafting," I announce casually, like it's something I do every weekend.

Margaret gasps. "You didn't tell me you were gonna do that. Aren't you guys too old for that?"

I slide my sunglasses down my nose to peer into her face. "We didn't tell anybody because we didn't want to hear 'Aren't you guys too old for that?'"

"Oh. My bad. How was it?"

"Exhilarating. Exhausting." I giggle like a school girl. "Harry fell in."

"Harry can't swim."

"There were life jackets."

"Oh. So no worries."

"Are you kidding? I was terrified. I thought I'd lost him. It was a great experience, but never again."

Margaret narrows her eyes and peers into my face. "I saw you get out of Harry's car just now. You two spent the night somewhere? Together? Same room? Same bed?" The gold in the back of her mouth twinkles in the sunlight.

"Don't you have an inquiring mind! We went for breakfast this morning. A sweet little place up in the foothills. Cinnamon rolls to die for."

Margaret leans in and speaks in a raspy whisper. "Did you do it?"

"What?"

"*It.*"

"No." I don't know why I don't want to confide in Margaret, my current best friend. She has told me she and Sam have had sex several times, but he won't let her stay overnight with him in his apartment. I know this hurts her feelings. He has told her he's not ready to commit.

"If you're not going to 'fess up, I'm going back in."

I encircle her shoulders. "Oh, come on, finish the walk with me."

"Can't. I promised Sam I'd watch his pickleball game."
"What does he need you for? To hold his pickle?"
Margaret blushes and I laugh. I am in such a damn good mood.

55

One morning, I wake up in Harry's bed to find his side vacant. He is already up making coffee. It's his habit to brew the coffee and bring it to me in bed, just how I like it, with a hefty splash of half and half and two-thirds of a pink packet of Sweet 'n' Low. This is a luxury I especially enjoy, not having to get up, get dressed, go to the dining room, and wait in line just to get my first cup of coffee. Plus, Shady Meadow coffee is pretty watered down, while Harry brews robust Peet's French Roast.

He enters the bedroom, bearing two steaming mugs and a good morning smile. I sit up and take the mug offered to me. "Thank you, my dear."

"You're welcome, my sweet." He takes his place alongside me in bed.

After the first delicious sip, I comment, "I just realized: I haven't been to my own room in five days."

"Why keep it?" Harry sips his coffee, which he takes black. "Move in here with me. Two can live as cheaply as one."

The offer is so abrupt, I burst out laughing. Does he mean it or is he just playing? "Not quite *as cheap*, but *cheaper*. What's your rent here anyway?"

"Oh, you wouldn't have to pay anything."

"Of course, I'd pay half."

He pats my knee. "Naw, save your money for extras, for our adventures."

"Hmm. You know what I've always wanted to do? Fly to Halifax and take the train clear across Canada."

"Let's do it."

"It would be a long trip, at least two weeks."

"So? What do we have to get back to? I'll tell you what I'd like to do. Tour Ireland. Fly into Dublin, rent a car, and drive counterclockwise all the way around the island, Dublin to Dublin." He raises his arm, and with his forefinger draws a jagged circle in the air. "My mother's side of the family are Duffys from up around Galway. I'd love to check out the area."

The idea of Harry driving all that way *on the left side of the road* is absolutely terrifying, but it's so pleasurable lolling in bed shoulder to shoulder, sipping coffee, and fantasizing about journeys we'll never take, that I say, "Sounds wonderful. I'd like to see Greece. Have you ever been?"

"No, but I'd like to go. Norway, too."

"Australia and New Zealand."

"And Machu Picchu."

"Oh! Just the thought of that altitude makes my head reel."

"And then there's the Galapagos Islands. We can't miss those. How about an African Safari?"

I twist my head to look him in the eye. "You want to shoot a lion?"

"Absolutely! With a camera."

I drain my coffee and settle back into Harry's arms. "It's fun to dream about going to such places."

"Not dreaming! Planning."

"Oh, Harry. It would be wonderful to travel together. I didn't think I'd get to go anywhere again."

He smacks me loudly on the temple. "Of course, we'll travel. Once we get you settled in here."

"Hmm." I never thought I'd cohabitate with a man again. I like my independence, and yet I like the idea of being half of a couple with Harry.

"Hmm, what?"

"What if we get on each other's nerves? What if we end up hating each other?"

"I don't think that would happen. But if it didn't work out, we'd just live separately again."

"That easy, huh? It's true I've never felt at home in my own dark, depressing little room. I'm much more comfortable here. But what about all my stuff?"

"We'll combine households. It shouldn't be that hard. I only use half of that walk-in closet. Our music cabinets can live side-by-side."

"The springs in my recliner are shot."

"Get rid of it. I have two."

I pat the bed alongside me. "My mattress is firmer."

"Then we'll move it in here. In fact, I know someone who can use mine."

I hoot to the ceiling.

"What?" Harry asks innocently, the corners of this mouth twitching in a suppressed smile.

"I can't believe we're talking like this."

"Well, we are. We love each other, why not live together?"

"Hmm, it's a pleasant thought, but…"

"But?"

I love what I have with Harry right now. I don't want to risk losing it. "Harry, it's too soon, and you know it. Let's give it a little more time."

"Whatever you want." He kisses me and bounds out of bed. "Bacon and eggs sound good?"

I know he means here in this apartment, in the luxury of our privacy. "I'd love it."

I lie back on the pillow listening to the clanking and scraping sounds coming from the kitchen. I give myself a couple of more minutes before sliding out of bed. Sometimes I think it's the hardest thing I have to do in an entire day.

Harry has already provided me with space in his closet and two drawers in his bureau. I take out clean underwear and socks, put on yesterday's jeans and T-shirt.

Then it happens, probably because I'm not concentrating on what I'm doing, indulging in a reverie about viewing the wilds of Canada from a whizzing train. I get my right sock on just fine. I raise my left leg, my baby toe catches on the rim of the sock, I teeter, I fall hard on my right hip with a thump. I remain sprawled on the floor, shifting my leg gingerly. The pain is deep, but I'm quite certain I haven't broken anything.

Harry appears at the doorway. "Oh, I thought we had an earthquake."

I groan. His comment irks me. He remains standing where he is, doesn't move to help me up, doesn't ask if I'm okay. Isn't that what a doting man is supposed to do? I roll over to my knees and pull myself up by holding onto the bed.

Still in the doorway, his hands on his hips, he suggests, "Why don't you sit down to put on your socks? It would be kind of hard to travel with a broken hip."

"I think I smell something burning."

"I turned off the stove, just in case I had to drive you to the emergency room." He saunters back to the kitchen.

Over the next several days I develop a bruise on the side of my hip, in variegated blues, purples, blacks, and browns, about three inches across and six inches long. I try to hide it from Harry, but one evening as I'm shedding my jeans, he gets a good look.

"Hmm. Kind of the shape and size of Lake Tahoe. You really ought to sit down to put on your socks."

"Okay." It really is. It's easier to take advice from Harry than my know-it-all daughter.

56

I reach far back into my closet and pull out my burgundy dress. Why not? Harry told me he is wearing a suit and tie for the talent show. I have an old school idea that dressing to attend a performance is a sign of respect; I would never wear jeans and a T-shirt to the symphony. But once the Sacramento Symphony performed in jeans to break down barriers. You don't have to be hoity-toity to attend the symphony. The idea attracted very few new concert-goers. You don't see many people under the age of sixty at the symphony, except music appreciation students who are forced to go as a class assignment. Anyway, I want to show Harry how performing his Bach fugue is a big deal to me.

The Shady Meadow staff has turned the dining room into a concert hall, shoving aside the tables and setting up rows of folding chairs. When Harry and I are settled side by side, I peruse the printed program. There's a lot of singing, dancing, recitations, skits, a recorder quartet, a stand-up comic, a juggler. Who knew Shady Meadow held so much talent? The list goes on and on. I flip the page over to find another stand-up comic, more singers, a saxophonist who will play the theme from *Star Wars*, a bird caller, a magic act. I wonder how Harry fits into all of this. There he is, second-to-the-last, Harold Beck, pianist, performing the Bach Fugue No. 2 in C Minor from the *Well-Tempered Clavier*. And then I am jolted into shock. I see my own name! Pianists Harold Beck and Colette Corbyn performing Debussy's *En Bateau*.

"Oh, hell, no," I announce.

Harry chuckles.

I turn to him. "It's not funny. How could you? Without my permission! You know how I feel about performing."

"You said it's the waiting that's the trouble, the weeks of anticipation. I spared you that."

I fold my arms and slump back into my seat, staring straight ahead. "I'm not doing it, Harry."

"Come on, sweetie. It'll be fun! We know the piece so well, it practically plays itself."

"I would die of stage fright."

"Look at all these acts before us. It's going on way too long. You'll see most of the audience sneaking out at intermission. Probably, we'll be playing to ourselves. Anyway, most of the audience doesn't know one note from the other."

"No!"

"Okay, sorry, sorry. I was afraid you'd take it this way. Let's just sit through all of this and then if you really don't want to play, just slip away after my Bach. I'll say you weren't feeling well."

"And Margaret and them will say I was just chicken, and they'll be right!"

"What's so bad about being chicken?"

"Nothing, I guess. I am what I am. Oh Harry, I could kill you for this!"

He bears a huge grin, and at last I'm able to calm down. I find myself smiling, a little. He's right. We do know the piece well and love to play it. And on the Yamaha grand! My fingers twitch in anticipation in spite of myself.

Harry leans into me, his breath warm on my ear. "Let's do it!"

"Oh, damn it, maybe. I can't decide. Maybe I'll just have a stroke and die."

"After you kill me?" I jab him with my elbow, a bit too vigorously. "Ooph!" he cries, and holds his stomach.

The show goes on. The singers sing pop songs with prerecorded accompaniment, "Mack the Knife," "Tie a Yellow Ribbon 'round the Old Oak Tree," for "our troops" of course, "Eat It," Weird Al Yankovic's parody of Michael Jackson's "Beat It." Ester Goldfarb delights and surprises us all with her rendition of "Aquarius/Let the Sunshine In" starting in the hippie clothes of *Hair* and ending in her bathing suit. The Ben and Jerry "Where's the ice cream?" Norton-Riveras tap dance to "Singing in the Rain," proving to be quite agile for men in their eighties. Julia and Ronald Bower present a hula, in traditional dress of grass skirt and pa'u loincloth, beginning with an informative mini-lecture on the meanings of the hand movements. Cyrus "Blessed-day Man" Dennison strums his guitar and sings "What a Friend I Have in Jesus," warbling on the long notes with more finesse than the bird caller had in imitating a warbler. I get to laughing and have to bend down and cup my brow with my hand. Every time a particularly long warble arises, Harry presses his thigh against mine, causing another ripple of giggles to bubble up, and when I try to suppress them, I erupt with one rather unladylike snort.

What brings down the house, however, is Margaret and Pandora, dressed as Yankee baseball players with prominent athletic cups, performing the Abbott and Costello routine "Who's on First" in a gruff Bronx accent. That is funny enough, but at one point Margaret flubs a line, and then another, and Pandora delivers one of Margaret's lines which Margaret automatically repeats. Neither of them can keep a straight face, and the audience is howling. Tears run down my face, and I realize what the talent show is: just a lot of fun with some good friends I have recently acquired.

I worry the crowd won't be able to settle down for Harry's serious performance, but by that time, there isn't much of a crowd. Harry is right in predicting many of the audience members have slipped out. A hush rolls over the room as Harry makes his way up the center aisle. Before the piano, he bows deeply with dignified aplomb, and my heart gets lodged in my throat. My dear Harry has worked so hard for this! I fervently hope he can get through it, that the audience can behave.

He begins with the lilting subject in the right hand. The left hand enters. The exposition is beautifully rendered. Harry has a couple of fumbles and one heart stopping memory slip from which he recovers after several seconds of gut-wrenching silence, although he lands several measures back from where he's supposed to be. I hear a little impatient talking in the audience. Folks just don't know when to shut up. Harry continues well enough, but the Bach sounds flat and dry. This piece is all wrong for this audience. Harry magnificently executes the *stretto* finish with all the voices sounding the subject in overlapping entries. The final chord rings out, strong and authoritative. He did it! I'm so proud of him! But next year I need to coach him in his selection of repertoire. More accessible would be a movement from one of the easier Beethoven or Mozart sonatas or maybe a Chopin Nocturne or Mazurka.

Harry takes a bow to polite but unenthused applause. He looks toward me, his arm stretched out, palm turned up. For an instant, I don't know what he means. And then, oh god, oh god! I have the sense to grab the Debussy music off the chair next to me. I stand and walk toward the front on wobbly legs, hoping I don't fall or faint dead away. I pass Margaret in her baseball uniform and she lets out a soft, but encouraging "You go, girl!" I am among friends.

Harry and I settle side by side on the bench. I quietly count us in. The touch of the keys sends chills up my arms. Yes, this is it. I know how to do this. The music flows along. Harry is right, it practically plays itself. I love playing this piece, I love playing with Harry. Our Debussy is going much better than Harry's Bach. I am clear-headed, projecting and shaping the melody, riding the wave of Harry's rippling broken chords. Yes, I do know how to do this. I have spent hours and hours of my life doing this very thing.

The applause is much more animated for our performance than Harry's. We take a bow together, and when I straighten, a spray of red roses is placed into my arms by a beaming Brooke. "Mom, you were wonderful!"

How did she know about this? Harry, of course. And then I have to cry.

Sam approaches us and slaps Harry on the back. "Pretty good piano playing for a blind man." He nods toward me. "But she's better."

"Why thank you, Sam!" I am filled with such goodwill some of it even spills over toward Sam.

Pandora in her baseball uniform gives me a big hug. "I knew Harry played, but not you! Why are you hiding your light under a bushel? You and Harry sound great together, but next year you should play a solo."

I have already thought about it. Perhaps I can resurrect a few movements of Schumann's *Scenes from Childhood* or dare I attempt Copland's *Four Piano Blues?*

<h1 style="text-align:center">57</h1>

Bridge is like piano: if you want to be good at it, you have to play a lot, you have to practice. I enjoyed the game in my younger years, belonged to a bridge club, but my teaching got in the way, someone else's teaching got in the way, or job, or family. So many cancellations and hiatuses, I threw up my hands and gave it up.

Living in Shady Meadow is different. Iris, Pandora, Margaret, and I have formed a solid foursome. We play with other folks sometimes, but mostly, it's just us girls, we call ourselves, because it makes us feel young. It's not just the cards. It's the friendships, the bonding, the sharing of our lives, the laughs and the fun. Margaret is the sharpest. She'll be yacking and yukking it up, throwing back her head in a display of her gold molars, appearing as if she isn't paying any attention to what's going on with the cards, but then she scores trick after trick. I don't know how she does it. Maybe by raising seven kids she learned to concentrate in chaos.

This morning Margaret and I are losing. Iris and Pandora are beating us bad. But then I finally get dealt a really good hand. I dare to bid five. Soon I have four tricks laid out before me. The game is getting really exciting. Margaret's pink encased phone sings out, "Let Me Call You Sweetheart," and I know who's calling.

She answers with a big grin. "Hi Hon. Yeah. I'm playing cards with the girls…I know you do, Sam, I was planning on it but—huh? Soon as we finish….Oh, another hour…" She glances at her watch as Sam talks some more. Her smiles slips. "Oh, okay…okay…yes, hon…okay, bye-bye." Margaret sets down her phone and rises. "Sorry girls, I've got to run."

"Right now?" I ask, "in the middle of a hand?"

"Sam wants me to go to Lowe's with him."

"You're playing cards with us." I counter. "Can't it wait?"

"He says he wants to get it done before lunch, cuz, you know, lunch hour the store gets crowded with workmen and…" She smiles apologetically. "You know how impatient men are, gotta get it done right now." She smiles proudly. "He's picking out lampshades. Needs a woman's opinion. You understand, right girls?" She turns to Pandora.

"Go, Margaret." She flicks her fingers reassuringly.

"Well, I don't understand!" I say. "Call him back. Tell him you'll go after our card game."

"I can't, Col, really."

My head feels like a pressure cooker about to blow. "Of course, you can't. You have to go scurrying off at a man's beck and call. Damn it, Margaret, are you gonna go to your grave thinking women are set on this planet to serve men? Call him back!"

She shakes her head.

"Yes, call him back, if we mean anything to you at all. Tell Sam to go fuck himself. He can damn well wait an hour. Have some self-respect."

Margaret juts out her chin. "I do have self-respect. Sam respects me, too."

"He sure as hell doesn't. That chauvinistic pig hasn't respected women a day in his life. He's just using you because you're so willing to be at his beck and call."

Immediately, I realize I have gone too far. Margaret is flushed fuchsia. Her mouth is working on words that don't come out. Finally she blurts, "Your boyfriend is married!"

I'm about to ask her what she means, but before I can say a word,

Margaret turns her back on me and stomps off.

Iris is staring at me wide-eyed. I was loud enough for her to decipher every word, which is very loud. Other card players in the room are peering over at our table, curious about the uproar I've caused.

I lower my voice and look at my friends out of the tops of my eyes. "She's crazy! Harry's wife is dead."

Pandora glances down at her hand as if she is studying her cards, then looks up at me. "She's as alive as we are."

"What? Harry wouldn't lie to me about a thing like that."

"No, he wouldn't." Iris leans into me. "Especially since she lives here."

"In Shady Meadow?" I pretend to need clarification while my mind is racing ahead. *His wife? Harry has a wife?*

Iris responds with a decisive nod.

"But…but…" Flustered, I run my hand through my hair. "I'm over at his place a lot, and—"

"They're separated," says Pandora. "Obviously."

"But married," adds Iris. "Everybody knows that."

"Everybody but me! Thanks for cluing me in!"

"We thought you knew. We thought you were okay with it." Pandora folds her cards and sets them neatly on the table. "You never bring it up so we thought you don't want to talk about it."

A slow burn sears my brain. I try to think back to what Harry actually said about his marriage the first day I went to his apartment, but all I can think is that he indicated his wife is dead. I'm in shock. Embarrassed, humiliated. A fool, the laughing stock of my community, my home. Harry—too good to be true. And, oh, god, *who is she?*

When I get into a muddle I usually give myself some time to think it through before taking any action. I imagine myself returning to my room, lying on my recliner, sorting through the past few months, maybe take a pad and pen and jot down some ideas to clear my head, but before I even come to my senses, I'm pounding on Harry's door.

When he answers, I plant my hands against his chest and shove him backward, step into his apartment and slam the door behind me with my foot. Words erupt from me in a low, guttural growl. "You're married!"

His mouth forms an O. "I thought you knew!"

"How would I know?"

He lifts one shoulder apologetically. "Well, Margaret is your friend and—"

"She hasn't said anything about it. I need to hear it from you."

"I told you right from the beginning she was gone from my life."

Gone! That's the euphemism he used, I remember now. "Gone isn't dead. You led me on!"

"Colette, no! I…" He slides his hands in his pockets and looks down at the floor. "I guess I kind of did."

"Kind of?" I roar.

He offers me a pleading look, his brow in waves. "I liked you so much, the moment you sat next to me and looked over my Bach. I wanted the chance to get to know you. And I did think you knew or found out eventually, or… oh, we never talked about it, but I assumed you were good with it. You're even friendly with her. Anyway, that's what she told me."

"Your *wife* is a friend of mine and I don't even know it?"

"Friendly, I said. She says you like her popcorn."

"Popcorn?" I try to think of the last time I ate popcorn.

"Yeah, when you guys watch TV together. She says—"

"Dottie! Your wife is Dottie?" I shake my head in disbelief. "Dottie is crazy."

"Not crazy. Addicted. She wasn't always this way, but we haven't had anything but misery between us for years, long before we moved in here."

"Does she know we're…we're—I don't know what we are now!"

"Together? I don't know. I haven't told her. Nothing I do matters to her. When she was working as an astrophysicist—"

"Astrophysicist? She did tell me she worked at JPL. I thought as a secretary or clerk."

"Nope. She was a good mom, we had some good years, but—"

"Shit!" I cut him off because I don't want to hear any more.

He looks at me pleadingly. "I'm sorry I misled you. I'm sorry about the misunderstanding." He reaches for my waist, and I take a step back. "I understand how you feel."

"Do you? That's great. Because I don't understand it at all."

"Can you find it in your heart to forgive me?" He pauses, but I don't respond. "If you can't…" The pained look in his eyes deepens. "If we can't go on as we have, I hope you won't cut me out of your life. I hope we can be friends."

"Fuck! That's what middle school kids say after they've gone together for a week." I'm not so angry anymore, just sad. Disappointed. Confused. Suddenly, the good relationship I thought I was in has morphed into something entirely different. I don't know what to think. I turn and quietly exit Harry's apartment.

58

A few days later, I pass the front desk after my early morning walk and notice three cards splayed out for the staff to sign: Cyrus "Blessed-day Man" Dennison, Susan Hartley, and a resident I don't know.

At breakfast, Betty Lambert says, "Cyrus has gone on to a better place."

"Right," I counter, "if you can call a hole in the ground better than this place."

"It doesn't matter," says Esther Goldfarb. "He'll never know the difference."

Betty sighs. "Cyrus buoyed me up when I saw him. I'm going to miss his, 'Have a blessed day.'"

The very same phrase that set my teeth on edge. I bend my head and get very busy stirring my coffee.

On *Fresh Air*, Terry Gross dredges up two past interviews with Susan Hartley, one from 2010 and another from 1984, the year she won the Pulitzer. That's what that show does when someone famous dies. People will remember Susan Hartley, they'll remember they haven't read her for a while, and they'll buy her books again, but the author won't be receiving any royalties.

Margaret has been avoiding me. When I text her, she doesn't respond. She doesn't pick me up to go to yoga together, but arrives to class only a few seconds before it starts, and rolls out her mat in a rear corner, as far away from me as she can get. I see her playing

215

bridge with Bonnie Sherman as a partner, who can't remember any of the cards that have been played. That's how adamant Margaret is about dumping me.

I try stalking her. One afternoon when I see her going out for a walk, I wait until she is a good ways into the park before I go after her and dash up to her from behind. She twists around to look at me over her shoulder, then quickens her step, but it's no contest. I glide up to her side.

"Hey," I say.

She purses her mouth.

"Come on, Margaret. Can't we talk about this?"

"Nothing to say."

"You always have something to say. Please forgive me for whatever transgression I committed to make you so mad at me."

"I'm not mad at you."

"You are. You're avoiding me. I miss you! Can't we be friends again?"

"We're too different."

"No, we aren't."

Margaret's feet come to a halt. She glares into my face, her eyes flashing. "You think you're better than me. You think you're better than everybody. You ridicule my religion. You think I had too many kids. You don't respect me because I was a stay-at-home mom. You think I'm stupid."

I'm flabbergasted. It takes me a few moments to realize she has stomped ahead at a pace much faster than her usual. "Margaret, wait!" I have to break into a run to catch up with her. "Where is this coming from? You're one of the smartest people I know."

"Yeah? Well, Sam doesn't want me hanging out with you. He says you're a bad influence with all your women's libber stuff."

"Oh! So it's Sam! Does he realize the Women's Movement happened over half a century ago? If you haven't caught fire yet, it's not gonna happen."

"There you go again."

"Let's not talk about women's liberation. I'll never say another bad thing about Sam, I promise, or Catholicism or what else? What else can't we talk about? Please, Margaret, take me back!"

She comes to a screeching stop. She looks in the distance as if she's considering my offer. "This is as far as I want to go today," she announces. "You go on, Colette. You walk faster than me. Another thing you put me down for."

"Margaret! I have never put you down!"

She turns and heads back. Shuffle, shuffle.

59

And then there's Harry. Actually, there's no Harry. No Harry is the problem. I see him around, in the dining room, on the grounds. If I catch his eye, he waves, tentatively. If we come face-to-face, he says, "Hi, how are you?" in automatic speak, his face blank, his eyes flat and noncommittal.

I actually thought he'd come running after me. I thought he'd be knocking at my door or at least texting, "I can't let you go." I thought my first boyfriend Mike would do the same. He started dating Sally instead, brought her to my senior recital. Come to think of it, the only guy who ever said those words to me was Tony, the guy I was only using as a companion to traipse through Europe, and he was a moron. That's how it goes: the guy you want doesn't want you, but the guy you don't want does. Surprisingly, this sad story of unrequited love carries through to old age.

I think I know what's going on with Harry. He's letting me decide what to do. I bet I could go over to his apartment right this minute, fall into his arms, and we could go on as before. But something's stopping me. Someone. Dottie.

I imagine having a heart-to-heart talk with her. "Do you mind if I date your husband?" Not date, exactly, sleep with, fuck. That would be called an affair, and I have always, always prided myself as a woman who does not date/sleep with/fuck a married man. After my divorce, when I got back into the dating scene, I met men who said they were married but didn't really have a relationship with their wives, or they were separated, or they were "taking a break." Uh-huh. Not my type. Go figure it out with your wife, and if your marriage ends in divorce, then give me a call. I shall not trespass on another woman's husband. That's what women are supposed to do for each other.

I think about Dottie a lot. I realize I have felt superior to her because she's an addict. I have read articles that say people don't become addicted to opioids if they stop taking them once the pain of a surgery or condition subsides. But what if the pain is chronic? What if a doctor gives you access to opioids for too long? What if Dottie is simply a victim of her own pain? It's true she's awful to Harry, but don't a lot of women, a lot of people, get fed up with the person they've been married to for too long? Dottie raised three sons. She was an astrophysicist and I was a third-grade teacher. Dottie is a genuine person with thoughts and feelings, the wife of Harry whom I can't bring myself to level with.

So that's where I am with the Harry thing. No Harry and no *Wheel of Fortune* and popcorn visits from Dottie. Harry and Margaret, the two people who have come to mean the most to me outside of family are gone, and I am miserable.

60

Margaret goes missing. She's not playing bridge with the girls—her new girls—she's not at meals or yoga. I don't see her out on the grounds. I go to the front desk to ask if she's checked out for a visit with family or friends.

Latrice offers me her tight little smile. "We aren't allowed to divulge any private information about our residents."

Of course not.

Around five, happy hour, I pop in the bar where Sam and Margaret have a beer together, nearly every day. He's drinking and throwing dice with the boys. I approach him, asking, "Hey, Sam. Where's Margaret?"

He squints at me and frowns. "Under the weather."

"She's sick? Is it a cold or flu?"

"She didn't say. Just told me not to call or visit until I heard from her. Says she doesn't look all that sexy right now." The other men laugh along with him.

"I'll go check on her."

"Will you?" He raises his eyebrows, hopefully. "Let me know?"

There's an urgency of concern in his tone, which alarms me. "Will do."

I go knocking on Margaret's door. No sound comes from the room. I knock again and press my ear against the door. There's a rustle of bedcovers, a quiet, low groan.

"Margaret?"

A cough erupts so fiercely that it sounds like she's trying to cough up a lung.

My pounding grows loud and desperate. "Margaret! Open up or I'm calling nine-one-one."

"All right already." More groaning, heavy footsteps. The door creaks open. Her hair is greasy and sticks up in all directions. The skin beneath her eyes is swollen in large, purplish circles. Her complexion looks as gray as death.

I push my way into the room. "Here, let me help you." She leans against my arm as I escort her back into bed. She falls against the mattress, and I cover her up. She kicks the blankets off and her whole body shakes as if she is feverish and chilled at the same time. She raises her head to break into another fit of coughing. I dash into her bathroom and return with a glass of water. I hold it up to her mouth, and she greedily gulps the liquid down.

I move the back of my hand toward her brow. I feel heat rising off her before I touch skin. "How long has this been going on?"

"Two days, three. Worse today."

I notice a potato chip bag and a candy bar wrapper on the nightstand. "When was your last meal?"

"Lunch yesterday? Day before? I don't know." She sinks back against the pillow and closes her eyes, her lashes fluttering.

"Are you vomiting?"

She shakes her head.

"You need to eat, Margaret. Did you test for COVID?"

She groans again. "If I have COVID, I don't wanna know."

"What? Of course, you do!"

"I don't!" She opens her eyes in a pleading, frantic look. "They'll send me to the hospital, and people with COVID who go to the hospital get put on respirators, and people who get put on respirators usually die, and if I do survive my kids will come get me, take me home, and when I get better I'll have to babysit the grandkids and the great grandkids and I'll never get my own life back or see Sam ever again." Her eyes flood to the brim.

"Margaret, no! You're not thinking straight."

"Brain fog."

"No, panic. You've been lying here miserable and hungry and thinking the worst. I'm going to get you some dinner. Hang on."

On my way out of her room, I grab a T-shirt draped over a chair and place it on the floor to prevent the door from closing and locking. I go to my room and rummage in a drawer for a fresh N95 mask and my stash of COVID tests. I slip the mask on, thinking I haven't worn one in months. The tests are at least a year old, but I hope at least one of them is still good. I stop off at the dining room and get a tray of chicken noodle soup and crackers and return to Margaret's room.

I help her sit up and spoon the soup into her mouth. After a few mouthfuls she takes the spoon from me and feeds herself. The nourishment seems to revive her somewhat.

The first test I open is dried up. The second one seems okay. I hold the swab before her face. "Get ready."

"Oh, hell, do I have to?"

"Yes." I press my hand against her forehead to tilt her head back, stick the swab up her right nostril and swirl.

"Ouch!"

"Sorry!" I go after the left nostril, I set the swab in its holder. In minutes, I announce, "Positive."

"Nuts!"

"Your boosters are up-to-date, right?"

"Yeah, sure."

"You should be fine quarantining right here." I pick her phone off the nightstand and hand it to her. "Call your doctor and tell her you tested positive."

Since it's after hours it takes a while for her doctor's service to relay the message, but eventually a prescription for Paxlovid is called in.

"I'm going to run over to Walgreen's and pick up your prescription."

"Run? You can run two miles?"

I laugh. "Walk fast."

"But it's dark."

"I'll be fine. Once you start taking your prescription, you'll feel better."

"Really?" Relief floods her face. She hands her empty soup bowl back to me and sinks back into her pillow.

"I bet you're up and at 'em by the end of the week."

"Colette, thank you so much."

"My pleasure." I fold her sheet under her chin and smooth her covers. "Rest up. I'll be right back."

On my way out of the building, I notify admin that Margaret will be quarantining. Outside in the warm and fresh air, my brisk walk is invigorating. I feel like a superhero on a mission to save my friend from serious illness. So happy to do it. I make it to the pharmacy just before it closes. On my way back into Shady Meadow, I stop into the bar where I find Sam watching baseball. "Hey, Sam, Margaret has COVID." I hold up the prescription bag. "This should fix her up."

"Can she have visitors?"

"Are you vaccinated?" I ask, knowing he's not, having heard him say he avoided the vaccine because it causes sterility. Why he believes such misinformation or cares about such things so late in life, I don't know. He shakes his head. "Then don't visit. Margaret will be in quarantine for a week or so."

"Send her my love. Thank you for taking care of her, Colette."

His sweetness surprises me. I have always thought the worst of him. "Don't worry. She'll be fine."

"Women are better at taking care of sick people."

I don't call him on his sexist comment. It's probably true.

I deliver Margaret's prescription and make sure she takes the proper dosage. "Sam sends his love."

"He said that?" She seems as surprised as me.

"Yep. You should have seen his face when I told him you had COVID. He's deeply concerned."

A big smile streaks across her weary face.

From the door, I say, "Sleep tight, don't let the snuffer-outer get you."

"Ah, Col, you know there's no such thing."

Yes, there is—COVID. But it's not getting our Margaret.

Margaret begins to feel better within a day.

"I'm so grateful for you, Colette," she says. "I haven't been a very good friend lately."

"I said some mean things that made you mad. I'm sorry, too."

"Can we forgive and forget?" she asks.

I hold her gaze an extra moment. "Only if you agree to still be friends with me."

"Agreed."

In the next few days, I spend a lot of time hanging out in Margaret's room, keeping her company and playing dozens of hands of gin rummy, which she usually wins.

An Instacart order is delivered from Sam. Inside the bag, Margaret finds Red Vines, Doritos, bean dip, and a fifth of Jack Daniels. We have a good laugh over it.

"Not exactly a dozen red roses," she comments.

"It's the thought."

"It's Sam." She twists off the cap of the whiskey, takes a swig, and passes it to me. "Cheers."

I hold up my hand. "Uh…I'll pass."

"Oh, yeah, right. Am I bad? I didn't know Sam knew how to use Instacart."

"Maybe one of his kids showed him how. Anyway, the gesture is very sweet. I'll admit I've misjudged him."

Margaret's eye pop. "You don't think he's a chauvinist pig?"

"Oh, yeah, I still do, but I'll admit he has some good points, too."

61

On day five of Margaret's quarantine, a dark cloud hangs over the residents of Shady Meadow, and it isn't because there's another card for the staff to sign. It's not a death, but a failure.

As I let myself into Margaret's room, balancing a breakfast tray, she's on her phone.

"Ah, gee, that's too bad. Uh-huh…uh-huh…uh-huh…such a disappointment…uh-huh…uh-huh…Well, she tried her best…uh-huh…uh-huh…yeah, she does! Spunk, I'd call it. Listen, Pandora, Colette just stepped in with my breakfast. I'll let you go. Bye-bye."

I set her tray before her. "So, you've heard,"

"Yeah. It's a shame."

"Is she okay? Do you know if she hurt herself? I hope she didn't break a hip."

"No, no." Margaret bats the air with a piece of buttered toast. "Her teammates anticipated the trouble she was in. At around forty minutes, Coral was turning the pedals slower and slower and when she stopped moving her legs entirely, they were there to play catch. She just fell right over into the arms of one of her gals."

"Forty minutes! So close. I suppose her ride doesn't count for anything since she was going for an hour record."

"Yeah, it does. Coral is the first one-hundred-five-year-old female cyclist to *attempt* an hour record."

I shake my head, laughing. "Close, but no cigar, as they say."

"Well, in my book, it counts. It counts like hell."

Later in the morning, over a hand of gin rummy, Margaret asks, "What are you gonna do about Harry?"

I sigh. "I haven't decided yet. I keep thinking I should talk it over with Dottie, but then I find I can't bear the indignity of it."

"What does *she* have to do with it?"

I grin sheepishly. "She's only his wife."

"So? She doesn't give a hoot about him. What is he supposed to do? Sit around lonely and miserable for the rest of his life because of that bitch?"

"Not a bitch, exactly."

"All right. I shouldn't use that word. But she left him. And she's still mean to him any chance she can get."

I nod. "I've witnessed that. Then why do I feel like Jane Eyre?"

It takes a beat for Margaret to catch the reference. "Rochester's wife was a madwoman living in the attic. Dottie is just an addict living in a separate room by choice."

I smile. "Why do women named Dorothy go by Dottie?"

Margaret shrugs. "Why do men named Richard go by Dick? If the name fits…"

We laugh some more. "I've missed you Margaret."

"And Harry misses you. You two are good together. You should go make up with him right now."

And just like that, it seems like the right thing to do.

When Margaret is well enough, the four of us go on a double dinner date. Sam picks the place—a steakhouse—but is slow to pick up the check, so Harry does. I want to pay for my own dinner, but Harry insists on treating us all. "I want to use up all my money before I die," he jokes. "I've already given enough to my kids."

It's a fun night out. I still don't like Sam, but I try not to let him grate on my nerves. He makes my dear friend Margaret happy. That's good enough for me. It has to be.

62

Beautiful Lake Tahoe! In August, it's sweltering in Sacramento so Harry suggests we head for the mountains and rent an Airbnb for a few days. I expect it to be a modest condo, but when we arrive I'm surprised to find a whole cabin with a deck overlooking the lake.

I wander from room to room, exclaiming, "Oh, wow! Oh, wow! Harry, this must have cost a fortune!"

"Not at all. Midweek rates are quite reasonable."

Harry introduces me to his favorite hike, the Rubicon Trail bordering Emerald Bay. We take all day, stopping frequently to enjoy views of the lake. We eat our picnic lunch on a small, secluded beach and take the high trail past the lighthouse on our return. Another day we swim and rent kayaks at Pope Beach. We ride the tram to the top of Heavenly Valley. Neither of us have an interest in the casinos at the Stateline, but we take a dinner cruise on the MS Dixie. On our last full day we rise at dawn to go fishing in the Truckee River, and that evening we grill freshly-caught trout on the deck. As we dine, we watch the sun set over the lake. We sip the last of the wine and watch a million stars pop out of the black sky.

I sigh. "Oh, Harry, I don't want to go home."

He takes my hand. "Isn't this great? It can always be like this, you know."

"We're moving to Lake Tahoe?"

He laughs. "I mean we can always be together. Why don't you give up your room and come live with me?"

Again we discuss which furniture we would move and what we would give away. We agree that the arrangement would boost our finances so we could take more trips like this. We divulge how much rent we are paying at Shady Meadow. I'm surprised to discover Harry's place is not that much more than mine.

"That doesn't seem fair!" I exclaim. "My dark little room!"

"You're in assisted living," he points out.

"Oh, right."

He kisses my temple. "Let me assist your living, honey. Come live with me."

"It's tempting."

"Say yes, Colette."

"I might. Let's discuss it later."

"How much later?"

"By the end of the year? My lease is up for renewal in January."

"Good deal! So you're moving in with me in January?"

"I said discuss. Let's consider it some more."

"Colette, why are you dragging your feet?" There's an edge to his tone.

I don't like to feel pressured. I look up at the stars. I squeeze his hand. "Oh, Harry, let's not ruin this perfect moment by talk of the future."

"Okay. But I'm not giving up on this."

I turn to him, his profile barely visible in the darkness. "I don't want you to."

63

Nearing the holidays, I finally make the decision to move in with Harry. He spends Thanksgiving in Bakersfield with his middle son George's family, and stays the whole week since George insists it's unsafe for Harry to drive all that way. George picks up Harry on the weekend before Thanksgiving, and plans to return him to Shady Meadow on the following weekend. Adult children are always calling the shots for we seniors, as if the tables have abruptly turned and now they're the parents and we're the kids.

I go to Brooke and Jonathan's house for Thanksgiving dinner. It's a bit vacuous sitting at their long, formal dining room table, just the three of us. Jonathan's parents are deceased, his brother and sister and their families live back east. I'm an only child, Brooke is an only, Carter is an only. Small families can feel lonely during the holidays. Today, Carter is MIA as usual, fighting for what he considers to be freedom, standing up for his version of the truth, lost somewhere in MAGA Land. Brooke looks youthful and pretty with a fresh face peel, light makeup, and new hairdo. She has finally given up her teen hair-to-the-waist look so that now her honey brown hair swings attractively over her shoulders in wavy layers. I compliment it over and over until she tells me to stop. Jonathan is jovial and welcoming, right about everything as usual down to the minutest detail. We are all relatively healthy and happy, so indeed, we have much to be thankful for as we gobble too much rich turkey and fixings and clink and drain our wine glasses.

I stay over at Brooke's for the long weekend because she loves companionship while elbowing her way through Black Friday shoppers, as if online shopping hasn't been invented.

When I return to Shady Meadow, there's decorations to put up, gifts to wrap, and parties that need attending. I still write and send Christmas cards as a way of keeping up on the current whereabouts of friends and extended family and finding out who died.

I'm also busy in my mind, thinking through the logistics of moving in with Harry. I'm going to junk my old recliner because Harry has two nice ones. He told me Dottie has coveted his bed ever since she decided she wanted a different one when she moved into her own room, so we'll let her have it and move mine into his place, along with my nightstand since he only has one. My music cabinet can slide in next to his. About my cat figurines, I can't picture them in any spot in Harry's apartment. Now I view them as being kind of sad and pathetic, a lonely old woman's trinkets, but I'm not ready to haul them off to the Good Will. I'll pack them away, each in its tissue paper nest, and if I miss seeing them, I'll find a corner in Harry's place to display them again.

It's amazing to me how much stuff I've acquired living in just one room for not quite a year. I'm going through all my cupboards and closet today, throwing out anything I don't want or need. I'm in a great mood, humming to myself, anticipating dinner at Harry's place. He's promised lobster tails, fudge cake, and a surprise. A surprise? What could be better than lobster tails and fudge cake? I'm in the back of my closet taking everything out with plans to put back only what I'll keep, when the phone connected to the landline rings. It startles me. I can't think of a time it's ever been used.

When I pick up, Latrice at the front desk says, "Hello, Colette? You're being paged to Conference Room C."

"What?"

"Your daughter asked me to call you. She's waiting there for you."

Did I forget a doctor or an accountant appointment? If Brooke needs to meet with me, why didn't she call or text me on my cell? My heart beats faster. "Did she say why? Is this an emergency?"

"I don't think so. Some family business." Latrice seems to know more about this than I do. Odd.

"Thanks. I'll be there in a few minutes." As I change out of my shabby work clothes, my mind races. Could this be about Carter? Has he been arrested for some alt-right protest? Is he hurt? Dead? Maybe Brooke is leaving Jonathan and needs to talk, but they were fine at Thanksgiving just a week ago, happy, seemingly, but you never really know what goes on in a marriage. Oh! Maybe this is about my Shady Meadow contract, up in January, and Brooke is here to renegotiate for next year. I haven't broken the news to her yet about moving in with Harry. I didn't want to involve her until it's a done deal. My hand holding my hairbrush shakes and my bowels rumble. What do I have to be so anxious about?

I find Brooke in Conference Room C at the head of a long oval table, closest to the door. At the other end are three middle-aged, burly men, one in a cowboy hat and jeans. Next to him is a woman in a pink denim jacket and matching cowboy hat studded with rhinestones. Another woman, who appears elderly, is face down on her folded arms heaving with sobs.

"Hi, Mom," Brooke greets me, her voice unsteady, her brow creased in agitation. She pats the empty chair next to her, and I slide into it. She gestures to the man in the big cowboy hat. "You know George."

"No, I don't. Sorry. I don't know any of these people."

George strokes the back of the sobbing woman and addresses me pointedly, "You know my mom."

Brooke continues the introductions. "This is George's wife Sharlene, his brothers Rick and Marty."

The realization of who they are comes on me like a slow burn. "Oh, god! Has something happened to Harry?"

"Not if we can help it," Sharlene snaps. She'd had too much sun over the years, her face like leather.

"The Becks invited me here to…discuss the situation." Brooke's eyes dart around the room uneasily. "I've been sitting here telling them you must not realize… I don't know how to break this to you, Mom. Your…friend Harry is *married*."

The sobbing woman sits up. It's Dottie.

"Divorce so late in our parents' lives," says George, "It just can't be."

"It's breaking Mom's heart." The best-looking one of the bunch, Marty—kind of a young Harry I see now—encircles Dottie's shoulders as she leans into him.

Brooke turns to me, her face splotched and stricken. "Mom, you have to stop with Harry. Look how you're upsetting his wife."

I'm sorely outnumbered here, no one on my side. Oddly, the very core of my being has stopped quaking. I'm perfectly calm. These people don't care about Harry's happiness, nor his best interests, if there is a difference. They probably don't care about Dottie, except she can make their lives a living hell if she doesn't get her way.

"The complication of a second marriage—" interjects Rick.

"The financial implications," chimes in the rhinestone cowgirl.

Oh, I get it. This is about money, Harry's money. Their assumed inheritance.

"Where is Harry?" I ask. "Didn't you guys think to invite Harry to the family powwow?"

George shakes his head in consternation. "He's already stomped out of here."

"Well, then, who said anything about marriage?" I ask.

"As if you don't know." Sharlene shakes her head in consternation.

"Dad did," says Marty. "He asked Mom for a divorce yesterday. I know they're separated and all. It may look like he's free to marry, but—"

"I never wanted to be a divorcee," Dottie whines, gasps, spurts fresh tears.

I look from one stern Beck face to another. Brooke is taking quick, shallow breaths, reminding me of the panic attacks she used to have as a teenager.

"What's my daughter have to do with this?" I ask.

"Dad's too stubborn to listen to reason," says George. "We're hoping Brooke can help with you."

"*Help with me?*" I repeat. "How'd you get her contact information?"

No one replies. I rear back and glare at Brooke. "Administration contacted me."

I roll my eyes. "So much for the legal right to privacy around here."

"I think a little too much privacy goes on around here," says Sharlene. "They seem to let you old folks do whatever the hell you want."

"Well, yeah." I don't like this woman, not one bit. Sadly, I'm not sure I like any of Harry's sons either. "We're not caged animals."

Brooke places her hand on my arm. "Don't you see, Mom? You're going to have to call the wedding off."

"*What wedding?*" My spine snaps straight in alarm. "I'm not marrying Harry. We just want to shack up."

Brooke gasps. Suddenly, a prude. "Mom, not really!"

"You see? You see?" Dottie exclaims.

"Oh, cut the crap, Dottie," I say. "You don't give a damn about Harry. You're verbally abusive and cruel to him." I mimic her high-pitched whine, "Stop playing the piano! You don't have any talent. I hate you! I hate you!"

"Our parents have their spats. They live separately," Marty explains to me slowly, like I'm a kid in a special ed class, "but—"

"We have our own shows we like!" Dottie blurts.

"Harry and Dottie are actually quite devoted to each other," says Sharlene. "Right, Mom?"

I stand up quick like a jackknife. "I'm done here. Nice to meet you all."

Sharlene slides forward in her seat, tips up her cowboy hat. "But nothing's been settled."

"The…trauma you've caused our mom," sputters George. "She

isn't well. She's beside herself with grief."

I look squarely into Dottie's puffy face. She actually flinches against my pointed glare. "No worries, Dottie. Things are looking up for you."

She slides her hands down to her lap, straightens in her chair in hopeful anticipation.

"You're about to get the bed you want."

"Mom!" Brooke collects her purse and coat and stands. I stalk out of the room, ignoring her pleading voice. "Mom! Wait! Mom!"

64

I hightail over to Harry's place, Brooke on my heels. "Mom! Can't we talk?"

I stop, turn, my shoulders up around my ears. "Brooke, go away."

"But, Mom, I really think you should—"

"I don't care what you think, not this time. You're the kid, I'm the mom. For once, let me do what I want."

Her head lilts to one side, her eyes flooded. "Do you know what you're doing?"

"I think so."

She takes a step toward me, clutches my upper arms. "You'll call me later? Let me know what's happening?"

"Of course, darling." She hugs me. I hug her back, kind of. I stand still in the hallway until she turns to leave. I think I'm rid of her, when she calls over her shoulder, "I could counsel you and Harry both."

"Goodbye, Brooke!"

I wait until she shuffles off. I go over to Harry's and pound on his door. He answers by opening his door only wide enough to show a long, glum face.

"I've been ambushed by a roomful of Becks!"

"Were they awful to you?"

"I could have used you in a unified front. Why'd you run off?"

"They made me too mad. What did your daughter say?"

"Aren't you going to let me in?"

"Oh, yeah. Sure, hon." He opens the door wider and I step in. Across the back wall of his living room are four red helium balloons with white lettering, a word on each one, "Will you marry me?" The last balloon is weighed down with something tied to the end of the ribbon. "They ruined my surprise," Harry says forlornly.

I point to the weighed object. "What's that?"

He grins sheepishly. "Go see."

I walk over and take in my hand a ring with a huge glittering diamond, how many carets, I have no idea. I stare at it for several moments, shifting it to catch the light at various angles.

"Well?" Harry asks tensely.

"It's gorgeous." I don't call it a monstrosity; it would hurt his feelings. My gaze locks with his across the room. "Don't tell me: you want to be engaged and married at the same time."

He slides his hands in his pockets, looks down at his feet, and then back up at me. "Well, Sam was in that situation once."

"Oh, hell! You're taking a page out of Sam's playbook?"

Harry looks down at his shoes again. "I wanted to make an honest woman of you."

"I already am an honest woman."

"You know what I mean: married."

"You're already married, and I don't need to be."

He looks up hopefully. "Yeah?"

"Yeah."

We step toward each other and fall into an embrace. We hold each other for several long moments. Harry rears back to look into my face. "I asked Dottie for a divorce."

"So I heard."

"The hypocrite! She acted all upset about it, like she cares about me, like she gives a damn what I do."

"I get it. She's comfortable with the status quo. I told your family and Brooke I don't want to get married. We're just going to shack up."

He drops his jaw in a goofy expression. "You did? You used those words?"

"Yep."

"You mean it? You're still moving in just like that?" He snaps his fingers.

"On one condition."

He raises his eyebrows, waiting.

I point to the ring. "You'll have to return it."

"Aw hon, couldn't we keep it in case Dottie changes her mind about divorce or if she…you know."

"Oh, hell, no! I don't want *that* hanging over my head! Anyway, the ring—it really isn't my style."

"It's not?"

He looks so crestfallen, I have to laugh. He joins in with a half-hearted chuckle. Suddenly, it seems our troubles are behind us.

65

The next morning, Harry and I make an appointment with the Shady Meadow administration to take care of business. Harry tells Latrice as of January first, we are giving up my room so I can move into his apartment. Of course, she knows the ramifications, that Harry is legally married to Dottie, that I would be exiting assisted living. I half expect her to try to deny our request, telling us that she will need to haul in our kids for legal permission, but no, she follows through with our directions as if we are two consenting adults, which we are. I'm pleasantly surprised to learn from Brooke that she has power of attorney only if I am incapacitated—essentially, she gets to decide when to pull the plug. How come I didn't know this? I guess it was decided while I was recovering from my TIA, when I was experiencing brain fog.

Harry and I agree we don't want to wait until January, but prefer to enjoy the holidays settled in together. We are of a DIY generation which doesn't pay others to do what we can do for ourselves or can recruit friends and family to help out. We can't manage the move ourselves; however, we certainly don't want to involve Harry's recalcitrant sons, who helped move him and Dottie into his apartment, and later was on hand to move Dottie into her own room. Harry and I agree that we have arrived at a point in our lives that we can afford the luxury of hired help.

The morning that the movers arrive, Harry oversees carting the bed he's been using to Dottie's room and the disposal of hers. He sweetens the deal by presenting her with a gift bag of three cartons of cigarettes. When I broach the hazards of heavy smoking, he says, "If Dottie slumps over dead next week or lives to be a hundred, there's bound to be a burning cigarette between her fingers as she draws her last breath. Not me, or the boys, or anyone else on God's green earth can get her to quit smoking. She's tried many times, especially when the boys were little, tried hard, I'd say, but she just can't kick the habit. Dottie just loves to smoke."

After my furniture and things are delivered and suitably arranged in Harry's apartment, I bite the bullet and go visit Dottie myself, also bearing gifts: a gourmet popcorn sampler, a pound of See's candy, and a miniature decorated living Christmas tree that will no doubt be dead within a month.

She seems delighted with her gifts. She breaks open the popcorn as we sit a while and chat. She brags about her grandsons and goes on about her holiday plans to spend a week with George's family in Bakersfield. She doesn't mention my relationship with Harry and I don't either. He, in fact, doesn't come up in our conversation at all, which is just as well.

Harry insists on buying us a full-sized live Christmas tree, which I haven't bothered with in decades. I inhale its delicious piney scent, the best thing about a live tree. We decorate it together with all new ornaments, no keepsakes from either family, a new beginning for us. With Bing Crosby's "White Christmas" on his old-school CD player, we are sitting back in the recliners, enjoying our first eggnogs of the season, when Brooke comes knocking, surprised to have found my room starkly empty and me settled into my new residence already. We offer her an eggnog, and Harry warms it up with a double shot of brandy. Cheers!

Harry and I would like to make our holiday visits to family as a couple, but we decide that it's going to take everyone a little time to get used to our living situation. Plans for Christmas have already been set so we agree to carry them out separately. I'll go to Brooke's, of course, and Harry will dine with Ricky and Lauren. We save New Year's Eve to celebrate together, by booking a four-day cruise from Long Beach to Ensenada, with a stop at Catalina Island, a sort of mini honeymoon without the bother of a wedding.

241

66

Christmas Day, Brooke is driving me to her house, when she says, "I have a surprise for you." Her eyes are bright, her mouth is wide, the tip of her tongue curling to touch her upper teeth.

"Carter is home."

"Aw!" She raps the steering wheel with the heel of her hand. "How'd you guess?"

I laugh. "You're wearing your my-boy's-home expression."

"He blew in last night, totally unexpected."

"Wonderful!" I clap my hands. It's been a long time, too long. "How is he?"

"Fine! Seems just fine, except for, you know…." She taps her temple with her forefinger.

"Still spouting conspiracy theories?"

"Oh, yeah. He started right in."

I sigh. "Ah, well. We've come to expect it. I can't wait to see him!"

At a red light, Brooke stares out the windshield, her chin dipped. "He wants something."

"Money?"

"Doesn't look like it. He came roaring up in a brand-new black pickup, the one the cat advertises. You know, Carter has never asked us for money."

I nod. Even in college he had a part-time job at the surf shop and stayed on full time the summer after his graduation. We thought

242

he might be settled in Santa Cruz for a while as a surfer bum, but after the death of his best friend-roommate Ankit Nadu, he couldn't get out of there fast enough. "He drove that truck all the way from D.C.?" I ask.

"I don't know. I don't even know where he's living. When I asked what he was up to, he just shrugged and said he'd eventually tell us all about it." Brooke pulls into her garage, and sets the emergency brake. She turns to me, grinning. "You can ask him a bunch of nosey Gram questions so we all get to know what going on."

Brooke has set her table with her Christmas china, which she uses about once a year if at all, two glowing gold candelabras, which make the room a little too warm, and a lush spruce pine poinsettia centerpiece, which makes it necessary for me to lean sideways in my chair to view my beloved grandson seated across from me. By the looks of him, you wouldn't guess he was among those fanatics who stormed the Capitol with straggly hair and beards, face paint, horns, sloppy paunches, camo pants, and offensive sweatshirts bearing "Camp Auschwitz." Not our Carter. No visible signs of rebellion, no tattoos or piercings, no facial hair. His auburn hair is clipped short, with a neat side part and shaved nape. He is of a slight build like his father and has difficulty finding shirts with a neckline small enough to fit him. He sits straight and tall in his navy-blue suit and red tie, more formal than his very formal dad who sports an open-collared Oxford shirt and a silly sweater vest depicting a Dachshund toting a candy cane in its mouth, a joke gift from Brooke, which I thought he would never wear.

"You're staring at me, Gram," accuses Carter. "Do I have cranberry sauce on my face?"

"No, darling. I'm drinking you all in because I hardly ever get to see you. You look wonderful."

"Thanks. You look good, too, Gram. Did you get a face lift?"

I chuckle. "You know that's not my style."

"Gram has a boyfriend," Brooke says with a singsong lilt. "She's living with a married man."

"You go, Gram. Where's his wife?"

"Same place," Brooke blurts.

Carter's eyebrows shoot up. "The three of you live together?"

"No," I clarify. "She lives at Shady Meadow, but she doesn't have anything to do with us. She hates Harry. She's a drug addict."

"And a soup thrower," Jonathan adds.

I turn to him. "Oh, you know about that?"

Brooke does a shimmy in her chair. She's high on having her boy home. "Mom, tell them about her hitting a policeman with a frying pan."

"I get it," says Carter. "You guys are gaslighting me."

"No, no. All true," I exclaim, "although, she didn't actually hit the cop, just threatened."

Brooke, Jonathan, and I emit peals of raucous laughter as Carter remains skeptical.

"What's going on with you?" I ask him. "Where are you living now? Still in D.C.?"

"Cedarville."

"Oh, is that in Iowa?" I ask.

"That's Cedar Rapids, Colette." Jonathan revels in correcting people.

"I've heard of Cedarville University in Ohio," says Brooke, "Highly reputable."

Carter grins. "Cedarville, California."

"Where's that?" I ask.

"Modoc County."

"That's way up there." Jonathan gestures to the north. "Nothing much up there except—are you a rice farmer now?"

"Dad. What I do I can do anywhere. I'm a crypto day trader."

Jonathan furrows his brow. "That sounds risky, son. Can you make anything at it?"

Carter rolls his eyes in a bored manner. "Sure. Nothing risky about crypto if you know what you're doing."

"Then why Cedarville?" I ask. "Do you have a girlfriend from there?"

"I knew you'd ask me about that, Gram. No. I came home because I have an announcement to make." He clears his throat and sips his apple-cranberry sparkling cider like a child. He peers into our faces one at a time, like he did in elementary school, when he was practicing an Odyssey of the Mind presentation. "Mom, Dad, Gram, I am running for Congress."

I dare to clarify, "What congress is that?"

Carter's lips tighten and flatten into a thin line. "The United States House of Representatives, California District One."

I can't believe my ears. "Are you even old enough?"

He huffs in consternation. "Gram, I'm twenty-six."

"Oh, yes, so you are. Time flies."

"What prepares you for such an endeavor, son?" Jonathon voice deepens in pitch as if he's interviewing a potential newcomer to his firm. "Do you have any political experience? Are you working through an online course for a law degree?"

Carter wriggles his fingers impatiently. "Lauren says you don't need any of that."

"Whose Lauren, a girlfriend?" I ask.

"A colleague, uh, um, an acquaintance, at least. She didn't have any political experience before she got into Congress, and she's a high school dropout." He pokes his breastbone with his forefinger. "I have a college degree."

"Oh, *that* Lauren." Brooke snorts to suppress a giggle.

Jonathan laughs out loud.

I hide my grin behind my napkin.

"I know what you guys are thinking, and you're wrong," says Carter. "Lauren is no lightweight. She was a savvy business owner. In her bar, she had all the waitresses toting guns. Very smart. Very sexy. Customers came pouring in."

"Luckily, no one started a mass shooting," comments Brooke.

"There are no mass shootings in this country," says Carter.

"They're all staged with actors."

"Holy fuck," says Jonathan.

I scramble to change the subject. "Well, then, what's your view on climate change?"

"Oh, that. Do you see any dinosaurs around? There's always been climate change. Humans have nothing to do with it." Carter straightens his tie, and I suddenly get the look he's going for: young Republican. "What other issues do you have in mind? Ask me anything."

"I don't think that will be necessary." Jonathan feigns a deep shudder. "I actually thought your showing up here might mean you've finally come to your senses. Please pass the wine, Colette."

"That's all you have to say?" Carter throws back his narrow shoulders against his chair. "You're my family. I came here to ask for your support."

Jonathan drops his head in his hands. Brooke throws her head back to drain her wine glass. I feel the need to say something. "It's wonderful to see you, honey. It's the best Christmas present we can possibly get."

"So no? Nothing at all?"

"You're our son, Carter." Brooke runs the back of her hand across his forearm. "We love you very much."

"We're proud of your ambition," says Jonathan, "but frankly, I wouldn't want you as my Congressman. I wouldn't want you anywhere near Congress."

Carter turns a steely gaze on me. "What about you, Gram? You've supported me in everything I've ever done."

I shake my head slowly, so sad to reject him. "Not this time, sweetheart."

Carter's countenance hardens in anger. "Mom, Dad, let me get this straight. You aren't giving me one dollar in support, but if I win, you'll be going around your fucking law firms and your fucking country club, bragging that your son is a United States Congressman."

"Cheers to that." Jonathan clinks his wine against Carter's sparkling cider.

We know the reason he doesn't drink. His best friend Ankit died not of a DUI, but of alcohol poisoning, age twenty-two. I know it's not easy being a member of Gen Z. We elders thought we were giving these kids every possible opportunity and material possession to succeed, but something went terribly wrong. College-educated and gainfully employed, Gen Z kids live in their parents' homes or they sofa surf among friends because they can't afford housing, health care, and sometimes food. Some of them are mentally ill or addicted to drugs or alcohol, some dwell in encampments for the homeless, "unhoused," they are called now, as if semantics puts them in a better situation, and some, like our dear boy, have gone down the rabbit hole of conspiracy theories, a grip on reality slipped away, gone, lost.

I reach across the table and squeeze Carter's hand. "Good luck, darling. California District One is as red as the blood in our veins. If you can beat the incumbent, more power to you."

"Agreed." Brooke raises her glass, which is now as empty as the bottle at her elbow.

"Same here. We just may have a congressman in the family." Jonathan clenches his teeth and pulls down one side of his mouth, which, thankfully, gets a laugh out of Carter.

We savor Brooke's once-a-year grasshopper pie. Carter helps clear the table before retreating to his childhood bedroom. Brooke is constantly redecorating the house with new color schemes, new blinds, new flooring, new furniture, but Carter's room remains at it was in his childhood, including his fourth-grade Carmel Mission model, X-box, razor scooter, science fair poster board on the first computers, the complete series of *Magic Tree House* books, Alien Ant Farm poster, Lego pirate ship, debate team trophies, the list goes on and on. It makes me wonder how many houses across America, throughout the world, hold such Museums of the Child. Perhaps parents are too sentimental to discard these artifacts of their kids' childhood, or maybe, in stepping into such hallowed spaces, they can imagine, for at least a brief moment, that their child is still present under their roof, still growing, still aspiring to a charmed adulthood.

I help Brooke and Jonathan with the dishes, then retreat to the guest room. I'm so tired that after reading a single paragraph, I doze off, my book slipping from my hands and conking me on the nose. I switch off the light and drift off. I am awakened by piano music, Debussy's "Girl with the Flaxen Hair." Obviously not a recording, but someone playing.

"Carter!" I hear Brooke exclaim, "your Gram is trying to sleep."

"No! No!" I call out. "Please, Carter, go on!"

He is out-of-practice, which makes me wonder when he last sat down at the piano. He plays the opening phrase, stumbles on the following chords, repeats the notes he missed. He keeps at it, and within a half hour or so, he is able to play the whole piece through with fluidity and expression. I lie there listening, the music enveloping me like a comforter. My grandson Carter will always have his piano, he can pick it up whenever he likes, and this makes my heart glad.

67

This cold January night is a long one. A branch scrapes against the side of the building, the wind roars in fierce gusts, the rain splatters against the window pane. I enjoy listening to the storm, but I'd rather be sleeping. No problem for Harry. He snores contentedly beside me.

"Ah-oo-ga!" His phone bleats out the sound of a Model A horn, an annoying ring tone in my opinion, but I've never said anything to him about it. He continues to sleep right through the call, but I nudge him with my elbow.

"Harry, your phone."

"Uh? Oh." He answers. "Hello? Yes, this is him. Oh? Uh-huh… about what time?" His tone is flat, serious. I can't hear the other side of the conversation, but when is the news at three a.m. ever good? He swings his legs over the side of the bed and hunches over. "Which hospital? Sutter? Yeah, I know it. We're on our way." He ends the call, switches on his nightstand light, and looks forlornly at me.

I bolt upright. "What is it?"

"Dottie ODed."

"Oh, shit!"

"I'm afraid she's really done it this time. A staffer heard some strange gurgling sounds coming from her room. He found her on the floor unconscious, face down in a pool of vomit. He called nine-one-one, and an ambulance rushed her to the hospital, but who knows how long she was down. Help might have come too late."

"Oh, Harry, I'm so sorry!" I feel just awful. I somehow feel responsible for this. Guilty. Should I take the blame, at least partly? Is it protocol to hug a lover when his wife might be dying? I remain still, at a loss of what to say or do.

"Let's get going. We need to get down to the hospital quick. I'll call the boys and let them know."

He starts jabbing at his phone, and I catch his forearm. "Wait! Do you think my going with you is the proper thing to do?"

"Of course. You're my partner. I need you with me."

"But Dottie's your wife. Won't it upset her?"

"From what I can tell, she won't know."

"Your sons will disapprove."

"I don't give a fuck what they think. Get dressed, Colette. Please."

I do what he asks. We have an argument about his driving to the hospital. As I try to talk him out of it, he continues to stalk out of the building, into the dark parking lot.

"Please, Harry, call a Lyft."

"I'm perfectly capable of driving at night. I can see even better than in daytime glare."

"Your driver's license says you can't."

"It says I'm not permitted. That's completely different from incapable." He clicks his fob, opens the passenger door for me, and hustles me in.

As we drive, I look out for traffic and sneak furtive glances at Harry. He seems determined, but calm. I'd like to know what' he's thinking. I touch his thigh. "Are you okay?"

He sighs. "Fine."

"How do you feel?"

He rolls his eyes toward me. "Want to know the truth? Nothing. I feel nothing. Do you think less of me for that?"

"Of course, not." I don't say so, but I don't believe him. Certainly, he's merely in shock.

He shakes his head slowly, as if he can read my thoughts. "Me and Dottie have been over for so long. Yeah, she gave me three sons, we had some good years. It's a sad, sad situation. She did this to herself. She let her life go to shit."

"But her back pain."

"Bullshit."

I don't know how to respond to that. We drive the rest of the way in silence.

When we enter Dottie's hospital room, I think she is on her way to recovery because her eyes are open. I expect her to turn and acknowledge us, but she lies frozen, staring up the ceiling. Her breath is so shallow, it is hard to detect.

Harry draws his hand back and forth over her face and calls out her name, but there is no response. We hold vigil until her presiding physician Dr. Aku and a nurse step in the room. He is a tall, thin Nigerian, who speaks with a British clip. After he explains Dottie's medical treatment thus far, Harry asks, "Is she in a coma?"

"Yes."

"But her eyes are open."

"It happens in these drug-induced episodes."

"Can't you give her something to snap her out of it?" Harry asks.

"We've done what we can. Now we wait."

"You know she's addicted to opioids," says Harry. "Perhaps a small dose would help."

Dr. Aku shakes his head. "If she can survive, she's going to have to go cold turkey. Her system is overloaded with drugs. She can't withstand any more. Now, if you excuse us, we must make another examination."

The nurse ushers us to the waiting room. And so we wait. Harry hears from his sons, one by one. Ricky says he'll be in meetings all day and won't be able to get away from work. He encourages Harry to call if there's "a change," meaning, I guess, if Dottie dies. Marty says seeing his mother in such a state might be a trigger for him to start drinking again, and he's been advised by his therapist to stay away. George says he'll try to make it, but it's a long drive from

Bakersfield and he doesn't see a point to it if he's going to be "too late" anyway.

I think Harry and Dottie's sons are behaving like selfish jerks, but he doesn't comment on their choices, so I hold my tongue. We wait some more. Around noon George and Sharlene burst into the waiting room, having made the drive from Bakersfield after all. In his large cowboy hat, George reminds me of Hoss on the old *Bonanza*. He hugs Harry like a big bear. Sharlene wears a denim dress, fur-lined knee-high boots with pompoms, a sheepskin jacket, and a sneer. Harry escorts George to Dottie's room, while Sharlene throws herself in a chair and glares at me.

"I see the future Mrs. Beck is right here, waiting in the wings," she snipes.

I try not to take her distain personally. She would dislike anyone whom she believes might come between her and Harry's money. I give her the stink-eye, but keep still. This whole fiasco has been a practice in self-control, and I'm beginning to feel the strain.

She crosses her legs and kicks out a foot, the pompoms on her laces bouncing. "There's nothing standing in your way to marry Harry now."

"Dottie is still breathing. Why don't you wait a while before you assess your future finances?"

Her eyes pop. She leaps up and stalks down the hall to make a phone call. Later, I overhear her telling someone that she'd "rather have the funds now rather than later." Harry and George return from Dottie's room. George's eyes are bloodshot from crying. He asks Sharlene if she'd like to see Dottie, but she gives a pert shake of her head. She takes out an emery board and goes to work on her long, pink claws.

"Dad, Colette, would you like some coffee?" George asks.

We drink coffee and wait. We get sandwiches in the hospital cafeteria. We drink more coffee. Harry and I go in to see Dottie again. No change. We drink more coffee. I'm not used to so much caffeine and get the jangles. My stomach feels queasy. Ricky makes a cameo appearance around six, apparently having completed all the important meetings of his work day. Harry takes him to see his mother. Afterward, the Becks and I go out to eat a fast food dinner. We return to the hospital. We wait some more. Around nine, Sharlee whispers in George's ear, and he announces they will retire to a nearby motel. Around ten, Ricky decides to leave also. I'd like to go home, too, but Harry seems glued to his seat, arms crossed, staring at the linoleum. He doesn't share his thoughts, and I don't ask about them. I wonder if he plans to wait through the night. By midnight, it's certain: Dottie lives.

68

I spot the sign just as we drive into Yuba City on Highway 99. I grip Harry's arm and exclaim, "Did you see that?"

"What?" Harry doesn't see much.

"It was a campaign sign for Carter!" As we ride along, I point, "There's another one and another one! And another!" Some of them read, "Carter Hughes for US Congress" while others say, "Hughes will make a difference."

"I saw that one," says Harry.

I slap my thighs. "This is really happening! I figured Carter would have only enough money for a couple of signs, but he must be getting funded by someone."

In Chico, we turn onto Highway 32, and then head east on 36, past Lake Almanor. It's early spring and the open terrain is filled with purple lupine, yellow mustard, orange poppies, and tiny white popcorn flowers, with snowcapped Mt. Lassen looming in the distance.

"Long ways up here," comments Harry.

"Yes, I'm enjoying the drive."

"Me, too, but don't be too disappointed if we can't find him, honey."

"Oh, I know." I pat his shoulder. "We're on an adventure. I've lived in California all my life and don't remember ever coming up here."

"Well, Modoc County isn't really on the way to anywhere."

At last, we arrive in tiny Cedarville, situated in the far north east corner of the state, nearly to the Nevada and Oregon borders. We

254

ask around, and eventually pull up to a spanking-new white travel trailer. I recognize the black pickup it's hitched to. Next to it is a large sign flapping in the wind, "Hughes will make a difference."

We slide out of the car and stretch. I roll my eyes toward Harry. "Here goes."

I knock on the trailer door, and Carter is quick to answer. His open, smiling face crumples at the sight of me. Clearly, he's been expecting someone else. "Gram! What are you doing here? Are you sneaking up on me?"

"Sorry for not giving you any notice, darling. I was afraid you'd run away."

"Why would I do that? Did Mom send you up here to check on me?" He looks over my shoulder as if he expects to see his parents.

"Oh, no. It was all our own idea. Well, my idea. It was a lovely drive. Long! Six hours!"

"Well, come in. You must be Harry." Carter reaches out to shake hands.

The interior of the trailer looks like a campaign headquarters and a home combined. There's a long folding table full of brochures, caps, T-shirts, and buttons, with lawn signs leaning against it. The compact kitchen is fully equipped and sparkling clean. The sitting area is spacious, and through a door I can see a bedroom and bath, everything in its place. Carter was a neat, organized child. When asking for peanut butter and jelly, he insisted that half of his open-face sandwich was spread with peanut butter—smooth, of course—and the other half jelly—never jam—which he would eat in alternate bites.

"Nice digs you got here," I say.

"I figured a trailer was the practical thing to buy. Big district. Lots of ground to cover."

"You own this?" I ask in surprise.

"And the three acres it sits on," Carter says proudly. "Property is cheap in these parts. Have a seat. Can I get you anything? Coffee? A sandwich?"

"No, thanks, dear. We had lunch and a bathroom stop a while back."

"You should've told me you were coming so I could make time for you." Carter glances at his watch. "I have a meeting with my campaign manager in twenty minutes and a town hall meeting tonight."

"Oh, we won't keep you," I say. "We just decided to go on an outing and thought it would be fun to try to look you up."

Carter asks about his parents, and we have a little chat about his campaign thus far. There's a knock on the door and a young woman lets herself in. She's short and squat with wide cheekbones and owl-like round glasses. Her shiny black hair is closely-cropped and she wears khaki capris and am oversized red "Hughes will make a difference" hoodie. She looks to be high school age, but all young adults look like children to me.

"This is my campaign manager, Sequoia Thunderhawk. This is my grandma Colette and her partner Harry."

The child offers me her small hand. It has a tattoo of a hawk in flight across the back; thunderbolts on her neck point to her earlobes. "Oh, you're the composer."

"That was my mother," I respond in surprise. "You know about her?"

She tilts her head toward Carter. "He told me all about himself." She wrinkles her nose playfully. "Do we have your vote?"

"He won't be on our ballot," I say, hastily. "We're in District Six, Sacramento."

Carter shakes his head, laughing. "Good excuse, Gram! She wouldn't vote for me anyway. She's a Democrat."

"So am I," says Harry.

I elbow him gently in the ribs. "Not much of one." I start to stand. "We'll get out of your way and leave you to it."

"Hold it." Sequoia places a restraining hand on my shoulder. "You could help us. The incumbent Wally Montgomery hasn't held a town hall meeting in decades. He's old and lazy with some baggage about campaign finance fraud and money laundering, but he doesn't have to do much of anything to get reelected time and time again. He knows he has a few vocal detractors and he's chicken. He fears being heckled at town hall meetings and he figures he doesn't need to hold them anyway."

"I'm putting myself out there," says Carter, "talking to as many people as I can. Alturas Town Hall is tonight, then Yuba City, Chico, and Redding come later."

"But he needs practice," says Sequoia. "Lots of practice. The Montgomery team is just waiting to pounce when our guy misspeaks. Will you ask Carter some questions, see if he can land on his feet?"

"Well, okay," I say. "Like what?"

Carter opens two lawn chairs, and he and his campaign manager sit opposite us. She begins typing on her iPad. "I'll start. Montgomery is a Bible thumper. We gotta address the far-right Christians up here." She turns to Carter. "Do you believe in Creationism?"

"Dinosaurs and people on earth at the same time?" Carter bares his teeth. "Chomp, chomp."

Sequoia turns to me. "See what I mean?" She looks at Carter. "Play nice."

"All right." He looks at the ceiling then back at us. "The Bible is the Word of God. In Genesis, when He speaks of days, it's really a poetic term for eons."

"Better!" says Sequoia. "Take out the word 'poetic' and you're on the money. Colette, you go next."

"All right. What do you think about gay rights?"

"Good one," says Sequoia. "Montgomery is both homophobic and misogynistic. There are LGBTQ Republicans, you know. They'd like to know how your views are different from the incumbent's."

Carter leans forward in earnest. "If same-sex marriage is against your religion, you shouldn't enter into it. If a gay couple comes asking you for a wedding cake, that's just business."

"What about free speech?" asks Sequoia.

"If a couple entering a restaurant are told, 'You can't eat here because you're Black,' that isn't free speech, that's discrimination. Refusing to bake a wedding cake for a gay couple is also discrimination."

Sequoia nods. "But also against my religion. That's the problem. We need to think about this more. Now you, Harry."

Harry is apolitical, so I wonder what he'll come up with. He creases his brow a moment and blurts, "Do you want to drain the swamp?"

"I don't want to drain anything," says Carter. "I want to fill reservoirs and lakes and rivers." He makes a wide arc with his long arms. "California needs water, and when it comes our way, we need to find a way to hold onto it, not just let it flow out into the ocean."

Sequoia pounds her knee with her first. "Oh, yeah, dude, you got this."

"Do you believe the twenty-twenty election was stolen?" I ask.

Carter waves away the idea as if it's a fly. "That isn't fashionable anymore, is it?"

"Among the MAGA folks, you bet! Use your pretty words, Carter," Sequoia coaches.

"Trump deserved to win. We have to be ever vigilant to make sure our elections are fair and free of fraud."

Sequoia raises her chin high, then lets it drop. "Now, you're getting it. Colette, you go again."

I look into my darling boy's lovely brown eyes and ask, "Why do you want to run for Congress?"

"To make the world a better place. Don't you know that about me, Gram? That's all I've ever wanted to do."

"Oh? What about that QAnon business?" I counter.

"Q was out after the bad guys, too."

"Who he *thought* were the bad guys," corrects Sequoia. "What about QAnon now? Are you still a believer?"

"Q hasn't made a drop in over four years, so whoever they were has completed their work. It's up to us now. We have to do whatever we need to do to protect our children and our freedom."

Before I leave, I write Carter a sizeable check, at least for me. I hand it to him saying, "I know this is a drop in the bucket."

"Gee, thanks. Are you just doing this because you're my Gram?"

"Nope. District One always votes red, and I definitely think you're better than the stuffy old incumbent what's-his-name."

He kisses my cheek. "Thank you, Gram. Your support means a lot."

Sequoia offers to give us a lift to the Alturas Town Hall, but we turn down the offer. My grandson is out in the world now, on his own, and besides, Harry and I are beat. We get a room at the Surprise Valley Motel and RV Park.

On our evening walk after dinner, Harry nods at a quarter-million-dollar Winnebago and asks, "Should we get one?"

"Oh, god, no! Not my style, even if you could see to drive it."

"It does look stressful, and a lot of work."

"Hook ups, sanitation dump, cleaning—get me to a motel any day." I squeeze his hand. "Thanks for this trip. It's so beautiful, and the big bonus was tracking Carter down."

"Do you think he can win?"

I raise my eyebrows. "I've been pondering that. With California's jungle primary, two Republicans can advance to the General, and then…"

Harry grins at me. "You could have a grandson in Congress. How about that?"

"I'll tell you what makes me even happier, happy and relieved. This campaign business has got him out into the real world. He's no longer stuck down the rabbit hole, talking only to other conspiracy theorists. He's listening to a lot of people with all sorts of opinions. He's facing reality for the first time in a very long time, and that makes my heart glad."

69

You wouldn't recognize Dottie if you knew her before. Gone are the gray braids, the puffy face, the vague stare, the slovenly dress. Her hair is dyed a chestnut brown, cut into a flouncy bob to the chin, parted to the far left so that it sweeps over lively, brown eyes. Today I visit her bearing a net bag of mandarins, her preferred snack now that she's become health conscious.

I rap on her open door and step in. "Hi, what's up?"

She doesn't answer right away, her attention shifting from her computer to the computations she's scribbling in the yellow legal pad at her elbow. She's wearing mint green leggings and a form-fitting T-shirt, rhythmically bouncing a silver flipflop on her pedicured toe.

"Hey, Dottie!" I call a bit louder. "Did I come at a bad time?"

"Oh, hi Colette. Come in. I'm working through an online course in baby calculus. I've forgotten all my math, but it's coming back now that I can think straight. Now that I can think at all."

"Baby calculus! I only made it through algebra and geometry, all that my all-girls Catholic high school offered, except for the algebra two class that only about six of the brainy girls took."

Dottie taps her forehead with her pencil. "I love what math does to my brain. I always have."

I hold up the mandarins. "I brought you these."

"Gee, thanks. Okay if we step out?"

"Sure." I've come prepared, wearing my carcoat.

Despite her new regimen of healthy eating and physical therapy, Dottie still smokes like a chimney. She gathers her cigarettes and lighter and leads me down the hallway, a bounce to her step. Outside the side door, we sit in a small patio area, in Adirondack chairs. It's gray out, but not too cold. She bends her head to light up against a breeze and tilts back to blow smoke up into the air, wearing that euphoric look smokers have on the first puff. It really must do something for them.

"How's the back pain?" I ask.

"Gone! No problem at all."

"Without a prescription?"

"None! It's all physical therapy now. It's all Raul! As long as I work through my exercises with my dear boy, I'm fine." She raises her shoulders and lets them drop, her face radiant. "Better than fine. I'm fantastic!"

I look askance at her. "You don't miss the drugs?"

"God, no! I'm released from them, I'm free. I never thought this would happen. I expected they would kill me, and I didn't much care. Well, they almost did."

"You wouldn't have become addicted if you didn't need them."

"Bullshit. I'll tell you, I've been living a lie for years. Ibuprofen would have been enough, but I liked getting high. I was miserable in my miserable life and the only way I could escape was with drugs." She straightens in her chair and bores a fist into her lower back. "Oh! And my dear boy! He does wonders. His fingers play my spine like an instrument." She bats her lashes, which are plied with mascara. She leans into me and says, "We're so in love."

What? I'm stunned. I hope it doesn't show on my face. "Raul— Dr. Martinez—is very popular around here," I comment.

"Oh, he's got to be nice to all the old hags to keep his job." Dottie lowers her voice to a hoarse whisper. "He's got a live-in girlfriend. He's admitted that much to me. He says he can't ask her to leave, not yet anyway, has to let her down easy. When she goes, I move in."

"He told you that?"

"Not in so many words. We don't always use words." Her eyes grow seductively wide. She appears ten years younger. "I never thought I'd have another romance, considering all the old duffers in this rat hole. A woman like me can't settle into bed against old, withered flesh. Oh, hell, no! Give me a fresh, strapping young man I can sink my teeth into, a firm ass I can smack, and have him crawling on his hands and knees begging for more."

My suppressed laugh erupts through my nose as a snort.

"What?" A naughty smile plays at the corners of her quivering lips. "Wanna know when old Harry started going downhill? Sagging jowls—" She pinches the skin around her mouth and tugs it down. "Paunch like a bowling ball." She slaps her lean midriff. "Age forty! I held my nose and stuck with him another twenty years. Along with his smelly fish and jangling piano. Ain't I a saint?"

"I guess we have different tastes in men." What else can I say? I won't tell Harry any of this, not because he'd be jealous, but because I don't want him laughing at her. I fake a shiver. "Brrr. I'm going in."

"Go on, I'm going to have one more cig." Dottie peers around herself furtively, like a teenager smoking behind the backstop. "My baby just hates to see me smoking. I'd quit for him if I could. I'd do anything for him. God, Colette, we're so in love it hurts. It's ecstasy and terror both. Love is torture!"

Love is comfort, but I don't debate her. Is it possible? Does a young man fall in love with a woman over twenty years his senior? Old men couple with very young women, so why is it so unbelievable the other way around? But really—Raul and Dottie? It's not just one-sided? I honestly don't know. I stand to leave. "Bye, Dottie."

"Bye. Say hi to your old duffer for me." Her tone hardens. "Thanks for not bringing him along. Just can't stand the sight of him. Don't know what you see in him."

70

I feel a little silly as I ice this cake, but I think I have to make a big deal about my scheme for Harry to go for it. I draw the message, "Happy Birthday Harry," with a tube of blue icing across the green cake top and scatter a few gold-foiled chocolate coins as the finishing touch. I start my clean-up by hiding the cake mix box in the bin under some other recyclables. I've always used cake mixes and feel guilty for being too lazy to start from scratch.

I've sent Harry off for the afternoon to run errands so that I get my surprise ready. I'm doing the cooking tonight: scallops wrapped in bacon, rice pilaf, and spinach salad. All my prep is done. The green and orange crepe paper streamers are hung, the balloon bouquet floats in the corner of the living room.

When Harry steps through the door, I throw my arms around him. "Surprise! Happy birthday, honey."

"Uh, thanks." He looks around, absolutely stunned. I know why, but choose to ignore it.

"Come on, I can't wait for you to open your present. You're going to love it." I lead him to the sofa and hand him a bulging package the size of a business envelope.

He gives me a quizzical look, and then with a tight little smile, unwraps my gift and stares at the travel documents inside.

"I booked this tour for us. Just what you wanted! We'll be spending St. Patrick's Day in Ireland. Can you believe it? Dublin to Dublin, around the whole perimeter of the Emerald Island. Transportation, lodging, breakfasts, all included."

Harry turns over the tour brochure in his hands, his brow furrowed, just what I was afraid of.

"You don't look that happy. You do want to go to Ireland, right?"

"Oh, yes. I appreciate the trip, but I thought it would be just the two of us."

"It will be just the two of us…in a busload of other tourists. We'll just ignore them."

"I thought we were going to rent a car, take our time, stop wherever we want."

"This tour goes everywhere." I point out, "Belfast, Derry, the Dingle Peninsula. Oh, and Blarney Castle—I want to kiss the Blarney stone—and Waterford—all that beautiful cut crystal! You can look up some Duffy ancestors in Galway."

"If there's time. A tour like this is usually rushed and regimented."

"Not this one. I've read the reviews. There's some organized things, and some excursions we can add or we can do our own thing. Oh, and we can arrive in Dublin early, ramble through the city for a few days before the tour."

Harry drops his head, then looks me full in the face.

"What's wrong, dear? You don't want to go?"

"I'll feel like an old fart riding in a big tour bus, like we're too old to travel on our own."

"Think about it, honey. Driving on the wrong side of narrow roads, not knowing where we're going. Think how stressful that would be. You'd be white-knuckling it the whole time, and so would I."

He gives me his crestfallen look. "You don't trust my driving?"

"Here, I do. You can drive me any place where we'll be on the right side of the road."

He taps the brochure with his forefinger. "This makes me feel like I'm no longer capable."

"Yeah? Well, now I sit down to put on my socks." I don't get the laugh I'm going for. He sighs deeply. I wait. "You want me to cancel?"

"No, no." He takes me in his arms. "Thank you, darling. This is a wonderful gift."

I'm relieved. I kiss him on the cheek.

"But…"

"But?"

"You know it's not really my birthday, right?"

"Yep. I just wanted to make a big fuss over this so you wouldn't turn me down."

"Are you going to get me something else in June?"

I playfully slap his shoulder.

He studies the itinerary. "Oh, look, the Cliff of Moher. I've always wanted to go there."

I clutch his arm. "Not too close to the edge, I hope. We can pack a picnic lunch that day—wine, baguette, cheese—then hike out into the wild."

Harry's whole face lights up. "Now, that's really living."

Harry and I press our heads together and look toward the future. I'm reminded of something Margaret told me: "You just keep living until you die. Make sense?"

About the Author

Janet Nichols Lynch's first published fiction appeared in *The New Yorker*, August, 1984, and she is the author of seventeen books. Her debut novel, *Chest Pains*, was published in 2009 and her short fiction has been included in *Seventeen*, *Baltimore Review*, *Writers' Forum*, *Highway 99: A Literary Journey through California's Great Central Valley*, and other publications. Her young adult novels include *Messed Up*, a 2009 ALA Quick-Pick for Reluctant Readers and a VOYA (Voices of Youth Advocates) Top of the Top Shelf Fiction for Middle School Readers; *Racing California*, a 2012 Society of School Librarians International Honor Book; *My Beautiful Hippie*; and *Peace is a Four-letter Word*. Janet has also written nonfiction for young readers about music including *American Music Makers: An Introduction to American Composers*; *Women Music Makers: An Introduction to Women Composers*; *Clara Schumann, Pianist and Composer*; and *Florence Price, American Composer*. Her most recent work for young readers is the historical novel *Ellen of Allensworth*, about a child growing up in the early Twentieth Century in Allensworth, the only town in California founded, owned, and governed by African-Americans.

Janet was born in Sacramento, California, and graduated with a BA in Music from California State University, a Master of Music Degree in Piano from Arizona State University, and an MFA in Creative Writing from Fresno State University. She has taught music and English at the community college, high school, and middle school levels, and private piano to all ages.

Janet lives in Visalia, California, with her husband composer Timothy Lynch, and they have two grown children, three grandchildren, and three cats. Janet has completed twenty marathons and numerous other races and triathlons. As an avid cyclist, her longest ride was from Phoenix, AZ to Washington, D.C., and she is nearing the completion of her goal of cycling in all fifty states. Find Janet on Facebook at facebook.com/jnicholslynch, Instagram at janet_nichols_lynch, and Bluesky at @janetnicholslynch.bsky.social. Her website is JanetNicholsLynch.com.

Acknowledgements

Writers can't go it alone. They need other writers for inspiration, encouragement, feedback, commiseration, and celebration. The outstanding writers in my life are Marion Wentzien, Barbara Kerr, David Borofka, Steve Yarbrough, Connie Hales, John Hales, Tanya Nichols, and Merrill Joan Gerber. I am grateful for the impact they have made on my writing and writing life.

I hold deep appreciation for the team at Legacy Book Press LLC, who turned my manuscript into a beautiful book and brought it out into the world: publisher/editor Jodie Toohey, book designer Kaitlea Toohey, and marketing assistant Tessa Stuhlhut. Kudos to Patricia Sullivan Steele for creating the wonderful cover art.

My workout buddies keep me sane and safe and laughing a lot: Richard Rodriguez, Chris Adams, Nancy Louviere, and Lori Nault. Chris especially gives me lots of great ideas; she was my first reader and convinced me that Dottie wielding a frying pan is funnier than a baseball bat. A shout out to friends Renee Saxman and Arvid Fristad for including me on their whitewater rafting trip. How else could I realistically create Colette and Harry's raging river adventure?

I am most grateful for my supportive, loving family: Tim, Caitlin, Sean, Lyndsey, Soren, Ranger, and Liam.